Her Tuscan
Summer

Per gli amori della mia vita, Fabio, Christian and Alessia

CHAPTER ONE

The wheels of suitcases graze waxed floors while I sit with a lapful of pencil shavings, drowning in a sea of crumpled paper balls bearing the lines of failed strokes. I'm wondering whether I'll ever be able to do this again.

For inspiration, I try to focus on all the things I should be thinking of when embarking on a trip to Italy: the taste of a ripe tomato, crowded piazzas and street artists. Art museums, fading frescoes, crumbling walls begging for restoration, and the comforting aroma of freshly brewed espresso. I think of all the ways I might be able to translate these things onto paper, but it isn't happening. Not how I need it to.

My stomach tightens. My pencil lead breaks. And then I hear my name being called.

'Mia Moretti, this is your final boarding call for flight seven-one-seven. Please make your way to gate twenty-six.'

All the doubts I have about heading on this journey evaporate as I slide my pencil between my teeth, haul my backpack over my shoulder and grab my sketchbook. I briefly pause in front of a departure board and gaze upwards at the letters and numbers flashing at me, reminding myself that life's meant to be sweeter in Italy.

Breathless, I reach the boarding gate. 'I'm not too late, am I?' I say, thrusting my boarding card towards the attendant.

Her crimson-coloured lips smile tightly as she runs my pass to freedom through her machine. 'You're just in time. Have a pleasant flight, Ms Moretti.'

Wedged between a Japanese businessman and a woman with a restless child, I read seventy pages of my Tuscan guidebook, too many pages of my Italian–English dictionary, and the first few chapters of a self-help book on how to achieve happiness through gratitude, which I tuck away in my seat pocket before drifting off to sleep.

When I wake, the little girl is sitting beside me. She reaches for my sketchbook, looks up at me and smiles. I take my pencil and hand it to her.

'I'm sorry,' says her mother, snatching the sketchbook from her daughter's grasp.

'Oh, I really don't mind,' I reply. I unlock the girl's tray table and watch her draw, uninhibited by judgement, unafraid of what she might see on the page.

Making a blank piece of paper come to life used to be effortless for me. I could close one eye, open myself up and capture one small moment in time: an expression of delight, a carpet of leaves the shade of pumpkin and ruby under an almost bare scarlet oak tree, a parched landscape full of cracks thirsty for a drop of rain. I could do all of this before.

'Your turn!' says the girl, waving the blunt pencil at me. She has reached the last blank sheet of paper.

I take the pencil and draw what turns out to be a cringeworthy sketch of a girl sitting on a suitcase, elbows on her knees, face resting on her hands. She's bathed in dappled light that's struggling to burst through the trees on the overgrown path she sits on.

'She looks sad,' says the girl, looking to me for an explanation of my drawing.

'She's looking for the light,' I tell her.

She wrinkles her forehead and giggles. I can't help smiling back. We land in Rome twelve hours later.

*

After having my passport stamped by a surly customs officer, I manage to catch the right train headed to Termini station and then on to Florence, after which I tug my luggage along the platform and line up outside for a cab. I should know the address off by heart by now because I've looked at it so many times, but I pull the worn-out piece of paper from the pocket of my jeans anyway.

'Via Monteluna fourteen, Impruneta,' I tell the driver. 'Do you know where that is?'

'Of course.' He tosses a cigarette butt on the ground, extinguishes it with the twist of his foot, and then heaves my suitcase into the boot. He's wearing a pair of shorts and leather sandals, and I decide that he looks like a Mario, or a Giovanni, or maybe even a Giuseppe with his olive skin and thick brown moustache.

'First time to Italy?' he asks in a thick Italian accent once we're sitting in the car.

'Uh, yes, can you tell?' I ask, gazing out the window in an attempt to soak in every intricate detail of the landscape. Not even the smell of stale cigarette smoke can bother me right now.

I grab my phone and send a brief text to my overly protective mum and dad, who are no doubt out of their minds with worry. *I've arrived. Safe and sound.* Within thirty seconds my phone is inundated with a barrage of texts and questions, to which I reply, *I'm fine. Please don't worry about me. I'll call you once I get a local SIM card*, before switching off my phone.

The cab driver, who actually turns out to be a Salvatore, turns on the radio. I recognise Dean Martin singing 'Arrivederci Roma', but I struggle to follow the conversational Italian. We take the Firenze Impruneta exit from the A1 Autostrada and now I can see signs towards the town I will call my home for however long it takes to find myself again.

Motorised scooters weave in and out of the traffic around us with stealth and precision. It's unsettling yet rather fascinating watching the organised chaos that is at work on these Italian roads.

'Impruneta. Right up there, *signorina*.' Salvatore is pointing to show me.

I shift to the middle of the back seat and lean forward for a better view of the quintessential cypress trees smattered over the rolling hills, symbolic of the Tuscan landscape. We pass a terracotta workshop with an aging sign fixed to the wall: Mariucci Terrecotte. Impruneta, a small hilltop town on the outskirts of Florence, is famous for not much other than the best terracotta in the country. I might have a fierce passion for art, but I can't say I'm that interested in pottery, even if it is resistant to cracking at temperatures below zero.

Salvatore slows down as we make our way through a narrow one-way street, where the balconies of the apartments are laced with colour from the flowers that occupy their pots. Women are hanging out their washing in the June mid-morning sun and I can't help smiling when I notice water dripping onto an unsuspecting passer-by below. The man looks up and snaps to life, yelling and gesticulating as the woman on her balcony defends herself just as fiercely. Irritated, she grabs a metal watering can and with one hand on hip she sloshes the water down on him.

As we approach the main piazza, I notice an elderly couple walking up the steep hill, taking care with each step. He's carrying a loaf of bread in one arm, and her arm is intertwined through his other one. If he falls, she'll follow. I let out a sigh as my shoulders lean back into the leather seat behind me. He's wearing a checked shirt and suspenders. She's wearing a loose-fitting floral dress and a scarf around her head, and I wonder why a couple might go to such trouble to dress this way for a trip to the local *panificio* for a simple loaf of bread.

Of course I know the answer. This is Italy. Land of style.

We slow down, taking a right-hand turn onto an unpaved road. Salvatore winds down the car window for me, and I struggle to hide my excitement. 'Is this really it?' I exclaim, shifting towards the window.

'This is it, *signorina*,' says Salvatore, glancing at me in the rear-view mirror.

The road leads up to a villa rendered a pale yellow with ivy covering the northern side of the home. Something catches my eye in one of the upstairs windows. The green plantation shutters are open, revealing a woman waving at the car from the balcony. I assume it must be Stella, my new housemate. She's wearing a red dress with a white scarf tied around her neck, looking impeccable.

'*Benvenuta*! Welcome to Florence, Mia!' she calls, as the car comes to a stop.

She disappears from the window while I get out of the cab. A minute later, she bursts through the wooden front door and locks me in a tight embrace. Stepping back, she kisses me on both cheeks. I'm not sure whether to move right or left or just stay still, but I'm pretty sure my awkwardness has gone unnoticed. She thanks Salvatore for me after I pay him and helps roll my suitcase up the path towards my new home.

'Is this all you brought with you?' she asks.

'That's it,' I reply.

Just me, a suitcase, 2,018 euros and a whole lot of invisible baggage.

'Welcome to Villa Belladonna!' she says, gesturing for me to walk through the arched doorway.

The tension in my shoulders vanishes as I enter my new home, Stella's warm welcome immediately putting me at ease. As my new housemate walks me through the ground floor of the villa, I'm thankful that she seems perfectly normal, given that we met online. I take a few moments to familiarise myself with the villa's rustic architectural embellishments. The voluminous living area lets in an abundance of natural light and opens out to an impressive outdoor loggia. Two potted lemon trees are positioned on each side of the bifold door that gives way to a heavenly backdrop of a small olive grove and undulating hills. Stella points out the laundry, main bathroom and kitchen, and then continues down the hallway.

'You coming?' she asks, glancing back at me.

'Oh yeah, sure. Just taking it all in,' I reply. 'Is this original?' I gasp, when I notice half of the ceiling covered in what remains of a faded fresco.

Stella looks at me strangely. 'Oh, that. Seventeenth century, I imagine,' she says, shrugging her shoulders. Stella's delicate facial features intrigue me. Freckles are dotted over her face and she has the most striking green eyes I've ever seen. Her auburn-coloured hair is certainly not typical of a girl with Italian heritage. Long, curly tresses fall perfectly down her shoulders. She's wearing red lipstick and she reminds me of an actress from a 1960s movie. Stella's only a year older than me but she exudes an air of confidence that I have yet to grasp for myself. Unlike me, Stella had little choice in coming to Florence. Her parents practically forced her to come and learn Italian here when she was younger. Much to her parents' despair, she loved living in Italy so much that she decided to stay, and from what I can tell, she has no plans to move back to New York anytime soon.

'This is your room, Mia,' she says, pushing open a door, revealing my spacious new bedroom and all of its Tuscan charm: cinnamon-coloured walls, terracotta tiles and a wood beam ceiling. 'I hope you like it.'

'It's gorgeous,' I say, glancing around the room. A small desk with a tiny lamp and a rickety wooden chair sit in the corner of the room. I'm particularly drawn to the three paintings on the wall, all oil, mounted in gilded wooden frames. One shows a beautiful young woman in a field of sunflowers; another features two lovers on a vintage bike riding down a steep hill, hair blowing in the wind; the third is of the same couple sitting on a rustic swing entwined in each other's arms.

'I'll leave you to unpack and freshen up and then I'll show you upstairs. I'm going to start preparing lunch soon,' she says.

The door clicks shut behind her. I want to leap onto my four-poster double bed and shriek with exhilaration, but I tone it down in case Stella can hear me. Not that I think she'd care.

'I hope you're hungry, 'cause I'm making *pasta all'arrabbiata*!' she calls out from down the hallway.

'Perfect,' I murmur as I push open the shutters. My bedroom window overlooks the front garden, where the most sumptuous view of the town centre of Impruneta lies before me, inviting me to explore its intricacies. It fascinates me how in Italy, the expansive countryside will always belong to its very own town centre, no matter how small. I admire the vintage swing in the garden. Two thick ropes are flung over the branch of an oak tree, attached to a weather-worn plank of wood, the mint-green paint peeling. It's the same swing from the oil painting.

I retreat from the window and flick open the clasp on my suitcase, letting the contents spill out over the bed, but I decide to delay my unpacking. Instead, I return to my open window, where I allow the invigorating breeze to penetrate my soul for what feels like hours. I feel like I've arrived somewhere I should be.

Actually, I know I have.

CHAPTER TWO

Peeling myself away from the bedroom window, I dig through my suitcase to find my toiletries so I can take a quick shower. I can hear Stella in the kitchen, singing as she prepares lunch. After spending more than twenty hours in the air, the hot shower feels good. I throw on whatever clothes I find at the top of my suitcase and gently dry my hair. I wonder whether I'd blend in as a Florentine girl if I had the accent and style down pat. I decide that my chestnut-brown hair and chocolate-brown eyes look Italian enough, but my pale skin needs some work. Too many months locked between four walls have rendered my skin a pasty shade of beige. Too many months that I should have spent getting on with my life, learning to live again.

A brick arched doorway leads to the rustic kitchen, where I join Stella. She's stirring a pot of pasta sauce that smells delicious.

'Let me show you upstairs,' she says, leaving the sauce bubbling away. A curve of steps leads us to an airy living area dry-painted in semolina yellow, with a charming brick fireplace and wine-red-coloured sofas. Stella points out her bedroom and the spare bedroom, and then nudges open a wooden double door, revealing a room that clearly used to be an art studio. Rows of glass jars, paintbrushes still in them, sit on a windowsill. Beams of golden sunlight burst through the slits in the shutters, and I stagger my way through the thick cobwebs to rub a patch of dust off of the window, big enough so I can see through it.

'Who did this house belong to?' I ask, making out the town centre through the cypress trees partially blocking my view.

'My great-uncle. He still owns it. He used to live here with my Zia Amelia. She passed away three years ago. He was left heart-broken and moved out the day after her funeral. It's been empty since then. I moved in about a month before we spoke about you coming. That's why I was advertising for a housemate,' she explains.

I notice the wooden trestles and sheets spotted with paint that must have once been white but are now a creamy yellow. 'Was she an artist?'

'No, he is, or was—he stopped painting when she got sick.'

The studio is stuffy and hot, yet at the familiarity of Stella's words, the hairs on my arms prick up, sending an icy chill through my body. It's then that I make the connection between the lovers depicted in the paintings in my bedroom and the original lovers of this home.

'You mentioned you turned down a spot at art school?' says Stella.

'Uh, yeah, well, deferred really,' I say, desperately hoping she doesn't pick up on the uneven tone of my voice.

'You're welcome to use the studio anytime.'

'I'll keep that in mind. Thanks,' I say, wishing I could tell her the truth.

We return to the kitchen, and I admit to Stella that I'm not hungry, but she insists I eat. '*Mangia*!' she commands in a thick Italian accent, winking at me. 'You can't *not* eat in Italy!'

'Okay, okay!' I laugh.

Outside, Stella has set the table with a yellow checked tablecloth and a bottle of red wine. I admire the round bottle, contemplating whether there's a purpose behind the straw basket it's wrapped in. She has set four places, so I assume we must be expecting company. I'm somewhat uncomfortable with the fuss

Stella has gone to in preparing lunch. There's fresh mozzarella cheese and tomatoes sprinkled with basil, drizzled with olive oil. Alongside that is a plate of rock melon and fresh prosciutto, and two bottles of mineral water—one sparkling and one still. In between them is an empty basket waiting to be filled with fresh bread. I pick up one of the green bottles. My Italian is decent enough for me to understand the fascinating health benefits that are described on the label. I raise my eyebrows, amused at how this naturally sparkling water has the potential to slow down the aging process. If I'm lucky enough to age gracefully without cancer ravaging my body again, I'll be happy.

'I need to go out to buy some bread and pick up Paolo,' says Stella, before darting inside to grab her keys.

'Paolo?'

'*Mio ragazzo*. My boyfriend,' she says. 'His cousin Luca will be here soon, too. He'll let himself in. He's practically part of the furniture.'

'Okay.' I nod, trying to mask my lack of enthusiasm. I've spent so long keeping to myself that I'm not sure I'm ready for mingling.

'Don't worry, he speaks English,' she adds, sensing my hesitation.

While I wait for our guests to arrive, I get cosy on the wooden swing in the front yard. I grab the sturdy rope and propel my legs forward, allowing the sense of freedom to course through my veins as I gain momentum with every leg extension. I arch my back, watching the clouds as I drift into a familiar meditation.

I mentally make a list of some of the places I want to visit before my trip is over: Rome, Siena, Pisa, San Gimignano, Venice. The swinging eventually stops, and I'm promptly interrupted by the sound of a voice. My gaze shifts from the blue sky towards the direction of the voice and I blink several times in an effort to regain complete vision.

I'm sure he's been watching me. He's wearing a pair of jeans and a light blue polo with the collar popped, not perfectly straight but with one side slightly higher than the other. His messy dark brown hair could do with a trim. He's wearing a pair of loafers without socks and I can't tell what colour his eyes are because he's wearing a pair of dark sunglasses. He's probably around my age, in his early twenties. My eyes trace the form of his clean-shaven face and my heart skips a beat when I reach the definition of his jawline. This guy is *beautiful*. My eyes travel down to his perfectly formed biceps, and I have to look away. I glance down at my old pair of jeans and ballet flats and wish I'd taken the time to at least iron my shirt and make a half-decent effort. I look so… Australian.

I stand up and try to smooth out the creases in my shirt. I may have just showered, but my hair is in a messy ponytail and my face is bare of makeup. He lifts up his sunglasses, and now he's squinting to get a better look at the girl who has come to stay here—the girl from Australia, with no fashion sense whatsoever.

'*Buongiorno, signorina!*' he calls.

I manage a small wave in response, and by the time I reach him, I seem to have lost my voice. I don't know whether to speak in English or to try out my limited Italian. 'Hi there! *Ciao!*' I blurt.

Oh my gosh, he's so incredibly handsome.

'*Ciao, sono Luca, Luca Bonnici.*'

'Nice to meet you, I'm Mia.'

He steps towards me, towering over me slightly, and I can smell his aftershave. It's subtle, but I recognise it from my brief stint at Myer's cosmetic counter; I know I'll never forget the scent of Gucci by Gucci Pour Homme again. He extends his hand and leans down until our cheeks touch. He kisses me once on each cheek. And in some completely inexplicable way, it feels familiar.

'Welcome to Florence, *bella* Mia,' he says, smiling as he winks at me. If any other guy back home were to wink at me like this, I'd turn the other way. I find myself wondering if he might have a girlfriend, even though we've only known each other for around forty-five seconds.

'So, where are you from, Mia?' he asks, with the slightest hint of an American accent.

'Melbourne,' I say, willing my cheeks to stop blushing. 'Australia,' I add, feeling the need to explain.

'I guess that means we haven't met before,' he says, his eyebrows furrowed together, as if he's trying to figure out the connection.

I shake my head.

'How long are you staying in Italy?'

'I'm not really sure; I guess it depends on how I find it.'

'So what are your plans?' he asks, just as we're interrupted by Stella and Paolo. I quickly try to ground myself as they make their affectionate greetings. I can't know for sure, but judging from his salt-and-pepper hair, Paolo seems to be several years older than Stella, possibly even in his mid-thirties, although I can see immediately that they make a sweet couple.

'Luca, you've already met Mia by the looks of it,' she says, nodding to the dark, handsome guy. 'Paolo, this is Mia.'

Paolo extends his hand. '*Piacere*, Mia.'

'Nice to meet you too,' I say, shaking his hand.

'She arrived this morning,' announces Stella. 'She booked a one-way ticket. We know what that means.' She nudges Paolo.

Paolo grins. 'Mia, you are in one of the most charming cities in Italy. It will capture your heart in a week. Just ask Stella.' He affectionately pinches his girlfriend's cheek.

'He's right. Tuscany will forever hold a piece of your heart, Mia. Just wait and see,' she says.

I glance over at Dark, Handsome Guy, who's leaning against the wall of the villa, legs casually crossed, glasses in his hand, watching us… err… *me*… intently. I'm convinced that if a photographer for *Vogue Italia* were to turn up in this moment, he'd have the perfect shot for the next Gucci spread.

'Let's eat! I'll be back in a second,' says Stella, turning to walk through the front door.

'Let me help you,' I say, trying hard to bring myself back to reality.

Please don't leave me out here with him.

'It's fine. Paolo will help me. Luca, *vino*,' she orders. I decide that I like Stella already. She's assertive and I can't help feeling relaxed around her, even if she is abandoning me completely with Luca.

Just breathe, I tell myself as I take a seat opposite him. He places his shades in the centre of the table and now I'm losing myself in his dark brown eyes adorned with eyelashes that would make any girl envious.

'*Rosso o bianco?*' he asks.

Red or white? Why is it that everything sounds better in Italian?

'Uh, *rosso, per favore*,' I mutter. What is happening to me? I'm nervous about speaking in Italian, but it's the mere presence of this guy that has turned me into complete mush. He pours me a glass of red wine and our eyes meet as he hands it to me. His eyes are sharp and intense yet kind. I'm in awe of how relaxed and comfortable he is in his own skin.

'So how was your flight?' he asks, leaning slightly forward.

'It was great. About twenty-one hours.'

Could I be any more boring?

'You were going to tell me about your plans,' he says.

I'm quiet as my mind scrambles to find the right words. Finally, I reply, 'I guess I needed a change of scenery.'

'Well, the scenery's good here.' His mouth twists into a smile as he waits for my reaction.

Is it ever.

I take my third gulp of wine and feel my shoulders relax.

'*Salute!*' he says, raising his glass. 'Here's to good food, good wine, good scenery and the best Tuscan adventure of your life.'

'Cheers.' I smile, lifting my drink. Our eyes meet over the rims of our glasses, his gaze lingering on me long after I settle my wine back on the table. 'So what do you do?' I ask, relieved that I haven't lost my voice for good.

'I'm a mechanic,' he says. 'I have an *officina moto* with Paolo. We sell and service scooters and bikes.' He gives me a smirk. '*Australiani*! Always thinking about work. Most of you live to work, not work to live,' he says, his hands frantically trying to keep up with his mouth.

'What do you mean?' My interest is piqued.

'In Italy we live *la dolce vita*. The sweet life. We don't just go to work and come home, go to work and come home to then complain about work and how busy our lives are. *Prendiamo la vita come viene,*' he says.

'*Prendiamo*, what, sorry?'

'It means, "We take life as it comes." Just like what you plan on doing here.'

'Gotcha,' I whisper, staring over the green hills. 'Making room for the unexpected is good,' I add, nodding as I let out an unintentional sigh. There I go, drifting into that space between reality and my thoughts, a habit I've never been able to shake.

'*Esatto*! For example, what are you doing tomorrow night? Let me take you out.'

I snap out of my bubble and see that he's…

He's actually serious.

'Are you always this forward?' I ask, shifting in my seat.

'Do you have other plans?'

'Um, no… but…'

'*Allora, prendi la vita come viene,*' he teases. So, take life as it comes.

I can't help laughing.

'Be careful of this one,' warns Stella as she places the freshly sliced bread on the table and nudges my shoulder.

I reach for my wine again and find I've almost finished my glass.

'More wine?' Luca asks, smiling. I'm certain my complete inelegance is amusing him.

'Oh, no thanks,' I reply too late. My glass is now full again.

Thankfully, the topic of conversation switches to food and soon the three of them are all too keen to educate me on today's menu in a fiery and passionate conversation about the origins of each dish on our table. The tomatoes come from Stella's kitchen garden and the olive oil from Paolo's uncle's most recent olive harvest last October.

'Why is it so green?' I ask.

Paolo explains that olives harvested early produce a greener and slightly bitter extra-virgin oil. Then Luca tells me about the fresh *mozzarella di bufala*. Although I'm as familiar with this cheese as any of them, I'm still captivated when he tells me it's made from the milk of water buffalos, which have lived in the hills of Campania, near Naples, for hundreds of years. Their milk is heated so that the curds separate from the whey, before being added to hot water until the cheese is ready to stretch and form into mozzarella balls, which are later immersed in whey liquid to keep them fresh.

I find it ironic that I'm in gastronomic heaven with a decreased appetite. Stella piles an enormous heap of pasta onto my plate, and I know there's no way I'll be able to finish it. She tells me about the simple pleasure of a *scarpetta*. 'This is where you take a piece of bread and relish the remaining pasta sauce on your plate. It's better for the dishwasher,' she jokes. When she sees that my plate is still half full I realise that despite my phenomenal effort, I've just subjected myself to a scurry of questions from Luca and Paolo about whether or not the meal was good.

Note to self: insist on smaller portions next time.

I'm grateful when Stella interjects with a one-word question: '*Caffè?*' to which the boys reply with a resounding yes. Of course.

I help Stella clear the table, but she doesn't let me wash the dishes. Instead, she tells me I can make the coffee. She goes to the cellar to hunt for some *liquore* to have with our espresso because the boys take their coffee *corretto*, which she explains is essentially an espresso with a splash of alcohol like sambuca or grappa. I hunt around for a coffee machine, but the only thing I can see on the bench are pots and pans, and handcrafted wooden spoons hanging from the tiled splashback. And then I see the same kind of aluminium moka pot that I remember from my Nonna Lina's kitchen. I unscrew the upper part and fill the base with water. I find the ground coffee beans in an elaborately hand-painted majolica canister and breathe in their delicious aroma. As I pat down a few spoonfuls of coffee into the strainer, I feel a presence. I don't need to turn around to see who it is because I already recognise his unforgettable scent.

'Here, let me show you, Australiana,' he says, taking the moka pot from me, his hand briefly brushing mine, the contact sending waves of butterflies through my stomach. 'If you pat it down too firmly like this, the water won't come out properly and the coffee will be burnt.'

'Ah, I remember now,' I say, nodding. 'My *nonna* used to remind me about that.'

'You're from an Italian background?'

'Yes, my dad's side, actually. He was born in Italy, but his family moved to Australia when he was very young. That's how I was able to get an Italian passport.'

'Ah. My dad was born in America,' he says, which explains his accent and his excellent English. '*Allora parli italiano?*'

Do I speak Italian? Oh gosh.

'A little bit. *Poco, poco,*' I say, in an attempt to exercise my cursory knowledge of Italian.

'So, did you come here to study Italian?'

'Not exactly… it's kind of complicated. I was going to study at university but I decided to defer my studies.'

'What were you going to study?'

'Art,' I reply, hoping he'll leave it at that.

He raises his eyebrows. 'You're an artist?' He sounds intrigued.

'Well, kind of, I suppose. I love to paint.'

Loved to paint. Not so sure anymore.

'Well, you're in the best place in Italy for that,' he says, turning away to check the coffee. 'I know where to take you tomorrow night.'

I study his profile, completely fascinated. He's so sure of himself.

'I never said I was free.'

'Oh, so you're busy?' He lifts the lid of the moka pot.

'No, but—'

'Then *si*, just say *si*.' He turns to me as he breaks into a smile, his eyebrows raised. '*E prendi la vita come viene.*'

I laugh. '*Si.* Yes. Okay.'

CHAPTER THREE

Four Years Earlier

At the sound of knocking on my bedroom door, I poked my head up over my quilt and forced my eyes open.

'You can't keep sleeping your days away like this, Mia. We've got an appointment—you need to get up,' said Mum. She ripped the covers off me, wincing when she found me curled up in the foetal position.

'No more doctors. Please, Mum.'

'It's not a doctor. Wear something comfortable.' She turned around and went to leave the room.

'Wait, where are we going?'

She turned back to face me. 'There's someone I want you to meet. She's a friend of a friend. I think she can help.'

'She can't,' I said, pulling the covers up to my chin.

'Mia, you think this is easy for me? To see you like this? Can't you see I'm trying to help you? Just let me in, trust me... for once.'

I sighed deeply. 'Who is she?'

'Her name's Sarah.'

'Therapist?'

'Meditation teacher.'

I rolled my eyes and flopped my head back onto the pillow. 'Mum, are you kidding me?'

'She's a warrior, too. Complete remission. Twelve years.'

'Good for her,' I said, staring at the ceiling.

'We need to stay positive, Mia.'

I sat up and looked her straight in the eyes. She swallowed hard, avoiding eye contact. I ran my fingers through my hair, effortlessly loosening strands from my head. I extended my arms out to Mum, the clump of hair hanging limply from my fingers. Mum simply stared, blinking at the orphaned strands.

'Adam, can you please come in here?' she called to my dad.

She stepped closer to me, and I noticed for the first time the way her clothes no longer fit her; they hung off her almost non-existent curves. Her eyes had become scored with extra creases around their edges. She sat down beside me and tried to hold my hands, but I pulled them away and ran them over my hair again, latching onto more clumps. I shook my head and balled up my fists. Something in me tightened, and through tears I yelled, 'How am I supposed to stay positive when this is happening to me?!'

The colour disappeared from her face and her hands rose to her temples.

I continued, 'This is what happens when you're dying from—'

'Stop! I don't want to hear it, Mia!' Tears pooled in her eyes.

I gasped, cupping my hands over my mouth. 'Is this how you think it's going to end? You don't believe I'm going to make it, do you?' When she didn't answer, I raised myself up to her level. 'Do you? When you sneak in here at night, looking at me while you think I'm asleep, you're just watching me to ensure that each breath won't be my last, that you can remember what this room looks like once the bed is empty. You don't even believe I can beat—'

'That's enough, Mia,' said my dad. He was standing in the doorway to my bedroom, toothbrush in his hand.

I averted my gaze and Mum straightened. She slid her hands across the sheets as she gathered the loose strands of hair between her fingers. Then she reached for my hands, pried my fingers open, and took away the clumps of hair that I was still holding onto. She got up and placed my hair in the wastebasket with such gentleness, you'd be fooled into thinking there was nothing destructive about the way they'd fallen out in the first place. Then she left the room, avoiding my dad's gaze on the way out.

'Get dressed, pumpkin,' he said. 'I'm taking the day off work. We'll do something nice after your appointment.'

I reached for a tissue, blew my nose and nodded. He left the room, following Mum down the hallway. A moment later I heard her let out a deep moan. The bathroom door clicked shut behind them.

Without bothering to dress, I headed for the kitchen. I was about to flick the switch on the blender—pre-loaded with the 'most amazing cancer-fighting' fruits and vegetables my mum had ever read about and insisted I drink in a smoothie that looked like it had been dredged up from a swamp each morning—when I caught my dad's raised voice carrying through the house.

I left the kitchen and stood on the other side of the bathroom door, frozen.

'You need to get yourself together, Julie! You're scaring her!'

'You think I don't know that? Do you think I'm not trying? Every time I look into those eyes and see sadness staring back at me, knowing that I can't do anything to make this better for her, I break. I break because all I want to do is hold her in my arms and kiss it better. That's what mothers are supposed to do. And I hate that I can't do that for her.'

'You *have* to find a way to be strong for her. You have to show her there's still hope.'

'How much hope can I have when my one and only daughter is wilting away? The withdrawal from it all, everything and everyone—the painting, her friends, you, me. It's killing…'

There was a long pause.

'You have to keep believing, Julie. If you don't, how will Mia? The stats are on our side. She's going to get through this.'

'How am *I* going to get through this if she doesn't?'

The house grew quiet. I wanted to walk away because I didn't want to hear his answer; I didn't want to think about what it might be like for them if I died, but I couldn't seem to move. It was like I'd been pierced with the numbing reality of what was actually happening to me, to them, to us.

'I don't know,' said Dad. This was what hurt the most—that he didn't know. He was supposed to know; he was the one who always had the answers.

Then the words became muffled, and I couldn't understand anything else until my mum opened the door to find me standing there. I looked past her tear-stained face to my dad, who stood there in his pyjama bottoms, electric razor buzzing in his hand.

An uncomfortable silence weaved its way between us until he held my eyes with his. He smiled. It was the kind of smile that was steeped in the deepest kind of love a parent has for their child. He switched off the razor and walked towards me. Taking one of my hands in his, he gazed at me with an unbearable look of desperation and said, 'We need you to fight, Mia.' He pulled me close and held me so tightly I could hardly breathe. When his hand touched the patch of bald skin on the back of my head, he buried his face in my neck. 'Just a few more rounds, pumpkin, and this will all be over.'

That morning, I agreed to attend my first meditation class with Sarah. The centre, located in the foothills of the Dandenong Ranges surrounded by mountain ash trees stretching up towards the sky, was quiet except for the calming music that was coming from a nearby room. I looked at my dad as he raised his eyebrows, and I couldn't help flashing him an amused smile. Sarah appeared and clapped her hands together.

'Ready to turn your eye inward?'

I shrugged. 'I guess so.'

'Come, I want to show you something.'

She led me to a garden fringed with sprawling tree ferns, and motioned for me to sit on a wooden bench. I waited for her to speak, but she didn't. I pulled my beanie over my ears and waited, my frustration escalating with each minute that passed. My thoughts twined themselves into a rope that knotted itself in my stomach, and when I could no longer feel my fingers and toes, I went to speak, except Sarah raised a finger to her mouth and the silence continued. I shifted my weight on the bench and sat on my hands in an effort to keep them still.

Eventually, Sarah stood up. 'You can go home now, kiddo.'

I felt my face twisting into confusion. 'But I thought…'

'That's the point.' She flashed me a hint of a smile. 'See you next week?'

'Yeah, sure.'

Over the next three months, I grew to look forward to my sessions with Sarah.

'You know the drill, Mia,' said Sarah one afternoon in the meditation centre.

I sat on my cushion, closed my eyes and started inhaling deeply the way she'd taught me.

'Breathing in through the nose and out through the mouth… Feel your body relaxing with every inhale. On the exhale, imagine your breath is releasing any worries or tension you might be feeling—let it all go with the breath.'

I let all the thoughts—large and small—of life and death and everything in between drift by with the smallest flicker of attention. I liked how the whole meditation thing helped with that.

'Now that you're completely relaxed, I'd like you to imagine yourself sitting on a lush green carpet of grass. It's a bright and sunny day and you can feel the warmth of the sun's rays on your skin. When you're ready, I want you to feel into your life as it is now. How do you feel?'

Empty.

'Can you name any of the emotions you're feeling?'

Sad. Scared. Lost.

'Now keep your eyes closed and continue breathing.'

Slowly, the image of two male hands appeared, their fingers pointing towards each other, not quite touching. I knew I'd seen this image somewhere before and that it was part of something bigger, but this perplexing thought drifted away when one of the hands reached out for mine. A feeling of complete safety and peace washed over me before the hand dissipated into nothing and then I was overcome with a strong desire to move towards it, long after it had gone.

That's when I remembered where the image was from. Michelangelo's *The Creation of Adam*.

I kept my eyes closed and imagined myself stepping through a door and into an airport. I looked down at my hands to find a boarding card with my name on it but without a destination. When I looked up, I suddenly found myself outside again, only I was now surrounded by hills dotted with olive trees and farmhouses that backed onto rows of vineyards. I turned around, trying to find some other clue of where I was, and then I saw it: a panoramic view of Florence, Italy.

'When you're ready, wriggle your toes and open your eyes,' instructed Sarah.

I turned around for one last glimpse of something that felt so distant yet so real and so comforting.

'So, how was it, Mia?'

'It was... amazing,' I said, stretching my legs. 'This might sound crazy, but I think I want to go to Italy.'

'Italy?' She smiled in surprise.

'Well, Florence, to be exact. After they give me the all-clear. If they give me the all-clear.'

I'd never wanted the all-clear as much as I wanted it right then.

By the time I'd battled it out for my last round of treatment, I tried to paint again. But no matter how hard I tried to dip into the right colours, my brush wanted to do other things. The only images that reflected back at me were formless dark shapes and shadows that were painted by a completely different version of myself—one I was scared could no longer recognise the pre-cancer version of Mia. One day after painting a completely horrifying swath of greys, I slammed my brushes down and pushed my easel over with such force that I stumbled and tripped and couldn't find the energy to get up again. As I lay there with my cheek to the floorboards, I thought that this was it; there was nothing left of me if I couldn't paint again.

My mum rushed in and dropped to her knees beside me. 'Did you fall? Tell me where it hurts.'

'Nowhere,' I said. The truth was that it hurt everywhere. She helped me sit up. My hands slid through the mess of wet paint as I scrambled for my brushes and held them tightly to my chest as though I was trying to channel one small glimpse of what life used to feel like.

My mum looked at me with scared, sad eyes and told me that she'd take care of the mess.

I brought my knees up to my chest, buried my head in my hands and yelled, 'I don't want you to take care of it, Mum! I don't want you to have to fix this! I have to fix this.' I just didn't know how to fix any of it. My mum winced at my words. 'Mum… I'm sorry.'

'Here,' she said, handing me a brush.

She took a cloth and started wiping the paint from my forearm before moving to each finger. I watched her wipe away every trace of paint, giving this task the kind of attention she might have given a younger version of myself when I came to her with a grazed knee or a superficial burn. I wasn't a mother, but in that moment she showed me what it meant to be one, and I became aware of how brilliantly she succeeded at being the best kind. When her fingers wrapped themselves around my wrist and put cloth to skin, I felt better, if only for a fleeting second. Here was my mum, conscripted to a life full of uncertainty, where she had no choice except to play the alternating roles of mother, wife, therapist, nurse, chauffeur and constant punching bag, all the while trying to maintain some shred of hope that I'd live to see my next birthday.

'You do make it better,' I whispered.

She folded the cloth and started hiccupping in silence, her chest rising and falling in an attempt to fight back the tears. She looked up at the ceiling as if she was drawing strength from above and then she brought her fingers to her lips, as if she was thinking about what to say to me.

'You don't need to say anything. I just wanted you to know,' I said.

CHAPTER FOUR

Stella potters around the garden while I fight the urge to nap and instead get ready for my first outing to Impruneta at a leisurely pace. After pinning back a handful of hair so it's out of my face, I put some makeup on for the first time in months, letting the artificial colour dusted onto my cheeks bring me partly back to life.

I grab my large-brimmed hat and make my way down the villa's pebbled driveway. Stopping halfway down the steep hill, I sit on the wall, admiring the country view, while my fingers rest on the warm stone. Here I am, upholding my end of the bargain in honouring my intuition, unable to fully explain what I expect from this adventure, but ready for whatever life might bring here. Awkwardly trusting, as I allow whatever glimmer of hope I have left to reignite my passion for life. My thoughts drift to what they usually do: worries about life expectancy.

It should be easy to focus on the survival rate for Hodgkin's disease, but it's not. The statistics haunt me like a dark grey cloud looming above my head, ready to burst open, showering my body with acid rain at any given moment. Let's face it: the statistics haven't really been on my side, given I developed lymphoma in the first place, only to relapse a year after the doctors told me I was in remission. After an autologous stem cell transplant and recovery following that, I was finally given the okay to travel, almost four years after my initial diagnosis at the tail end of my last year of high school.

I start to focus on my breath, just like Sarah taught me. *Breathe in, hold the breath... and release*, and eventually the thoughts evaporate. Approaching the town centre in my somewhat relaxed state, all I can hear is the buzz of the odd scooter and the curious little three-wheel trucks called *api* that rattle by every so often.

A warm northerly breeze brushes my skin, dislodging wisps of hair that dance around my face as I drink in the seconds of what is right now. I hear Sarah's words echoing in my head: *Mia, just focus on the present, because this is what really matters.* My heart expands and an immense sensation of gratitude washes over me. Right now, I am not just a girl who has overcome her battle with cancer. I am not a girl who doesn't know who she is anymore. I am not a girl whose nightmares wake her at night with the terrifying feeling that she might not live to see her next birthday. In this moment, I am just *me*. I find myself singing out loud until a sky-blue Fiat Cinquecento zips past.

As I approach the piazza, the smooth asphalted road turns into cobblestoned one-way streets. It's just before four o'clock, and the sleepy town is waking up for the afternoon as the shop merchants of Piazza Buondelmonti hoist up the metal roller doors to their shopfronts, ready for the second half of the day's trading. People venture into the main square after their naps, having pulled down their shutters at midday for the *riposo*.

Vintage cruiser bikes are lined up in a row beside the large basilica. It's Tuesday, and people of all ages are filtering out from the afternoon mass, congregating in small groups. The passionate rise and fall of the Italian language carries through the air. Between the men smoking cigars and the young children kicking a soccer ball in the middle of the piazza, I'm unsure of which group to watch first. I'm intrigued by them all: their mannerisms, their appearance, their accents.

The priest trails behind the last group of churchgoers and begins his own animated chat with a few of them under one of the five large arches. The Basilica of Santa Maria, according to my *Fodor's*, dates all the way back to 1060 and was restored after a bombing destroyed its baroque ceiling during the Second World War. I'm at my most comfortable amongst artwork, and, used to the silence of my own company, I easily spend an hour here, taking in the basilica's rich history and beauty. A fleeting thought about the future passes in my mind as I wonder whether studying at the Academy of Art in Florence might one day be a possibility for me. Thinking too far into the future sends an uncomfortable feeling into the pit of my stomach. Trying my best to ignore it, I make my way to the church exit. A strong feeling wills me to turn back.

'If you're unsure of any emotion or feeling, just sit with it,' Sarah would say.

I take a seat in the back pew and sit in silence, the uncomfortable feeling growing stronger with each passing second. It doesn't dissipate until I acknowledge what it is that I'm feeling. I think about the battle I was forced to fight, and like a pipe that's bursting with anger, something in me unlocks. I want my life to feel the way it *used* to feel: full of possibility, untarnished by fear. I feel an intense need to get back to that, except I don't know how. Tears start pouring out of me as if the heavens have burst, staining my face and tickling my neck as they slide past my collarbone onto my cotton shirt. By some unknown force, I'm brought to my knees. I drop my head into my hands, my spirit grieving for what should have been one of the best years of my life. I sob and sob and sob for what was ripped away from me, and as I break down in the privacy of this holy space, I look at Jesus, fixed to the crucifix, palms bleeding, head drooping, and beg for myself back.

'Show me the way,' I whisper.

I wipe my face against the clammy skin of my arm and take a few minutes to compose myself. The priest, who has been watching me, dressed in his cream-and-gold-embellished robe, cautiously shuffles towards me.

'Are you okay, *signorina*?' he asks, his eyes trying to meet mine.

I nod because the words are too hard to find, especially if I have to find them in Italian. He passes me a tissue, which I graciously accept. I clean myself up, blow my nose and see that he's still waiting for an answer. My mouth opens and closes, only no sounds come out. He rests the weight of his small, bony hand on my shoulder.

'I'm Father Damiano,' he says.

I place my palms together and nod, the only way I can express my thanks right now. And then I turn my back on the father and rush out the doors, hoping my prayer will be answered.

Sarah always said there'd come a time when I'd admit my feelings to myself even if I wasn't yet ready to talk with her or anyone else about them. 'When that happens, honey, you'll know you're on the road to healing what's causing you all that pain in your heart.'

I find a fountain in the square and splash the cool water on my face, washing away the residual streaks of tears and any last traces of makeup. I don't feel like going home yet, so I figure it might be a good time to grab a coffee. The seats outside the bar are mainly occupied by men wearing flat caps, blissfully people-watching or playing a heated game of cards. They don't look like regular playing cards, and I recognise one of the games they're playing: Scopa. My Nonno Aldo taught me to play Scopa with his deck of Sicilian playing cards when I was eight years old. He let me win every time because I'd throw the most livid tantrums whenever I lost.

I take a deep breath and ask the barman for a cappuccino in my rusty Italian.

'Cappuccino is for breakfast!' he teases. 'You foreigners, you drink *caffèlatte* in the afternoon. This is like eating Coco Pops for dinner,' he says, chuckling.

Point taken. Short macchiatos from now on.

The barman is probably in his mid-forties and reminds me of an animated Roberto Benigni from *Life Is Beautiful*.

'Ah, *sì*. Could you change that to a *macchiato, per favore*?' I ask, trying to act as local as possible.

'*Come ti chiami, bella*?'

'My name's Mia.'

'Silvio,' he says, breaking into a friendly smile as he points to his badge. 'Nice to meet you, Mia. Let me guess, I bet you're from America.' He raises his eyebrows. 'Chicago!'

I shake my head.

He purses his lips, pretending to think. 'Los Angeles!'

Again, I shake my head. I'm smiling now.

'New York!' His eyes are alight with humour.

A barman steps out from the kitchen and twirls Silvio around.

'Aah! "New York, New York!"' He breaks out into the famous Frank Sinatra tune.

'Matteo, this is Mia—she's from…' Silvio winks. Matteo has white hair and looks as though he should be at home and in retirement, even though he has the moves of a twenty-five-year-old.

'Melbourne,' I reply, finishing Silvio's sentence.

'Australia? Now that's a long way from here.' Silvio rubs his chin.

'Pleasure to meet you. Are you enjoying your holiday?' asks Matteo.

'I only just got here, but so far so good,' I reply.

'We know the ones like you, Signorina Mia. Just wait until you fall in love,' teases Silvio, as if he's seen my life played out before him.

I smile politely and tell him I'm not looking for love right now.

'Ah, but you haven't gotten to know the irresistible Luca yet,' he says, winking at Matteo.

Their small-town behaviour is amusing, yet I nonetheless feel my embarrassment escalating as my cheeks flush until they're prickling hot. Surely they can't be talking about the same Luca. My irrational heart sinks at the thought of him being the local heartbreaker. It would be just my luck to fall for the wrong guy. Without letting the conversation get any more uncomfortable, I go to sit down before remembering Stella's words cautioning me about not sitting at a table unless I'm ordering a meal. She's right; everyone around me is drinking their espressos at the bar, standing up.

'Actually, I'll also have a… *piadina*,' I say, pointing to the nearest thing I can find in the window. It looks like my early dinner is going to be a flatbread sandwich with cheese, prosciutto and rocket salad. I hate the bitterness of rocket salad.

'Toasted?' asks Silvio.

'*Sì, grazie.*'

I wait for my *piadina* at a small uneven table overlooking the buzzing piazza and its honey-coloured buildings. I make the connection between *macellaio* and butcher, *erboristeria* and herbalist store, *salumeria* and delicatessen. Pulling out my pink-and-grey Moleskine, I scribble down these new words.

Across the square is a motorbike workshop that hasn't yet opened for the afternoon. A large scooter pulls up in front of it. It's a cherry-red Piaggio. The broad shoulders of the rider look familiar. He takes off his helmet and there's no mistaking him. Luca. Town Casanova. He's now wearing a pair of dark jeans and a tight-fitting black T-shirt that accentuates the muscles of his sun-kissed arms. He hasn't seen me yet, but he's walking towards the bar.

I stare down at my notebook when I sense him approaching, looking up only when he stops in front of me.

'*Bella* Mia, *buonasera*,' he says in a delicious tone, tilting his head slightly, his eyes on my half-eaten *piadina*.

Is it totally Australian to be eating a piadina *at five in the afternoon?*

He grins at me and our eyes lock, a magnetic force holding them in place. The world closes in around the two of us. My heartbeat quickens, and I unwillingly tear my gaze away from him as my lips purse together.

Mia, just breathe.

'Silvio giving you trouble?' he asks.

'*Salve*, Luca,' says Silvio.

Salve. Just another word for *ciao*. Another word for the Moleskine.

'Silvio,' he nods, '*un caffettino per favore*.' He pulls up a chair beside me.

I guess rules can be broken.

'Wasn't it any good?' asks Silvio, appearing concerned that I've left most of the *piadina* on my plate alongside a pile of untouched rocket.

'It was great, but I'm a little full. We had a big lunch.'

'You eat like a sparrow,' says Luca, leaning forward in his chair. 'Silvio, this is Mia, Stella's new housemate. The one I was telling you about.'

'I know. We already met,' he says. 'He couldn't stop talking about you, Mia!' he calls as he walks away, carrying a full tray of plates and cups.

Luca grins and raises his eyebrows.

Does nothing faze this guy?

'You were talking about me?' I challenge. I can't seem to help it, I want to shake his confidence somewhat.

'You're hard not to talk about.'

I almost choke on my saliva, and my mind scrambles as I try to find something to say. 'So… you work over there?' I ask, pointing across the street.

He doesn't follow the direction of my hand; he just nods with a cool expression on his face.

'Uh... do you live close by?' I ask.

Silvio returns to the table with Luca's espresso. 'We don't do table service, you know. But I'll make an exception for you today, seeing as you're in the presence of a *bella donna*.' He winks at me as though we're old friends.

Luca throws back his espresso in one shot. 'Not too far from here. I share an apartment with Paolo. I moved to Florence when I was eighteen. I've been here five years.' He pauses, his eyes travelling across my face. I'm sure he's studying every detail of the redness in my eyes and the puffiness in my cheeks.

'Are you okay?' he asks, frowning suspiciously.

'I'm fine. Must be allergies.'

He gives me a slow nod that says, 'I know you're lying,' but he goes with it and points out that there's a *farmacia* across the road.

'Where are you originally from?' I ask.

'Orvieto. There's not much work there, so when Paolo asked me to join him in the *officina* I decided to move here,' he says.

'Do you miss your family?' I ask, thinking about my parents and how far away they are.

In the blink of an eye his expression hardens as he clenches his jaw. 'More than you can imagine. My parents were both killed last year in a car accident. Drunk driver. My sister lives in Orvieto with her husband and my two young nephews. I don't see them much these days.'

I don't know how I feel about him sharing intimate details of a life I don't yet feel privileged to know about. The whole conversation makes me uneasy. 'I'm sorry to hear about your parents. That must be really hard.'

'It's life, I guess. It can be ripped away from us at any given moment, for no good reason at all,' he says, spinning his cup on its saucer.

Boy, don't I know it.

My heart goes out to him. '*Prendi la vita come viene,*' I whisper.

'Every day, as if it's your last.' He leans across the table, takes my hand and plants a kiss on it. '*Bella* Mia, I need to open up the shop.' And with that he gets up from the table. 'Don't go meeting any handsome Italian guys between now and tomorrow night,' he warns in a voice so smooth I want to bottle it up.

By now he's walking backwards across the street as he calls out, 'Seven! Your place!'

I can't help laughing.

Yes, this is what it feels like to laugh again, Mia.

'*É cotto!*' exclaims Silvio from behind our table. I have no idea what that means, but I scrawl the words in my Moleskine so I can look it up later.

I do know what '*mia*' means and I do know what '*bella*' means. Together, they mean 'my beauty', or in the case of my name, 'beautiful Mia'. From the intonation of Luca's voice I know he means the latter, although I can't help admitting to myself that I wouldn't mind the former.

I spend the next hour or so exploring the shops, quaint streets and alleys before heading home, where I find Stella preparing *panzanella*, a typical Tuscan salad made with pieces of tomato and soaked stale bread. I help her throw in some red onion, cucumber and basil, and we sit down to eat at eight thirty. I force what I can down since I already had an early dinner in town. She tells me I'll need to get used to late dinners this summer. Afterwards, we retire to the sofas to watch a game show with numerous glittering dancers dressed in skimpy clothing.

'Discreet,' I say, raising my eyebrows.

'Mmmhmm,' she says, rolling her eyes. 'More wine?'

'No thanks, I'm pretty tired. I'll be heading to bed soon. It's been a big day,' I say, yawning.

'What did you think of the town centre?'

'It was… nice. Actually, I bumped into Luca again.' I picture his beautiful face. 'What does "*è cotto*" mean?'

'It's cooked.'

'Huh?'

'It also means… Oh, Mia!' she says, eyes widening. 'I *knew* it!'

'Knew what?'

'It means he's smitten. A crush! I can't believe it—I've been trying to set Luca up with girls from work for months. He hasn't been interested in anyone. Not since…'

I wait for her to continue, but when she doesn't, I finish the sentence for her. 'His parents?'

'What? He told you about his parents?'

'Yes.' I nod. 'Why?'

'He never talks about it. With anyone. Ever. He took it pretty hard. It's been difficult to watch. You know what Italian families are like—very close. He used to go home every month to visit his parents, but he hasn't been back since the funeral,' she says. 'Who told you he was *cotto*?'

'Silvio. Barman guy. He reminds me of Roberto Benigni.'

'Ha! Totally!' She laughs.

'We're going out tomorrow night.'

'You're going to love Italy, Mia. I just know it,' she says, rubbing my leg affectionately. She switches off the TV and turns to face me, her eyes sparkling. 'I had a good feeling about you, you know.'

'That's good, because I thought the same about you,' I say, choosing not to tell her that I'd made a list of local hotels before I arrived in case I didn't like what I found here at the villa.

I retreat to my bedroom, flop onto my bed and switch on my phone.

Mum has sent me a message asking if I've managed to get a SIM card yet.

I can't wait to hear your voice again. How is it there?

Better than I could have imagined. Look at the furniture, I respond, attaching a photo of the living-room furnishings. I try not to think about how Mum had to put her interior design business on hold because of me when I got sick.

Love! That light fixture! The wall art! Imagine all the things you'll be able to paint over there! (If you let yourself try.) I packed two boxes of paint sets for you. Bottom of your suitcase. Make sure you unpack!

She follows this with a series of messages telling me how much she loves me, how much she misses me and how much she wishes she could be here with me. I choke back the lump in my throat. I miss her, too. I just don't know how to say it. So I text back, *I love you too, Mum*, and hope that it's enough for now.

I get changed, slip under the sheets and rest my head on the pillow. My mind drifts to a certain dark and handsome guy. For the first time in months, I'm asleep within minutes, the last thought that enters my mind one of hope, not fear.

CHAPTER FIVE

The unmistakable sound of roosters crowing wakes me just before six in the morning. I'd usually resent the sound of farm animals waking me at the crack of dawn, but I'm as fresh as a set of clean sheets this morning, having slept through the night without my usual nightmare.

'Okay, so Italian breakfast—you have two choices here. Breakfast cookies or a Kinder Colazione,' says Stella, tossing me a bar that resembles a sponge cake.

'Any chance of something a little more savoury?'

'You could try these,' she says, handing me a packet of toast-like crackers called *fette biscottate*, which are so bland that I end up reaching for the jar of Nutella to make them more palatable.

'Sweet it is,' I say, shrugging my shoulders.

Stella fumbles around in a drawer and hands me a map of Florence. 'You can get your bus ticket on board or from the local *tabaccaio* in the piazza.' She explains that the local tobacconist in Italy sells more than just cigarettes: stamps, postcards, lotto and bus tickets. 'There's a shop at the end of the piazza where you can buy a SIM for your phone.' When she offers to meet me for lunch during her break, I tell her not to worry. I have some other plans in mind.

There's no point in venturing out yet, so I spend some time flicking between TV channels before I take a book out to the garden, losing myself amongst the pages of a previously untouched copy of Natasha Lester's *The Paris Secret*. Once the traffic begins to pick up on the main road, I prepare my portable sketch box easel and tuck my pad of watercolour paper into my satchel. My mind wanders to the last attempts I made at painting after I had finished the chemotherapy, which feels so very long ago now. Before I received my diagnosis, a painting I'd been working on as part of my art unit at school, *The Floating Leaf*, was one of forty-two pieces selected to be featured in the National Gallery of Victoria's StArt Up: Top Arts exhibition. My painting, which explored the relationship between nature and our emotions, caught the eye of one of the gallery curators, who invited me to show her my future work for consideration in a forthcoming exhibition. Only, by then, I had become incapable of producing the usual artwork that inspired me. The style of my paintings had changed, from work that generally incorporated smooth lines and gentle brushstrokes to work that was monstrous: dark, heavy, sombre. It frightened me, and after several failed attempts at painting, I eventually stopped altogether.

I lock the door behind me and consider going back to return my art supplies, but I know that if I want any hope of getting Mia back, I have to take this step. After I follow Stella's instructions and organise my new SIM from the phone store, I head to the bar. My eyes scan the *officina* across the square for a glimpse of Luca.

The mere thought of him makes my cheeks flush. I haven't felt emotion like this in so long, and the intensity of it reminds me that I'm alive and that it is possible to feel again. There's no sign of Luca; however, I can see Paolo having a lively conversation on the phone complemented by elaborate hand gestures.

The smell of fresh *cornetti* wafts from the bar full of locals, who stand against the counter waiting for their first shots of coffee for the day. Silvio greets me with a bubbly, '*Buongiorno*, Mia!' as if we're now the best of friends and it's been a lifetime since we've last seen each other. A familiar body turns around to face me at the sound of my name. He grins. I melt.

Luca's lips twist into an irresistible smile. '*Ciao, bella* Mia.'
So. Incredibly. Charming.

I'm holding my breath. His eyes are staring right through me, pinning me so intensely that I can't look away.

'*Ciao,*' I reply quietly.

'*Caffè?*' he asks.

'Uh, yes please.'

'*Silvio, un cappuccino per la signorina.*' He takes the liberty of ordering for me.

They don't call it a romance language for nothing.

'*Grazie.*'

'You're welcome. So, what are you up to today?' he asks, glancing at the easel I'm carrying over my shoulder.

'Well, I can hear the Piazza del Duomo, Santa Croce and Piazza della Repubblica all calling my name,' I say, feeling proud of the amount of information I've retained from my handy pocket guide to Florence.

'Wait, what about the Ponte Vecchio?' he says.

'The Ponte Vecchio?' The name doesn't ring any bells.

'The Old Bridge. The famous Florentine bridge! Over the Arno River,' he says.

'Oh, right… I'll make sure I look for it.'

'It's only one of the most romantic spots in Florence,' he adds casually. 'I'll have to take you there sometime.' He pauses, waiting to see my reaction.

I'm lost for words, my attention turning to the fluttering in my stomach. Luca and the word 'romantic' cause me to blush yet again.

'You're blushing, Australiana,' he smirks.

I purse my lips together and shyly look away.

'So you're going to do some painting, too?' he asks, pointing to my easel.

'Uh. Yeah. I'm going to try.'

'What do you paint?'

'Mainly watercolour, sometimes oil. It's been a while since I...' My voice trails off, and I wish I could take back the words.

He looks at me curiously, squinting as though he's trying to work out the meaning behind what I've just said.

'I took a bit of a break from painting, so things are a little dusty,' I add, shrugging my shoulders.

'Word is that Picasso once said that the purpose of art is to wash the dust of daily life off our souls.'

'Really? He said that?' I feel myself smiling at him. Somehow I'm not surprised he would know this.

'Yes, he did.'

'Well, I hope he was right,' I murmur.

I finish my cappuccino and then he says, 'Let me walk you to the bus stop.'

'Oh, it's fine,' I say, amused by his tenacity. The bus stop is less than a hundred metres away and he knows it.

'Let's go,' he says, winking. He places his hand on the small of my back as he guides me out of the busy bar, his touch sending warmth through my entire body.

We walk to the bus stop, and he warns me to be careful of pickpockets. He asks for my phone number, and when he's recorded it in his phone, he sends me a text message so that I have his in case I get lost, and then he waits until my bus arrives. 'Have a good day,' he says softly, his lips brushing my cheek.

Gucci by Gucci Pour Homme. Heaven.

'You too...' I reply, still thinking about how that just felt.

'Don't forget about tonight!' he calls as I step onto the bus.

No chance.

I take a window seat and can't help smiling. Luca occupies my thoughts for the entire trip into Florence as I daydream about what could be. And in the most bittersweet way, it scares me.

I disembark close to the Piazza del Duomo along with most of the other passengers. The square is swarming with tourists, locals riding bicycles and pristinely dressed traffic police strolling around in groups of three. Facing the huge Cathedral of Santa Maria del Fiore, referred to by Italians as 'the Duomo', I let out a gasp. I can't believe I'm really here. I venture over to the octagonal Baptistery of Saint John, which dates back to 1059. Its sophisticated Florentine Romanesque style is mesmerising, as are its three bronze doors, but I'm especially drawn to the *Gates of Paradise*, as coined by Michelangelo. These doors on the east side of the baptistery particularly intrigue me. This masterpiece tells the story of Adam and Eve and took Ghiberti a mere twenty plus years to finish. I spend the next hour or so studying every superb detail of the artwork in the church, pulling myself away only when I hear the mid-morning bells ringing from the adjacent Giotto's Bell Tower.

As I head down Via dei Calzaiuoli, one of Florence's most elegant and famous streets, I see rows of street sellers displaying imitation Prada bags alongside mass-produced prints of Raphael's signature cherubs. They appear in almost every Florentine street, on calendars, postcards, diaries and posters. It disappoints me to think that these adorable male *putti* have been taken from the larger painting of the *Sistine Madonna*, without acknowledging the much bigger work of art they belong to.

The cobblestones take a little getting used to, even if I am wearing flat sandals. Through windows illuminated with artificial light, I admire Furla handbags, handcrafted shoes by Ferragamo and the prettiest Austrian crystals in the Swarovski store. When I reach the end of the *via*, I find what I'm looking for. There it is, the statue of David, and to his right, the Uffizi Gallery. I soak in the beauty of this magnificent replica of the original statue and take a seat on the cool stone steps, where I observe silently, trying to decide whether certain parts of his anatomy are in fact out of proportion. Carved from a single block of marble, a frustrated Michelangelo was unable to reproduce one of the muscles in David's back due to an imperfection in the medium. Despite its flaw, this statue has been accepted for centuries as a symbol of perfect Renaissance art. Flawed yet still able to defeat Goliath. I'm tempted to visit the Uffizi Gallery, desperate to see Botticelli's *The Birth of Venus* amongst numerous other paintings I adore, but the queue is already enormous. On either side of the Piazza degli Uffizi, painters dip their brushes into pigment and layer by layer bring their depictions of Florence and Tuscany to life. Scenes of fields amassed with sunflowers, stone farmhouses amidst bales of hay and winding country paths. A watercolour of an antique bridge catches my eye.

'It's beautiful.'

'Thank you, *signorina*. It's the famous Ponte Vecchio, just around the corner,' says the man. 'You paint, too?' he asks, nodding at my easel. He's an old man, frail, possibly in his eighties, faultlessly dressed in a grey suit and tie with a white flat cap from which contrasting silver tufts of hair protrude. I can tell that in his youth he would have exuded a certain exuberance. His deep-blue eyes have a gentleness to them that intrigues me.

'I thought I'd try to,' I say.

'*Bene*. Straight down there you'll find the magnificent Arno. Turn right and you'll see the Ponte Vecchio,' he tells me in his Florentine accent.

I follow the man's directions. The bridge is dreamier and more captivating than Luca could have described. Rows of quaint jewellery stores are lined up on either side, one after the other. As I stroll along the gentle rise of cobblestones, I feel as though I've stepped into a different time and place in history. After taking in some of the details, I return to a quiet spot on the bank of the Arno and set up my easel. I spend some time studying the bridge's contrasting hues of yellow and sun-baked orange, its three lower arches and the rectangular and square mismatch of windows, most of which are fitted with rust and dark green wooden shutters. I carefully take out a sheet of paper, realising in this instant that I'm not so different from it. For a painter, the paper is an integral part of the work itself. White paper lends itself to the brightest images, and longevity is dependent on it being acid-free. My sick body was everything except white, bright and acid-free; however, today I am a clean sheet of paper, ready for a new picture, for a new story to be brought to life.

After such a long break from painting, my brush feels unnatural in my hands, so for several minutes I stand, simply playing around with it, running my thumb over the soft tuft. Then I close my eyes, sliding my dry brush over the paper, letting the rhythm come back to me. I centre myself with my breath, knowing that opening myself up to this fearful experience means that I'm upholding my end of the bargain in my quest to find myself again. I wet my brush and begin painting. My brushstrokes sweep across the paper, and in my mind, the soft sounds of 'shh, shh', repeat themselves, as if I'm lulling a baby to sleep, though in reality I'm willing the voice of self-doubt to quiet.

I slip into a meditative state; even though I can hear the French, German and English chatter of tourists around me, inside I am still. There are two lovers standing in the middle of the bridge, locked together in an embrace, watching the river flow. They come to life on my sheet, a snapshot of their love captured forever. Taking my time, I add more colour: browns, yellows, burnt oranges, and then finally a bright, clear sky-blue that promises no chance of showers. It's early afternoon by the time I finish. I take a step back to assess the picture I've created. My hands cup my mouth as I marvel at my work. It's anything but dark and sombre. It's a direct reflection of the love and beauty I witnessed today. An enormous sense of relief settles in my heart, lifting away months of doubt.

I pack up my gear, my heart bursting with a giant thank you to the universe for second chances and for the small part of myself that I rediscovered today. On the way back to the bus stop, I pass the painter near the Uffizi again. Most of the paintings that were on his stand this morning are no longer there, having been sold to eager tourists, keen to bring home a slice of Florence in watercolour.

He nods, recognising me. 'How did you do, *signorina*?' he asks with a gentleness that matches his facial expression.

'I'm Mia, by the way,' I say, extending my hand.

'Giovanni Fiorelli,' he says, reaching out a hand mottled with age spots.

'Lovely to meet you, Signor Fiorelli.'

'So, your painting. Was it all you'd hoped for?'

I nod thoughtfully. 'Yes… I think it was.'

'*Bene*,' he says as he slowly turns back to his work. I stand there, watching as Signor Fiorelli brings to life a bustling piazza of tourists with meticulous, confident brushstrokes. The central focus of his painting is the statue of David, but then I see a woman appearing. She's sitting at the café on the periphery of the piazza, reading a book. Although it's subtle, the attention of the painting is actually focused on her.

'Your work really is beautiful.'

'A lifetime of love,' he says casually, not lifting his gaze.

I slip away unnoticed, elated with how my first afternoon in Florence has unfolded. Inside I feel invigorated, as though something dormant has been stirred to life; I am, however, exhausted. I nod off to sleep on the bus ride home and am awoken by the sound of my phone ringing.

'*Pronto*! I just wanted to make sure you're okay. How's your day been?' Luca asks, his deep voice as smooth as honey. It feels as though we've known each other for a lifetime rather than the mere twenty-four hours since we met.

'I'm about to get off the bus. Lucky you called, because if you hadn't, I probably would have ended up back where I started. I fell asleep.'

He laughs. It's the first time I've heard him laugh and it makes me feel all kinds of happy.

'See you soon, painter girl,' he says, before the line goes silent.

Back at the villa, I find a note from Stella telling me she's working late tonight because she has to catch up on a heap of visa applications at the consulate.

It's a warm night so I opt for a dress and sandals. I try several updos before deciding on a low chignon with a side-swept front. I play around with the pillow until it's as perfect as I can get it. Deciding not to go overboard with makeup, I fumble through my beauty case for some lip gloss and mascara. I don't have time to find my perfume because the toot of the scooter tells me he's already here.

CHAPTER SIX

Straightening my shoulders, I tell myself I can do this. I really can do this.

I can't do this. What was I thinking when I decided to wear a dress?

I open the front door to see Luca leaning against the archway, legs crossed in his signature position, one hand in his pocket. I let the breezy summer air fill my lungs, and my mouth turns upwards into a smile. It's like I have no control over what I'm feeling right now, and I can't explain the logic, but he's more beautiful than he was this morning.

'*Buonasera, bella* Mia,' he says. Two kisses. One for each cheek.

He smells so good.

He's wearing a pair of cream capri pants and a melon-coloured twill shirt with rolled-up sleeves and he looks so… Italian.

'Ready to visit Firenze, City of Art, painter girl?'

'Yeah, sure. I'm just going to get changed first,' I say, pointing to my dress.

'*Ma sei bellissima,*' he says.

He thinks I look beautiful.

'I'll be back in a minute,' I say, turning around.

Luca reaches for my hand and twirls me around to face him. 'Mia, you're in Italy. Women here wear dresses and skirts much shorter than that one every day, even when they ride scooters,' he says, his eyes shifting to my legs. 'Besides, you've got very beautiful legs,' he murmurs, gazing back into my eyes.

I clear my throat. 'Fine. Where's the helmet?'

'That's the way, Australiana! You know, I've never dated an Australian girl before.'

'Who says we're dating?' I ask, almost dropping my helmet.

'Isn't this a date?' he counters innocently.

'I guess so…' I say, trying to keep a straight face. I can't help smiling back into those irresistible chestnut eyes as I return the stare. I put on my helmet in an effort to distract myself and end the conversation before it gets any hotter.

'Then, *bella* Mia, that means we're dating,' he says, clicking the strap shut under my chin. He keeps his captivating eyes locked with mine for what feels like minutes. It takes all the effort I can muster to look away. 'So… I'm guessing you've never been on a scooter before?'

I shake my head. 'I'm… uh… scared of…'

'You'll be fine. It's much safer than a motorbike. I've been riding since I was sixteen. In seven years, not even a parking ticket,' he says. 'Well, actually, maybe one or two.' He winks as he mounts the scooter.

'Jump on!' he says, adjusting his helmet and breaking into a luminous smile. He has perfectly straight white teeth and I'm convinced that if he wasn't a mechanic, he'd have no problem being a model.

Despite my reservations, I do as I'm told and climb onto the scooter.

He turns his head over his shoulder to face me. 'Relax,' he whispers, which makes it impossible to do just that, and not because I'm thinking about how scared I am of bikes. He turns on the ignition and now I need to touch him. Well, actually… embrace him. I'm too nervous to do either, so I place my hands on my legs, pulling my dress down as far as it will go.

'You're going to need to hold on,' he tells me.

I gingerly place my hands on his shoulders. He turns his head around to look at me again, half smiling, before he faces forward and reaches behind his body for my hands. My palms are completely sweaty and my heart feels as though it's going to burst out of my chest at any moment. My legs are complete jelly. Luca places my hands around his waist so they meet at the front and I'm forced to move in closer behind him.

'You smell nice,' he says as he releases the stand. I can see his mouth curl into an amused smile in the side mirror. I'm sure my cheeks have just flushed crimson and I hide my face behind his back in case he catches a glimpse of me in the mirror.

As we take off slowly down the path I call out, 'Where are we going?'

'It's a surprise!' he replies over the thrumming of the scooter.

His body is warm and strong and I'm willing myself to breathe deeply to slow down the pace of my heartbeat. We make our way down the winding roads through expansive countryside and rich green vineyards passing through the small suburb of Galluzzo, when he calls out and asks whether I'm okay.

'I'm fine!' I reply. Surprisingly, I am fine.

We pass an old monastery and a few restaurants, and shortly after we reach the city centre. We begin darting in and out of traffic and I close my eyes, holding on tighter. We stop at a set of traffic lights and he checks on me again.

'How are you doing back there, painter girl?'

'I'm doing okay,' I reply.

He takes one of my hands that is gripping his waist and holds it in his, placing it gently back around his torso when the light goes green.

Eventually we stop, parking the scooter close to the Arno, which is even prettier by dusk than it is by day. There's a lazy vibe to the city now, as tourists tuck away their cameras and head back to their hotels to freshen up, and the local artists along the Arno pack up their supplies.

We reach a medieval city gate and Luca explains this is the Porta San Niccolò.

'Can you tell me where we're going now?' I ask.

He smiles. 'Piazzale Michelangelo. The most stunning view you will ever get of Florence is from that square,' he says.

As soon as we pass through the gate we find ourselves on a steep and winding road. When I almost lose my footing, Luca is there to catch me. He leaves his hand on my back long after I'm steady, and I'm unsure of whether to squirm away or leave him be. We chat a bit about the differences between Melbourne and Florence, and he reels off ten reasons why he's sure I'll fall in love with Florence, his main compelling arguments being the food, the art and the people.

'You won't go home the same person you are today,' he tells me. 'That's guaranteed.'

'That would be nice.'

He glances at me curiously. We continue to walk up some stone steps and take a rest midway.

'Why did you really come to Florence?' he asks, his eyes piercing mine. I can tell his question goes much deeper than a simple getting-to-know-you one.

'What do you mean?' I ask, taken aback by his directness.

'I can see it in your eyes. You're hiding something.' He shrugs, looking at me intensely, his dark brown eyes seeing right to my soul. 'I don't think you're here just for a change of scenery.'

'Well, maybe you're wrong.'

'And maybe I'm not…' He blinks a couple of times, and before I can look away, he says, 'Am I?'

Without reflecting on them, the words tumble out. 'I wanted to start afresh. I mean, I'm better now… in remission… but for a while they… I… we all thought I wouldn't make it.' My eyes begin to glaze over as I move from my body to that familiar space in between. That space where I don't have to think, or feel, or whatever, because it's all too hard.

Luca's silent for what feels like an eternity. I try to bring myself back into my body. With each passing second, the familiar lump forms in my throat and instantly I regret telling him.

He knits his eyebrows together as if he's trying to work it out. 'Cancer?' he finally asks.

I nod without meeting his gaze. He looks surprised, and without me commanding it to, my body subtly shifts away from him. He waits patiently for my words to surface. 'Hodgkin's lymphoma. It's hard for me to talk about it. Like I said, I'm okay now, but it's like I've missed out on years of my life. I'm trying to figure out how to start a new life for myself. I spent some time working in a school office—it was only part-time but I've been a bit directionless since I got sick.'

I can't help but glance over to check his reaction. His jaw is clenched, and I can sense he's holding his breath. I wish I could take back the words. The last thing I want or need is pity. He takes a few moments to blink away the surprise, and when his breathing returns to normal, he moves closer to me. He reaches out a hand and gently tilts my chin so that our eyes meet. I feel almost naked, as if he's looking right through me. He plants a gentle kiss on my forehead and moves some loose strands of hair away from my eyes.

'Is that why you were crying yesterday?' he asks, his voice low.

I let out a deep breath and search his face for a reason—any reason—not to trust him, to keep my guard up, to give myself permission to retreat and keep the gate to my soul closed. I find none.

Defeated, I nod. 'I'm still working through some stuff. Emotional stuff. It's kind of messy. I suppose I don't see life the same way I used to and I'm trying to feel my way through that. Today was the first time I painted in a really long time.'

'Well, that sounds like progress. It also sounds like you're a bit of a fighter, painter girl.'

'I'm not as strong as you think.'

'I get the feeling you might be.'

'It scares some people,' I whisper, as I play with the hair elastic that's wrapped around my wrist. 'The whole cancer thing, I mean. I lost a lot of friends because of it. It makes people uncomfortable… the whole idea of potentially losing someone.'

He shakes his head. 'It doesn't make me uncomfortable. You said you're better now, right?'

'Yes, but…'

'But what?'

'There's a chance it could come back, especially since I relapsed.'

'There's also a chance it won't come back though, right?'

'What if I'm unlucky?'

'What if I get hit by a bus tomorrow?'

The thought makes me shudder.

'Tell me… what did you paint today?' he asks, changing the subject.

'The Ponte Vecchio.' I smile as I think about how good it felt.

'*Benissimo.* Wait until you see it by night. *Hai fame?*'

'I'm starving,' I reply, feeling sweet relief at the conversation moving to food, but not only that, I'm delighted that I have an appetite.

'Me too. There's a restaurant in the *piazzale*. La Loggia. We should go there,' he says. 'Let me warn you though, the views will be pretty average.'

My forced smile doesn't go unnoticed.

'Hey, what did I say to you yesterday?' he asks softly, tilting my chin up.

I search his face for answers. I'm not sure what he's referring to.

'Take life as it comes, remember?'

Oh yes. Of course. Do as the Italians do.

'I'm trying.'

'You're doing a great job so far—I mean, you said yes, right? You're here, with me, right now,' he says, grinning. 'And tomorrow night, I'll take you to the Ponte Vecchio.' His eyes sparkle mischievously.

'Oh, really?' I tease. 'And what makes you think that I'll say yes?'

'This,' he says as he leans in and plants a series of slow, soft kisses on my mouth, holding my face tenderly as though I might break. He stops and allows our eyes to meet.

'So what's your answer?' he murmurs.

'*Sì*. My answer is yes.'

'I knew you'd say that,' he says, tickling me.

I squirm and giggle; I feel about fifteen, but it feels good. So good. And I know that I want more of this.

'Stop it!' I squeal, defending myself. He's ticklish, too. He takes my hands and places them around his neck, moving his own hands around my waist. He's smiling as his face draws closer to me. His lips brush over mine softly and unhurriedly, and once our kiss comes to an end, I almost have to remind myself to open my eyes again.

'Let's go eat,' he says, pulling me up from the steps.

'*Perfetto*,' I say.

Everything is perfect. Too perfect. Scarily perfect.

We walk to La Loggia, and Luca pulls out my chair at an outside table on the terrace, the live music drawing me deep into the moment. We spend the next hour chatting about the vast contrast between our two lives. Luca grew up on a farm where his parents owned an olive grove, and he'd spend his weekends helping out in the family business. After he moved to Florence, he eventually became part-owner in the business he and Paolo built up together. He's always had a love for cars and bikes, so making the move was an easy decision for him, especially since he considers Paolo to be the older brother he never had.

I tell Luca about my life in Australia, skipping the dark parts of the most recent years completely. I tell him about how I used to find joy in painting everything from café-lined inner-city streetscapes to pristine ocean coastlines and sunburnt plains and ancient gum trees, only to turn down my chance to study art at university once a place was finally offered to me.

I want to tell him how terrifying my life was during my illness and how scared I still am, but I can't. Not yet. Maybe not ever. My attention turns to the flickering candle between us; however, before I can drift into my usual space in between, he reaches over and strokes my hand.

'Why did you turn down your spot at art school?'

'Um… well… I couldn't paint anymore.'

'What do you mean?'

I take a sip of wine and consider my words. 'When I was sixteen, I applied for entry into the Victorian College of the Arts Secondary School. They only offer fifteen places for visual arts students, but I wanted a place more than anything. I'd been working on my portfolio for a year—a series of paintings that explored all the hidden places we can find beauty. A broken chair, a piece of bruised fruit, a wilted flower, even a pair of worn-out boots. It turns out I was lucky enough to be accepted.'

'That's amazing. You must be good.'

'All I know is that I loved studying there, and I learned so much. Before my diagnosis, I felt like my paintings were a translation of what I used to be able to see in my life…'

'Go on…'

'After I got sick my style changed. I couldn't see things the same way, and it scared me, you know, to think I could paint pieces that were so… dark and depressing.'

'There's nothing wrong with that though. Look at expressionism. We all go through dark times. Your emotions manifested onto canvas. Your emotions were dark at the time. We all need to experience the darkness to recognise how beautiful the light is.'

'How do you know about expressionism? I thought you weren't so into art, Mr Mysterious.'

'I had a crush on my middle school art history teacher. I paid attention to what she had to say.'

'Oh? You were *cotto*?' I joke.

'*Eh, sì.*' He laughs. 'But nothing like this.'

My heart skips a beat and my eyes dart away. There's no way I can meet his gaze now without coming undone.

'*Dolce*?' he asks.

'Sweet?' I say, unsure of my translation.

'Dessert. I meant dessert. But you're much sweeter than dessert.'

'Dessert would be great,' I whisper, feeling my cheeks glow.

By the time we finish dinner, I'm giddy from the wine. Luca intertwines his fingers through mine, and we take a stroll in the piazza, illuminated by a handful of street lamps. A string of tourists, adorned with their Nikons and Canons, file back onto their tour buses, after which a quiet lull fills the square. I lean over the stone railings as Luca wraps his arms around me from behind, resting his chin on my shoulder.

'This is so beautiful. I've never seen anything like this before,' I say, letting the panoramic view of the city cast its mesmerising spell over me.

'Me either,' he says, his attention on me.

I try to push aside the feelings in my head that tell me this is wrong, that whatever it is I'm feeling can't be possible or rational. Yet my heart doesn't care that we've known each other for less than forty-eight hours. When he leans in and pulls me close to his warm, strong body for a kiss, I'm his. And it feels anything but irrational.

We stand there in silence, entwined in each other's arms, the infancy of our love weaving its foundations in the stillness of the moment, until finally, he whispers, '*Bella* Mia. I wish you were *mia*.'

I'm petrified to think that I already am.

CHAPTER SEVEN

Stella's still awake by the time I creep through the front door.

'You're home late, *signorina*,' she teases. She's in the living room reading *The Florentine*, an English newspaper.

'Yeah.'

'Yeah? Just yeah?' She raises her eyebrows.

'It was nice,' I say, shrugging. I can't hide my smile.

'Mia, are you *cotta*?' she asks, waving her finger at me. 'C'mon, tell me all about it!' She gestures for me to join her on the sofa, patting the cushion beside her. She shifts one of the large pillows and crosses her legs as I take my spot. 'So, where did he take you?' asks Stella.

'Piazzale Michelangelo. Dinner at La Loggia.'

'That's a winning first date. Impressive. Okay, and...?'

'He's... just... beautiful,' I say dreamily, picturing him in my mind.

'Yes, he's hot. We all know that,' she says impatiently.

'I don't mean it like that! I mean, yes, he's completely sexy and good-looking, but he's just... a really nice guy.' Although I know my eyes are glazing over, I can't help it.

'Kiss?'

'Mmm. Incredible.'

'Oh, Mia. You're falling for him already, I can see it in your eyes,' she says, her own eyes wide.

'It's insane, isn't it?'

'He's a catch. Go with it,' she tells me. 'He has girls lining up at the door. Like I said to you yesterday, he hasn't shown interest in anyone since his parents died. Nothing. *Niente*. Zip. Until you.'

'Maybe it's not a good idea,' I say, feeling myself plummeting from the clouds into reality, albeit relieved that he isn't actually the local heartbreaker of Impruneta.

'Oh, please—don't overthink it.'

'But I probably won't be around for long. And it's too rushed,' I say, dropping my head to my chest so I don't have to meet her gaze.

'Wait until you fall in love with Florence. Then talk to me,' she says. 'I've seen many a holiday turn into a lifetime love affair with Tuscany,' she adds with a chuckle. 'In fact, I see it every day on my desk over on Lungarno Vespucci, where a pile of visa applications sit waiting to be processed.'

I smile, wishing I could tell her that's not what I mean.

'Listen, I'm beat. Time for bed.'

'Yeah, me too. I thought you'd never arrive,' she says, glancing at her watch.

'You waited up?'

'Bet your ass I did!' She giggles.

I grab a pillow and toss it at her as we both burst out laughing.

Hours later, I'm awoken by a particularly frightening nightmare in which Luca is walking on a soft blanket of grass, carrying a bunch of colourful flowers in his arm. I'm smiling and waving and then suddenly the surface he's walking on turns into a gravel road, and the crunching beneath his feet gets louder as he approaches me, until it's almost deafening. When he's an arm's length away from me, the sky turns grey, and everything around me turns from vivid colour into black and white. The flowers wilt away and it becomes apparent that we're now in a cemetery. He walks right past me, a distraught look on his face. I reach out to touch him, but he walks right through me.

'Luca!' I scream, suddenly jolted out of my dream.

'He's not here, Mia. It's me, Stella.'

'I can't breathe,' I cry, reaching for my chest as I gulp for air.

'It's okay. You're okay, Mia. It was just a bad dream.' She reaches over me and switches on the lamp, and I squint from the sudden influx of light.

'I'm so sorry. It felt so real.'

'You were crying.' She tilts my chin up. 'You were reaching out, calling Luca's name.'

'I don't know if I can do this.' I untangle myself from the damp bedsheets and make my way into the en-suite to splash some water over my face. Stella follows me in.

'Do what? Mia, what are you talking about?'

'I'm sorry I woke you; it was nothing.' I pat my face dry and return to bed.

'You were thrashing around and telling me you didn't want to die.'

A desperate plea escapes my lips. 'I don't.' I look at her long enough to catch her expression, which tells me she can sense something is off.

'You should get changed, you're soaking wet. I'll go get you some water,' she says.

'Honestly, thanks, but I'm fine.'

She ignores me and begins to get up. Before she can stand, I reach out for her hand because I feel like I owe her at least some kind of explanation. 'They happen pretty often. Just so you know.'

'Right.' She waits for me to continue.

'I usually wake up and fall back to sleep. You don't need to check on me.'

She stands up and begins to make her way out of the bedroom. When she reaches the door, she turns around and faces me. 'If it's all the same to you, I'd prefer to check on you.'

I change into a fresh pair of pyjamas and lie down, wondering why my past continues to haunt me even when things seem to be going right. Stella returns a few minutes later with a glass of water. 'You know, Mia, you can trust me,' she says, placing the glass of water on my nightstand.

I pretend I'm already asleep.

'Hey, I need to look for a job today. Where do I start?' I ask Stella at breakfast.

'Already?'

'Yep. And I'll do anything. After paying my share of the rent, if I don't find a job soon, my time here will be a lot shorter than what I'm beginning to hope it will be.'

'Try going into Florence. A lot of the stores advertise for staff in their windows. Look for the *cercasi* signs.' She pours herself an espresso and asks whether I want one, too.

'No, thanks, I thought I might grab one at the bar this morning.'

'And that you might just bump into a certain someone across the square,' she teases.

'Enough!' I giggle.

'I'll walk with you. I'm taking the bus today.'

Our stride to the square is filled with mindless chatter until Stella stops walking. She pierces me with her emerald eyes and I immediately know what she's going to ask me. 'Mia, the nightmare you had last night—something must be causing them if you're having them regularly. Were you… I don't know… assaulted or something?'

I swallow down the rapidly forming lump in my throat.

'No, it's nothing like that,' I reply.

She waits patiently for me to elaborate, but I can't seem to find the right words.

'I'm sorry. It's really none of my business. You can tell me when you're ready.' She moves towards me and gives me a kiss on each cheek outside the bar, then points to the *officina*. 'You should go say hi,' she says, before giving me a wink and turning on her heels as she rushes to catch the bus.

I catch a glimpse of Luca in the *officina*. He's talking to a customer who's showing him something on a scooter. As I study the movement of his body, my lusting is interrupted by a bubbly Silvio, who has come out to open the umbrellas at the outside tables.

'*Salve*, Mia! Let me guess—a *macchiato*?' he asks.

'*Sì! Grazie.* And a *cornetto* too, please,' I say, feeling like a local already. I'm surprised at how *cornetti*, sweet pastries and biscuits form such an integral part of the Italian breakfast.

'Of course,' he replies.

'Mind if I take a seat out here?'

'Go for it, Australiana,' he says, pulling out a chair for me. He opens up the red-and-white umbrella and switches on some background music, which he hums to as he stocks the fridge with fresh bottles of water. I can see why Silvio enjoys his work so much. A social butterfly, he greets almost everyone who walks past, and receives packages of fresh produce from at least two passers-by in addition to a wrapped package from the butcher. He delivers espressos to shops on the other side of the square, and I'm almost certain that in the short while I've been watching him, he has spent more time chatting with the locals than behind the bar. Everyone seems to love him.

I drop my sketchbook on the table and sharpen my pencil. I open and close my hand to get the circulation going. The first pencil stroke lacks the smoothness I'm accustomed to and my hand feels heavy until I change my grip. In frustration I toss away three attempts at sketching the busy square. Discouraged, I take a short break while I finish my coffee. Rolling the pencil between my fingers, I contemplate going home, but I want to prove to myself that yesterday's painting wasn't a fluke. I think about the girl on the aeroplane and tell myself that I have no expectations of my work, that I will accept whatever ends up on the page, no matter what. Wiping the perspiration from my brow, I lift my head to get the right perspective on a different subject matter.

The morning sunlight is streaming across the square into the *officina*, bouncing off the metallic bikes and scooters. Luca's working on a bike through the open roller door, the rays of the sun highlighting the curves of his toned body. I start creating a light map, cross-hatching for the right amount of tonal depth I'm looking for. Silvio asks me if I'd like a drink, which I decline, unable to pull myself away from my drawing. By the time Luca's body comes to life on my page, I have an intimate knowledge of how he carries himself, which contributes to my growing attraction to him. I'm heavily focused on my work, just as he is on his. He stops only once to answer the phone, giving me another glimpse of the radiant smile that lights up his face.

Ninety minutes later, I rest my pencils on the table and study my work. I relive the emotions I felt while sketching and a strong sense of relief sweeps through me like a warm hug. Silvio brings me a bottle of water and asks if I'll share my drawing with him. Nervously, I hand over my sketch.

'This is amazing,' he exclaims, praising my work, his eyes widening.

'*Grazie*,' I reply.

He's right. It is amazing. He's amazing. Everything is amazing. And now, I just need to find a job.

*

While I'm on the bus to Florence, I check my phone to find a couple of text messages from Sarah, asking how I'm doing. When I was at my lowest point during treatment and recovery, Sarah was one of the only people who really *got* me and wasn't afraid for me when everybody else was. I didn't have to be strong for Sarah or open up to her completely, but she was one of the few people who was strong for me. I reply, telling her that things are going great and that I've started drawing and painting again.

She texts back three smiley faces and too many love hearts to count.

I disembark close to the train station and start scouring the streets of Florence for the *cercasi* signs taped to the windows of various shopfronts. First up, I try a restaurant. The lunch crowd has dissipated, and I approach the cashier, lifting my head up high. Discreetly clearing my throat, I give it all I have.

'*Buongiorno, mi chiamo Mia.*' I explain that I'm looking for work.

'*Ah, sì.* Gisella!' she calls. Her indifference causes me to shuffle uncomfortably to the other side of the counter. A woman in her forties appears.

'Gisella,' she says, extending her hand.

'Mia, nice to meet you. I saw the sign outside. I'm interested in the job.'

'Where are you from, Mia?'

'Australia.'

'Experience?'

'Ah, well, not so much waitressing, but—'

'How many languages do you speak?'

'How many?'

She nods impatiently and strums her manicured nails on the counter. It's hard to not be distracted by her rudeness.

'Uh, just one. I speak a little Italian. So that would be two, I suppose.'

'We need someone who speaks English, German, French and Italian.'

I struggle to hide my shock.

'We deal with many tourists here,' she says bluntly.

'I understand. Thanks all the same.'

The next *cercasi* sign I find is advertising the need for a *commessa*, or shop assistant, for a clothing store. This experience is marginally more pleasant as the manager invites me to have a chat in the back room of the store. She introduces herself as Loretta, pulls out a chair and we exchange the usual details about where I'm from, how long I've been in Florence, and what brought me here. She glances over my résumé.

'I see you worked as a shop assistant for a while. Cosmetics. What's your interest in fashion?'

'Well, I enjoy working in customer service, and I've always loved Italian fashion,' I say, only slightly bending the truth. My mind immediately turns to the fashion-conscious Luca.

She looks at me as if she's waiting for me to expand on my interest in fashion, but I can't think of another thing to say. 'Who doesn't love Italian fashion?' I smile weakly.

'Do you speak Italian?'

'I can get by.'

'And any other languages? French or German?'

'No, but I'd be willing to take a course. I'm a quick learner.'

'How long are you intending on staying in Florence?'

'Oh, well, I don't have any plans to go back home just yet.'

She uncrosses her legs, then sets her pen and clipboard on the desk beside her. 'I'll be honest with you, Mia. Finding a job here in Florence isn't easy. There are hundreds of foreigners like you competing for work. I need someone with solid sales experience who's going to be around for the long term. We see a lot of girls coming and going. Since you've only recently arrived, it might be best to see how you like it here first. If you're still here in six months, come back to see me.'

Clearly, I do a terrible job of hiding my disappointment because she suggests, 'Why don't you try teaching English?'

'I'll try that, thanks,' I reply, knowing that isn't possible for me without the right qualifications.

I hand my résumé to various stores on the way back to the bus stop, and return home to the villa deflated. Without a job, by the time I pay this month's rent and other living expenses, I'll only have enough funds to see me through the next six weeks. I scour the classifieds section of an online newspaper, hoping I can manage to secure at least a couple of interviews. I make a note of three jobs that might be a good fit. When I call for an interview, two out of three jobs are taken, but I manage to get an interview for the third, a receptionist role for an export company.

In an effort to take my mind off the pressures of finding work, I head upstairs to water the frangipani on the balcony when I notice somebody slipping through the gate. It's Luca. He's carrying a bunch of flowers.

He brings his hand to his mouth and calls, 'Signorina Mia!'

The watering can I'm holding in one hand is spurting water all over the washing on the line below, and I'm blissfully ignoring the problem because it's *him*.

'What are you doing here?' I call out from the window, unable to hide my smile. I almost drop the now empty watering can. Bouncing down the stairs, I stop at the front door to regain my composure. I fan my face and move the stray hairs out of my eyes.

'You going to open the door, painter girl?' he asks through the door.

I smile to myself and open the heavy door to see him leaning in the doorway. He places one of the rose stems in his mouth and waggles his eyebrows. Grinning at his own cheesiness, he takes the rose from his mouth and hands it to me as he breaks out into a melodramatic rendition of an Italian classic: 'Rose rosse per te'. Red roses for you.

I laugh, shaking my head at how charming this guy is.

'For me?' I ask, playing along. He nods, handing me the most beautiful roses I've ever seen. In fact, they're the only roses I've ever been given by a guy.

He doesn't answer, but instead leans in and gently takes hold of me around my waist, knocking the breath out of me. He tilts my chin up and brings his lips down on mine for the most passionate kiss ever, which takes several seconds to recover from.

He pulls away and winks at me. 'I couldn't stop thinking about you, *bella* Mia,' he whispers.

A smile creeps over my face. 'Shouldn't you be at work?'

'*Sì*.'

And with that, he spins around and walks away, leaving a trail of lust behind him.

CHAPTER EIGHT

'Any news on the job front?' asks Stella, joining me on the sofa, where I've been spending the early evening amusing myself with Italian game shows and barely dressed ballerinas who break out into dance routines before every commercial break.

'Nope, but I've got an interview tomorrow. I actually meant to ask you—where's Empoli?'

'You sure you want to travel that far each day? It's over an hour away.'

'You're kidding! Maybe I should cancel the interview.'

'Something has got to come up closer to home.' She glances at her watch. 'We better make a start on dinner.'

'Stella, there's something I need to tell you. It's about last night. You know, the nightmare I had. I just need you to not make a big deal about it.'

'What is it?'

'I'm in remission from cancer—lymphoma.'

'What? You're okay now though?'

'I'm okay now.' I nod, reassuring her.

'All right, so if and when you want to talk about it, I'm here.' She gives me a gentle smile.

'I know, but I don't think I need to talk about it again. I just want you to know.'

'Okay,' she says in a kind of dismissal. 'Let's get dinner ready.'

'Oh, I already prepared something for you,' I say, following her into the kitchen, where I open the pot of *ribollita*, letting the aroma sweep through the room. 'Just thought I'd try a typical Tuscan dish.' I smile proudly. Earlier today I dusted off an old recipe book and mastered this tomato-based bean-and-vegetable stew, to be served with bread. For dipping, of course.

'Smells delicious! I'm impressed. Hey, where did those flowers come from?' she asks, pointing to the windowsill.

'Um, well…'

'Mia!'

'I know, I know. We're going out again tonight,' I say, my lips forming a timid smile. I have no power over the physical responses that overcome me the second I think about Luca.

'What about dinner?'

'I guess I'll eat something in town,' I say, biting down on my smile.

'You're falling hard, girl!' she teases.

There's no use denying it. Just then, someone knocks on the door.

'You go,' I whisper.

'No, you go,' she says, ushering me out of the kitchen.

'Too nervous. Please, Stella.'

She chuckles and then bounces through the living area, while I follow behind. I race into the main bathroom to fix myself in the mirror. In a frenzy, I apply some lip gloss and smack my lips together, and when I glance up I notice Luca's reflection, standing behind me. Grinning.

Uh-oh. I bet he saw all of that.

'I knew that dating an Australian girl was going to be fun,' he says, smiling.

That smile undoes me every time.

'You look perfect. Ready?' he asks, giving me the customary kiss on each cheek. I assume he's going for the left, but he goes for the right and our lips almost meet in the middle. My mouth twists into a nervous smile as our eyes meet. He smiles affectionately, as if he's enjoying this. He squeezes my hand and we make our way to the front door.

'Bye, Stella!' I call.

She licks the back of a wooden spoon and beams at us from the doorway of the kitchen like a proud mother hen.

'*Ciao, piccioncini*,' she calls. 'Don't be home too late!'

'*Ciao*, Stella!' calls Luca, closing the door behind us.

'*Piccioncini*?' I ask.

'Lovebirds.'

'Oh,' I murmur, suddenly feeling shy.

'Oh?' he asks, tilting his head to the side.

'You're having way too much fun teasing me, you know.'

'Can't help it. You couldn't be more adorable if you tried.'

It's a cool summer evening, and I'm glad I've opted for a pair of jeans. I mount the scooter, and this time, when my arms wrap around Luca's body, he brushes his hands over mine before starting the ignition.

Approaching the city centre, we make our way through the Porta Romana, which once formed part of the city gate around Florence. We park near Piazza Santa Croce and I ask him to wait while I admire the Franciscan basilica.

'Michelangelo's tomb's inside there,' I say. 'And in the Bardi Chapel there are these incredible frescoes by Giotto that depict the life of Saint Francis. I mean, I haven't seen them yet—only in photos, but—'

'You really do love art, don't you?'

I nod, running my fingers along the pink, green and white marble facade of the basilica. I explain there are supposed to be tidemarks on its walls that date back to the 1966 flood of the Arno River. 'They lost so much precious artwork in that flood...' My voice trails off when I notice he's stopped nodding and is now gazing at me in an admiring stare. 'You're not really that into art, are you?' I ask, embarrassed at my rambling.

He shakes his head. 'Not really, but I'm really into you.' He moves closer to me, planting a series of soft kisses on my mouth. My stomach flutters in response. We kiss as if we're the only couple in the buzzing square, and I wish this feeling would never end. When our lips finally part, he asks me, 'Now, what was that you were saying about destroyed artwork?'

'Oh, so you were listening?'

'To every word.'

He waits for me to finish my story. Once I stop talking, he doesn't say a word, just kisses me tenderly on the head. He takes my hand, intertwining his fingers with mine.

'So, tell me about your day.'

'Well, I did some sketching… and I guess the highlight of my day was when this charming guy I recently met gave me a bunch of the prettiest flowers I've ever seen.'

'Oh, really? You need to be careful of charming, random strangers in Italy, you know. They prey on breathtakingly gorgeous Australian girls.' He stops in his tracks to kiss me again. As we continue walking, Luca asks me how the job hunting is going.

'Not so great,' I reply. 'If I don't find a job soon, I'll have to go home in six weeks.'

He stops walking and his expression turns serious. 'But you can't go home anytime soon.'

'Why is that?'

'Because… us. This is only the beginning.'

I take a deep breath, my stomach somersaulting.

Is it possible that this could be something real after such a short time?

As if reading my mind, Luca interrupts my train of thought. 'There's something about you, painter girl. And whatever it is that I'm feeling right now, it's very real.'

I retreat into my safe space, eyes fixated on the horizon, confused by the flurry of conflicting emotions that are swirling through me. I don't want to think about how logical this is. It doesn't make sense, yet the rightness of it all is what makes it so darn special.

'We barely know each other, Luca,' I say in a weak attempt to appease the left side of my brain into thinking it's in charge. As soon as I speak the words I regret them.

'That doesn't matter to me,' he says, not fazed in the least. 'Want to know why?'

'Why?'

'Because I decided that time is overrated.'

'Since when?'

'Since you.'

I start fidgeting with my watch, my eyes now fixed on a group of illegal street sellers packing up their wares as the *carabinieri* stroll through the square.

'What does your head say?' he asks.

I snap out of the zone as quickly as I drifted into it and look up into his perfectly rounded chestnut eyes, knowing there's no way I can lie.

'That it's too quick.'

'What does your heart say?'

'That…'

He nods with a half-smile, knowing what I'm going to say.

'… it feels right.'

'Then it's right. And it's real,' he says, raising his eyebrows, flashing his gorgeous smile, which quickly turns into an intense gaze.

I study his face, contemplating his beautiful mind, when he winks at me.

'So, what did you sketch today?' he asks.

'Uh, it's a surprise,' I say, deciding that I should wait for the right time to show him my work.

He moves my hand around his waist, where my fingers slip through the loop on the side of his jeans. He places his arm around me and we stroll down a small cobblestoned street. The faint smell of leather drifts through the air; the hallmark scent of Florentine craftsmanship. Soon we are in Piazza della Signoria, passing the replica of the statue of David. Further ahead, near the entrance to the Uffizi Gallery, Signor Fiorelli is packing up his paintings.

'*Buonasera, signorina,*' he greets, smiling. 'Nice to see you again.' He turns to face Luca and reaches out to shake his hand. '*Luca, da quanto tempo. Tutto bene?*' He's happy to see Luca, though I can still sense a loneliness in Signor Fiorelli's voice. I quickly try to translate the words into English: *It's been a while. Is everything well with you?*

'Signor Fiorelli,' says Luca, smiling. 'Good to see you again. This is my *amica*, Mia.'

'We've already met,' says Signor Fiorelli. 'Aah, Mia. You're in good company with this young man.'

We're interrupted by a French couple who want to buy some of Signor Fiorelli's paintings before he packs them away. As they contemplate their selections, he asks us what we're up to tonight.

'Luca's giving me a tour of Florence. We were on our way to the Ponte Vecchio.'

'Make sure he shows you the padlocks,' he says. 'Young love. Precious young love.' He winks at the couple, who smile fondly at us.

'See you soon, Mia. Luca, send my regards to Stella.'

Luca nods and we say goodbye.

'How do you know Signor Fiorelli?' he asks.

'I met him the other day when I came to paint. His work's impressive.'

'Do you recognise it?'

'Recognise it? From where?' I pause to think about where I could have seen Signor Fiorelli's work before. The loose and expressive brushstrokes seem familiar. Then I remember I have seen them before—in the three paintings in my bedroom.

'Signor Fiorelli is Stella's great-uncle?' I shake my head in amazement.

'Yes, he is. Didn't you notice the paintings? Amelia's in every one of them.'

Luca's right. The same woman appears in each painting.

'I thought he didn't paint anymore.'

'Well, apparently he picked it up again,' says Luca, shrugging his shoulders.

Signor Fiorelli intrigues me and so do his paintings: the way he can no longer live in the home he shared with his wife because there's so much pain attached to it; the way he breathes life into her with memories and brushstrokes. I suppose that's what true love does. It carves a space so deep in your heart that it can never die. Once one person goes, the other, in some capacity, follows. It dawns on me that my own fear of dying is becoming more complicated.

Unsettling thoughts float through me during our short walk to the Ponte Vecchio, which is illuminated by the city lights in anticipation of sunset. Gold bracelets and charms glisten through the windows of jewellery stores, their wooden shutters bearing the decorative emblem of the Florentine fleur-de-lis.

'Have you heard of the love locks?' asks Luca.

I shake my head. 'No, I haven't.'

'Well, tradition has it that when two lovers fix a padlock to the bridge and toss the key into the Arno, they're locked together by their love… for eternity.'

'Really? That's like the most romantic thing I've ever heard. It's beautiful.'

'Just like you,' he whispers, tucking some loose strands of hair behind my ear. I shift uncomfortably, worried that he might notice the hair extensions used to mask my painfully slow-to-grow hair.

'Everything okay?'

Without meaning to, I momentarily drop my gaze. 'Everything's perfect.'

He continues telling me about the bridge. 'This is the only Florentine bridge that wasn't destroyed during the Second World War bombings.' I study the way Luca's eyes come to life, the way his mouth smiles ever so subtly as he talks. 'So if you're ever going to attach a love lock to a bridge in the hope your love can withstand anything, I'd say this bridge would be a good one.'

'That is so utterly romantic,' I say as I crouch down to admire the impressive number of padlocks fixed to the railing that surround a statue of Benvenuto Cellini, who, according to the plaque at his feet, was an Italian goldsmith and sculptor. Everlasting love. So romantic.

We stroll over to a space on the side of the bridge where the lovers that I painted yesterday were standing. Our timing is perfect, with the pink-orange sun being minutes away from setting. Luca wraps his arms around my waist from behind and nestles his chin in between my neck and shoulder as we wait for the light to change over the horizon before it disappears completely. Being held this way feels safe. Right. Meant to be. I argue internally about whether I can actually *let this be*. I don't know if I can do it to him. He doesn't deserve to see a girl he cares about wilt away and die any more than I deserve to be that girl.

Two small tears escape from my eyes. They glide down my cheeks, past my nose, tickling my skin on their way down. They eventually drop off my chin onto his hand. He turns me around and wipes away the residual tears.

'It's okay, Mia. You can feel safe here.'

'Sorry, I'm just a bit emotional.'

'Shh,' he whispers, placing his finger on my mouth. 'No need to explain.'

'Bet you think I'm a basket case.'

'No… just a bit emotional,' he teases. 'Let's go. I know what can make this better.'

I desperately want to tell him the things that overwhelm me, but Luca's kiss washes away every thought, rational or irrational.

*

Tables at the piano bar are filled with locals sipping aperitifs, singing along to live Italian classics. Luca hands me a menu. 'I should have told you they don't actually serve dinner here. Although they do amazing Nutella crêpes,' he says, grinning.

'Great!' I say, folding my menu. 'Perfect cure for volatile emotions.'

He laughs, watching the ice cubes slide over each other in his glass as he takes a slow sip of his Rosso Antico. Then he says, 'So, I've just shown you my favourite place in the world. Where's yours?'

'After I got the news of my remission, my mum took me to see a musical at the Regent Theatre, because that's what we did whenever we had something to celebrate. Afterwards, we had dinner at the Langham Hotel, where the city was glittering below us and piano music was playing the whole time and you could see the most incredible view of the Yarra River, which was painted with the reflection of the skyline. Maybe I'll take you there some day.'

'I'll hold you to that. Before we even get to that, though, we'd need a padlock first,' he says, raising his eyebrows and breaking into the most irresistible of grins.

We polish off our crêpes and spend the next few hours chatting, lost amongst the melodies of the piano, alternating between periods of comfortable silence and meaningful and not-so-meaningful chatter. Luca teaches me how to roll my r's, and once he's satisfied with my intonation, he teaches me a string of terms of endearment in Italian.

'*Tesoro*. Treasure.'

'*Teh-soh-ro*.'

'*Dolcezza*. Sweetheart.'

'*Doll-cheh-zah*. How am I doing?'

'You're doing great. *Ti voglio baciare*.'

'*Tee*—'

'No, I actually mean I want to kiss you.'

'Like right now, right now?'

'*Sì*—right now.'

He leans towards me and his lips meet mine. His mouth tastes sweet, like a delicious infusion of citrus and vanilla. Any inhibitions I might have had about public displays of affection dissipate into nothing as the warmth of Luca's mouth ignites life in me again. He gently pulls away and rests his forehead on mine. He smiles. I smile. He kisses me again. And again. And again.

We arrive back at the villa at almost one in the morning, and as our perfect-as-it-ever-could-be date draws to an end, I tell Luca to wait for me at the front door before going home. I lift the paper off my desk, swallowing the excess saliva in my mouth. If I have any chance of moving forward, of healing, I know I need to do this. Sharing my work is almost as important as trusting myself to paint again. Determined to resist the temptation to change my mind, I command my feet to move forward.

'I made this for you,' I say, handing him the sketch. My eyes peek up at him, watching his eyes dart over the page. He forms the words to speak. Nothing comes out. He tries again.

'You seriously have big talent, Mia. This isn't something that just happens.'

When I don't answer, he looks up at me.

'I didn't know whether I'd ever be able to get that part of me back.'

'Sometimes we have to let the past go…'

'But what if the future scares you even more than the past?'

He looks at me penetratingly, searching for clues. When he doesn't find any, he asks, 'What is it you're scared of?'

'Dying. I'm scared of dying.'

Luca's eyes soften. He blinks, his Adam's apple moving as he swallows. Here we are, standing at my front door, and I've quite possibly chosen the absolute worst timing to admit my biggest fear to this wonderful guy I barely even know.

'Nobody ever knows what can happen tomorrow.' Even his voice has softened now.

'But it could come back. There's a chance I might die if I get another recurrence.'

'But, Mia, you're here now. You can't control what happens tomorrow.'

'I know, but I can't stop thinking about it,' I whisper. 'Every day, hundreds of times a day, it's always at the back of my mind. And then there are the nightmares...'

His eyes are intense, taking in all of my brokenness.

The words keep rolling off my tongue. 'I don't know if I could go through it again... I don't think I'm strong enough to face being sick again.'

'Who says you have to?'

He wraps his arms around me and places his hand behind my head, encouraging me to lean into him. As soon as my face nestles into that warm space on his shoulder, I come completely undone. I let myself unravel in his strong embrace, my tears flowing as though a river's banks have burst. A series of quiet sobs from deep within release themselves onto his chest and he holds me tighter than ever. Not letting go of me, he closes the door gently behind him with his leg and he swiftly lifts me into his arms as if I'm as light as a feather. He carries me to my bedroom, shifts the curtains of my four-poster bed and places me onto the softness of my mattress. He reaches for a box of tissues on the nightstand before nestling his body against mine, stroking my face tenderly.

'I didn't realise I was this scared. I'm really, really scared.'

'You can let go and relax into life now. Focus on what's working, what's beautiful, what makes you feel alive. Surround yourself with more of that. You know, we humans can only control a small percentage of what happens to us. The rest is... I don't know, destiny... or stuff that just happens. Most of the time we never know why. Which is why we have to live one day at a time, Mia. Making the most of every minute.'

I lie still, trying to catch my breath, trying not to question why what happened to me did.

'I'll be back in a second,' he says.

A short time later he returns with two cotton balls on a plate in one hand and a cup of tea in the other.

'The world lights up when you smile, *bella* Mia.'

'What are they for?' I ask, pointing to the cotton balls.

'Your eyes. Wild chamomile does wonders, you know. You don't want them puffy for your interview tomorrow, right?' He winks at me.

'Who taught you that?'

'An ex-girlfriend who used to cry a lot when she didn't get her own way.'

The thought of Luca with another girl sends pangs of envy through my stomach. 'Have you had many girlfriends?'

'Let's just say I've had enough to know that this is nothing like I've ever had before.'

'But we're only dating.'

'I'm not really fussy when it comes to labels.'

'Tonight was... *perfetto*,' I whisper.

He kisses me on the forehead. 'You made it perfect.' His lips move to my neck as he guides me onto my back, the weight of his body pressing against me. His mouth gently explores mine while his hand unhurriedly travels over the curve of my waist. He slides my top up and the breath knocks out of me in response.

It becomes impossible to control the reaction of my body. All of me wants this, yet something is holding me back.

'I can't. Not yet… not ready…' I whisper, releasing my grip around his neck. I look up at the ceiling, sink deeper into my pillow and let out a sigh of frustration. I'm in my early twenties, yet I've missed out on all the things my friends experienced after secondary school, including boyfriends.

Luca shifts over to his side, rests his head on his elbow and rolls my body towards him. He blinks at me thoughtfully, as if he's taking me in, trying to work me out.

'Okay,' he murmurs, a soft smile forming on his lips. 'I'll wait for you. However long it takes.'

Without dropping his gaze, he reaches for my hand and holds it against his chest. Before I can say a word, he closes his eyes, leaving me to contemplate the accelerated beating of his heart through the palm of my hand.

We lie on top of the sheets until morning, when we wake up to the roosters crowing and the golden sunlight streaming through the shutters, closer and more united than yesterday.

CHAPTER NINE

'Good morning, *bella* Mia. Sleeping with you was the best thing I've done in a long time.'

I grab my pillow and toss it at Luca's head. He retaliates. Our pillow fight is short-lived as I plead with him to be quiet.

'Stella,' I whisper, raising my finger to my mouth as I try to hold back the laughter.

'Eh, it's Stella. She's like a sister,' he says.

'But she'll think…'

'Think what?'

'You know…'

'You know what?' he teases.

'I'm not like that.'

'Not like what?'

'You're unbelievable.' I fling the pillow at him again. He grabs me and flips me onto my back. Now he's kissing and tickling me all over, intentionally making a heap of noise.

'Stop! Please! Stop it!' I beg, trying to catch my breath. The laughter feels so incredibly good.

He feels so incredibly good.

He stops only to plant the dreamiest of kisses on my mouth and I'm lost in the moment until a fleeting thought about work crosses my mind. In a panic, I pull away and Luca rakes his fingers through his hair, as though he's trying to bring himself back to reality outside our bubble of intimacy.

'What just happened?' he asks, his eyes twinkling at me in surprise.

'I need to get ready for my interview!'

'Whoa, settle down, Australiana. It's five thirty in the morning. You've got plenty of time.'

'But I don't know what I'm going to wear,' I say, jumping up from the bed. I'm not usually too concerned about my appearance; however, my future depends on the outcome of this interview and I know I should be making an effort.

'Relax. You're in Italy. And in Italy, we start the day with a nice, strong *caffè*,' he says.

'What will Stella think?' I don't know how she'll react to someone staying the night, even if it is someone she knows.

He doesn't answer, and instead walks out of the bedroom door, stands at the bottom of the stairs and calls out, 'Stella! *Alzati*! Get up, you're late for work!' A playful grin spreads across his face.

In the kitchen, Luca gets the coffee ready while I reach for the *fette biscottate*. Ugh.

'I hate those things,' he says.

'Me too,' I groan.

'Try the third drawer. That's where the good stuff is,' he says, smirking. 'I've raided it enough times to know.'

I open the drawer to find a stash of no fewer than eight boxes of Kinder Colazione cake.

'Told you,' he says, popping open a packet with a single hand. He slides it out and hands it to me. 'Try this.'

'I know what they are,' I tell him. Nutella crêpes for dinner and this for breakfast. My mum would be horrified.

'Don't throw out the boxes when you're done. Stella saves the points. Everyone always saves the points,' he says, pouring three cups of coffee. 'Stella! *Caffè*!'

I turn the box around and find the square perforated coupons. Fifty points will get me a free toaster, and a hundred coupons will get me a set of brand-new bedsheets.

Stella enters the kitchen, her hair dishevelled. She snatches her coffee and gives Luca a light slap across the back of the head. 'Thanks very much,' she says.

He grins. '*Prego*,' he replies, giving me a wink. He finishes his coffee, places his empty cup in the sink and makes his way to the bathroom.

Stella grins broadly at me, her eyes demanding answers.

'It's not what you think,' I mouth desperately.

She raises her eyebrows and steps in closer to me. 'So was he good?'

'Quiet!' I warn. 'I told you, it wasn't like that,' I whisper under my breath.

'Looks like Tuscany isn't the only thing that's stolen a piece of your heart, *bella* Mia,' she says, exiting the kitchen.

I bury my head in my hands.

Luca comes out of the bathroom, freshly showered, looking more gorgeous than ever. Stella was right when she said he and Paolo were part of the furniture. He throws a cardboard packet in the bin.

'What's that?' I ask.

'A new toothbrush,' he says, grinning. 'Figured I might be needing it.'

'Oh, really?'

'I want to make sure those nightmares don't haunt you anymore.'

My stomach does a series of flip-flops.

'Meet me outside the *officina* once you get back from Empoli,' he says, planting a kiss on my forehead. '*In bocca al lupo.*'

In the wolf's mouth? I must have the translation wrong. 'Huh?'

'You're meant to reply "*crepi*",' he says.

'Die? You want me to wish you to die?'

'It's a colloquial expression. It's like saying "good luck" or "break a leg", to which the person is supposed to reply "*crepi*" or "*crepi il lupo*", which kind of means you're wishing the wolf to die,' he explains. 'Actually now that I think about it, the Italian-to-English translation doesn't work that well.'

'No, it doesn't,' I agree on a laugh. 'But I need all the luck I can get. So *crepi*!'

I reluctantly walk Luca to the front door. As he leans in to kiss me goodbye I get the overwhelming urge to apologise. 'I'm sorry I broke down last night,' I blurt. 'And I'm sorry I couldn't…'

'There's nothing to be sorry about,' he tells me firmly.

'But I barely know you. You must think…'

'When you're ready, I'll tell you what I think.'

He kisses me as if he'll never see me again and then slips his helmet over his head. And just like that, he leaves me hanging.

Stella's gone by the time I'm showered and dressed. I manage to arrive in Empoli by train, and the interview goes smoothly until the role-play in Italian, which is followed by a language test that I'm certain I failed, given the expression of disdain from the stodgy old man who has interviewed me. He stubs out his cigarette with his yellow-stained fingers and gives me my score: seventy-five per cent.

'We need a pass rate of ninety per cent,' he informs me, lighting another cigarette. He inhales deeply and exhales a puff of toxic smoke in my direction. By now I'm feeling defeated, albeit slightly relieved. Given the correlation between cancer and smoking, I'm not sure I would have taken the job anyway.

During the bus ride home, Stella calls me.

'Hey, girl, I have some good news for you! My friend recently resigned from her job as a nanny. I made some calls and Clara, the mother of the twin boys she was watching, wants to meet with you. Great family—she's a top art dealer, originally from London. Her husband's away a lot. Anyway, she wants to see you this afternoon at three if you're available. Grab a pen, here's the address,' she says, before reeling off the address for me, along with some directions.

'Okay, got it,' I reply.

Oh, gosh. Can I actually do this? Care for two kids? What on earth am I thinking?

Back at the villa, I tidy my hair, put on some light makeup and grab my bag for another stroll through the square and to the Balducci family residence. The villa and its grounds are enormous, reminding me of something out of *Architectural Digest*. I'm interrupted by the sound of laughter just as I ring the doorbell. I turn around to see where it's coming from when the cold spray hits me, soaking my hair, my face, my shirt.

I frantically sift through my bag for something to wipe my face dry, hoping the little mascara I'm wearing hasn't smudged down my cheeks. I shake the drops of water off my clothes, turning around to see if I can catch a glimpse of the tiny offenders. Hiding behind a large terracotta planter is a little guy with dark brown hair and huge brown eyes. He's beaming at me, proud of his efforts to drown me at the door. I expect his brother to be identical to him, but they're complete opposites. This child's green eyes pierce mine, his curly blond hair bouncing around his head as he jumps out from the planter, yelling, 'We got you!'

I burst out laughing just as a woman, tall and slender with porcelain skin and shoulder-length blonde hair, opens the door. Her straight hair is so smooth and silky that she looks as though she could be in a shampoo commercial. She's immaculately dressed, just like her boys.

'Oh, Mia, I am so sorry,' she says as she guides me through the front door into the safety of her home.

'Oh, that's fine. Kids.' I shrug, not knowing what else to say. 'I wish I hadn't worn a white shirt,' I say, trying to make the best of an uncomfortable situation.

She ignores my attempt at cracking a joke and extends a manicured hand to meet my semi-wet one.

'It's lovely to meet you, Mia. I'm Clara,' she says in her enchanting British accent.

'It's a pleasure.' I suddenly feel far too casual and insignificant around this woman, with her perfect accent and pristine demeanour.

'Boys, please behave while I chat to Mia,' she says, as the twins scramble upstairs in a race to reach the top. 'In the meantime, I'd like you to think about your behaviour.' Her voice lacks the firmness that I was used to growing up, and her reprimand sounds more like a polite request than an order.

'Lemonade?' she asks, gesturing for me to sit at the rectangular wooden table in the middle of her enormous rustic kitchen.

'Yes, please, that would be lovely.'

'So, Mia, you're a long way from home. What brings you to Florence?' she asks, filling my glass with ice cubes, which she takes from a bucket with a pair of silver tongs.

'Uh, well… I was hoping for a new experience,' I reply. At least I'm half telling the truth.

'Well, that you will have,' she says. 'Florence is an enthralling place to explore. Stella told me a little bit about you. Is it true you're an artist?'

Commonality. I should have known she'd ask me this question. I wish I'd better prepared myself. 'Yes, I suppose so. I love art. I paint, mostly.'

'What kind of painting do you do?' she asks, placing her hand under her chin.

'Mainly watercolour. Occasionally oil. I also like to sketch.'

'How lovely. I'm intrigued. I'd love to see your work sometime,' she says.

'Of course. I'd love to share it with you,' I lie. Showing a sketch to friends is completely different to sharing my artwork with a successful London art dealer, even if it is in the most casual of circumstances.

'I look forward to it. Are you studying art here?' she asks, eyeing me over the rim of her glass as she takes a sip of her lemonade.

I shake my head, unsuccessfully masking my disappointment. 'Maybe one day. I mean, I'd love to. I was offered a spot back home in a Fine Art programme, but I had to turn it down.'

She raises her eyebrows. 'I might be able to make a recommendation for the academy when you're ready,' she says.

'That would be great, thank you,' I say, relieved that she hasn't asked any killer questions.

'Mia, let me get straight to the point and tell you what I'm looking for. I need a nanny three days a week for split shifts. Nine until one and then four until seven. Cooking, washing and ironing for the boys only, and light household chores as needed,' she says.

'That… It all sounds great,' I reply, thinking that it sounds perfect.

'Do you have any questions?'

'How old are the boys?'

'Five. And I should warn you—they're a bit of a handful. The last six months or so have been particularly challenging. What they need is some… stability, shall we say.'

'I understand,' I reply, thinking that I don't really understand what she means at all.

'You do plan on staying for a while?'

'I hope to.'

'Right. Well, Stella spoke very highly of you, and I trust her judgement. This is what I'm proposing for a weekly salary,' she says, grabbing a fountain pen and scribbling down some dates, times and a figure. 'Thoughts?' she says, turning the paper around to face me.

I scan the page and nod. 'That all looks great.'

'Could you start by doing a trial morning shift tomorrow?' she asks, her hands clasped on the table.

'Really? I mean, of course, I can't see why not.'

'Wonderful,' she says, the slightest hint of a smile spreading across her lips. She reaches out to shake my hand as though she's performed some kind of business transaction in a boardroom.

'Let me introduce you to Massimo and Alessandro.' She calls out to them from the bottom of the staircase. *Bambini*! Come down, please. I want you to meet your new nanny!' A minute later, looking dishevelled and extremely guilty, the boys tumble down the stairs.

I stand up from the table. 'Hi, I'm Mia. Now, which one of you is Alessandro?' I ask, trying to sound as bubbly as possible.

'Me!' replies the dark-haired boy.

'Massimo!' barks Clara. 'That's Massimo, and this is Alessandro,' she says, keeping a tight grip on the Alessandro's shoulders in an effort to still him.

I want to laugh at Massimo's mischievousness, but I hold every muscle in my face tight in an effort to stop myself.

'Nice to meet you, Mia,' says Alessandro, piercing me with his emerald eyes. I smile back.

Clara then reaches for Massimo and steers him towards me.

'Nice to meet you, Mia,' he says, eyes on his feet.

'Can we go now?' asks Alessandro innocently. I already have a soft spot for this gentle soul.

'Don't you think you owe Mia an apology first?' asks Clara, the sternness in her voice now more apparent.

'Sorry, Mia,' says Alessandro, fidgeting.

'Yeah, sorry, Mia, but it's just water,' says Massimo.

As much as I feel like laughing at his response, I hold myself back. Clara sighs deeply.

Without waiting for another reprimand from his mother, Massimo takes off up the stairs, Alessandro trailing behind him.

'It's the attention… or lack of it,' she says, sighing again. 'Bert, my husband, who you may get the chance to meet before Christmas if his job permits, isn't around much these days. I suppose, to some degree, the boys miss their father.'

Christmas is six months away. Clara briefly drops her gaze before she asks whether she can drive me home. I tell her I prefer to walk.

'Well, it's been lovely meeting you. I'll see you tomorrow morning,' she says.

'I'm looking forward to it,' I say, meeting her eyes.

She returns a gentle nod and closes the door behind me.

I text Luca.

I got a job. I get to stay.

CHAPTER TEN

When I arrive at the Balduccis' the following morning, I close my eyes and wait for the shower of water that never comes. Instead, the boys both jump out from behind the planter with a loud, 'Boo!'

'Oh, you scared me!' I say, dropping my art satchel on the ground. I clasp my chest and stumble backwards, playing along with their game. They both dissolve into hysterics. Clara opens the door to find us giggling uncontrollably but refrains from joining us. Underneath the mask of makeup and pretty lip colour, she looks tired this morning.

'Boys, boys, boys,' she says, shaking her head. 'Good morning, Mia. I've left all the numbers you might need on the fridge. If you can prepare lunch for the boys at twelve, that would be perfect. I'll be back exactly at one. There's some coffee in the pot if you'd like some.'

I nod at each instruction, hoping that it will all go smoothly. She takes her phone off the charger and picks up her leather briefcase. Outside, she gives each of the boys a kiss, ruffling their hair as she leaves. I'm astounded when a minute later she drives off on an almond-coloured Vespa, heels and all, her briefcase positioned between her ankles.

I clap my hands together. 'Okay, boys, what should we do first?' There's no answer. 'Boys!'

'We're playing *nascondino*!' shouts a voice from somewhere in the garden.

'Um, what's *nascondino*?'

'Hide-and-seek! You have to find us, Mia!'

'Right! I'm counting to twenty, watch out!'

We spend the next hour playing games amongst the manicured lawns of the English garden. When my stomach aches from laughing so much with the boys over the silliest of things, I think to myself that maybe this is the perfect job for me right now. Once I catch my breath, the boys start showing off their dance moves. I can tell they've been craving attention by the way they're competing with each other for mine and the slew of 'look at mes'. After a game of soccer, we sit down under a tree and sip on lemonade.

'So, boys, tell me about your dad. Do you get to speak to him much?'

'Not that much. Just sometimes on the phone,' says Massimo.

I turn to look at Alessandro. 'He's got too much work to do now,' he says, shrugging his shoulders.

'And before?'

'Before, he wasn't always at work. Just sometimes,' says Massimo.

I don't press them any further for answers because keeping them still is impossible, and Alessandro is already running off, challenging his brother to yet another game of hide-and-seek.

It's almost eleven by the time I call the boys inside for some downtime, but it takes another fifteen minutes to get them to actually listen to me. 'How about we make a deal? Every morning I will play with you. Whatever game you want. But when I call you inside for morning tea, you have to promise to listen and you need to behave. No tricks, pranks or making a mess like this,' I say, pointing to the remainder of their breakfast, now splattered across the kitchen floor. 'Or this,' I say, picking up the toy cars surrounding my feet.

'Or what?' asks Massimo.

'What do you mean?' I ask, surprised at how he's already pushing boundaries with me. I thought this would be straightforward.

'If we don't listen, what happens?' asks Alessandro.

'There'll be consequences. Big ones. And I don't think you'll like them very much,' I warn.

'Like what?' asks Massimo.

'Well, I'll have to take away your toys, and there'll be no TV or playing outside,' I say, trying to sound as firm as possible. I'm hoping my spur-of-the-moment rules are convincing enough.

'Oh, yeah. We know this stuff.' Alessandro shrugs.

'Good,' I reply. 'Now listen, while I get you a snack, you can watch some TV,' I say, trying to figure out the remote.

'Here, like this.' Alessandro takes the remote and shows me which button to push.

'Thanks,' I say.

He smiles as he settles on the sofa. His brother, on the other hand, is jumping all over it.

'Massimo. That's strike one. Get to three and you're out. That's your warning,' I threaten as I turn my back, ignoring the questions he calls out in an attempt to test me.

I slice fruit and give it to the boys to eat, tidy the kitchen and make the boys' beds. Strewn across the floor is a pile of dirty clothes. By the time I finish the household chores and put on a second load of washing, it's time to prepare lunch. By now the twins have grown tired of watching TV, and I manage to come up with a strategy to keep them entertained.

'Who likes cooking?' I ask.

'Play cooking's boring,' says Massimo, screwing up his face.

'No, I mean *real* cooking. I need some help from two chefs. *Proper* ones. But if you're not up for it…'

'Yes! Yes!' shouts Alessandro, jumping up and down. 'We have aprons here.' He slides open a drawer. I tie one of Clara's aprons around his neck and do the same for reluctant Massimo.

The boys help me prepare a salad, and I fry the *polpette* Clara prepared in a pan while they do an average job of setting the table—a must-do, because we are, after all, in Italy.

'Who wants another *rissole*?'

After lunch I tidy up the kitchen before joining them outside.

I almost drop the jug of water I'm carrying when I see them throwing stones at each other. They're covered in dirt.

'Boys! Come here, right now! What are you thinking? Your mum will be here any minute. Let's go upstairs and get changed.'

'No!' says Massimo, running away.

'Okay, well I guess I'll have to cancel your surprise.'

Alessandro approaches me and I crouch down to his level. 'What's the surprise?' he asks, his eyes wide.

'Go call Massimo, and I'll tell you both together.'

He dashes off and soon both boys are standing in front of me, ready for the news.

'Who's heard of Picasso?'

'Me!' says Alessandro.

'How about Botticelli, da Vinci and Michelangelo?'

'Yes, yes, yes!' they both exclaim.

'Okay, well, who likes painting?'

'Yeah, I love it!' says Massimo, bouncing up and down.

'Me too,' says Alessandro, who is now as fidgety as his brother.

'I need some painters to help me make some works of art. I've got some special brushes and paints that I'd love to show you. But I don't know if I can trust you both to take this job seriously.'

'Yes, we will, we promise,' says Massimo, speaking on behalf of his brother.

'Putting together an art exhibition is a big job, you know. It's going to take us a few weeks of work. We'll need lots of practice to get things just right. Do you think you're up to it?'

They both nod with such eagerness that it makes me want to reach over and cuddle them.

'All right, let's scoot upstairs and get changed, and I'll see whether you're going to be able to help me with this next time I see you.' Upstairs I take the opportunity to tell them a few stories about Italian Renaissance painters, which they listen to with intrigue. By the time we return downstairs, Clara has arrived, looking more drained than she did this morning.

'It looks like everything is under control here,' she says coolly, her eyes darting around the pristine kitchen. She nods in approval, and my shoulders relax.

'Mamma!' says Alessandro, tugging at her top. She scoops him up, plants a kiss on his cheek and places him back down. Massimo hasn't even bothered saying hello and is out playing in the yard.

'It's been great. It's pretty busy, but a good busy.'

'Ah, yes, they'll certainly keep you on your toes,' she says.

'How was your morning?' I ask, sensing something is off.

'Oh, the usual.'

I'm not sure what to make of her response, so instead I tell her about my plans for some art lessons for the boys.

She seems happy with the idea. 'If you'd like to take them on an outing to the Uffizi or the Accademia sometime, they'd love that,' she tells me.

'Sure, that would be great.'

'It would be good for them. It's been a while since we last did something together like that as a family.'

After a long silence, which I assume is due to her pensiveness, I excuse myself from the discussion as I remember I'm meant to be meeting Luca at the *officina*.

She looks up from the photograph on the mantel she's now staring at, and absently responds, 'So, I suppose I'll see you again on Monday, then?'

'He's still there,' says Silvio, startling me as I stroll past the bar.

'Oh, I was just—'

'Can't take your eyes off him, can you, *signorina*?' He chuckles as he wipes down a table. 'Hold on a second,' he says, dashing into the bar. He comes out holding a shot of coffee in a disposable cup.

'Here you go, a *caffè corretto*, just like he takes it every other day.' He hands me the coffee to take across the road to Luca.

'*Caffè*?' I ask Luca once I enter the *officina*.

Luca wipes his brow with the back of his hand and flips around to face me.

'Silvio?' he asks as he tucks a spanner in his back pocket and wipes his hands on a nearby cloth.

'Yes.' I titter, handing him his coffee. He takes it from me and sets it on the bench beside him. Then he takes a step forward and places one of his hands around my waist.

'How was your first morning on the job?' he asks, his voice low and smooth. He doesn't wait for an answer as he guides me closer to him. He cups my cheek, presses his forehead against mine and whispers, 'It was a long morning.' He's smiling as he tilts my head up and kisses me.

He pulls away gently and he's smiling with his eyes now. They wander into mine, almost in slow motion, taking me in, saying all the things that can't be spoken but can be felt. He blinks twice, slowly, then says, 'So... the job?'

'The... what?' I'm still floating. I try to clear my head, to recover my equilibrium. 'Oh... yeah... I've got a new-found respect for people with kids now. Even if they are a little exhausting, I really like the boys. Doesn't help that I've only had about four hours of sleep, though.'

'I've got the perfect solution,' he says, tossing his empty coffee cup into the bin. He grabs my hand. 'Let's go, Australiana.' He leads me out of the *officina* and pulls down the metal roller door.

Given I have no other place to be and no other person I'd rather be with, I take my spot behind Luca on the scooter. Soon we're cruising up and down winding country roads through the expansive Chianti countryside with postcard-perfect sunflowers that carpet faraway fields. Luca slows down and we park on the side of a gravel road.

'What do you think?' he asks, helping me off the scooter.

'I love that you knew I'd adore this spot.' My attention shifts to the hundreds of sunflowers highlighting such a picturesque landscape. The yellow tones instantly stir something in my soul, as if the flowers are talking to me.

Luca moves his arms around my waist. My arms reach around his shoulders and play with the curls of hair at the back of his neck. He plants a trail of soft kisses from my forehead to my collarbone before taking my hand in his. 'Come with me.'

He leads me through a space in between the sunflowers and when we reach the other side, we throw ourselves on the grass, under the shade of a tall cypress. We lie down and I let my head rest on his chest. I don't want to think about cancer today. My fingers doodle tiny swirls over his torso as I try to concentrate on how good it feels to be here right now with him. Luca stops my hand with his free one and slips his fingers through mine, before resting our clasped hands on his chest. Then he closes his eyes and together we doze off.

I wake up when Luca starts stroking my face. 'How often do you have the nightmares?' he asks.

His question is completely unexpected, and my muscles tighten in response. I sit up and lean my back against the tree. I take a deep breath and start to pick at the seeds of a dry sunflower. I've already shared so much with Luca, and I don't know if I'm ready to share anything more.

'Talking about it isn't going to make it worse,' he says.

'It's just… I've never told anyone about them before. I mean, my mum and dad knew I had them, but I never spoke to them—I couldn't tell them. It's not as bad as it used to be. Before I came here they'd happen most nights. Usually I feel like I'm suffocating, but there's this one dream where I'm at my own funeral and I watch the casket being lowered into the ground. The terrifying part is when I look around and see the faces of people I know. My friends all look so sad. Then I see my mum and dad. They're completely devastated, crying their eyes out, like they've lost part of themselves, like they'll never be the same. That's when I usually wake up screaming,' I finish, staring at the sky.

'You were worried about the people close to you—about hurting them?'

'Am.' I look him straight in the eyes. 'I think I still am.'

'You shouldn't have had to go through what you did, but the worst is behind you,' he says.

'I want to believe that. I just can't seem to let go of the possibility that it could happen again. It's like that messy web of my past is still wrapped around me and I can't—don't know how to—shake it off.'

'What's it going to take for you to realise how strong you really are, Mia? Look at where you've been and where you are right now. Those nightmares, they'll be a thing of the past before you know it. I promise you.'

I bite the inside of my lip. 'I hope you're right.'

I reach across and run my fingers over his eyebrows. I trace his perfectly rounded eyes and stop at his lips.

'Hey, can you sit with your back against the tree? I want you to look at me, exactly like you did then.'

'You changing the subject?'

'Nope. I'm just facing a fear,' I say, pulling out paper, brushes, and a bottle of water from my satchel. 'Can you take off your sunglasses?'

'Anything else?'

My brush quivers in my hand and I don't reply until I have a steady grip on it again.

'I'm trying to work here,' I murmur, determined not to lose focus on the definition of his torso. His arresting gaze makes it difficult to concentrate on anything other than what he's just asked me. As difficult as it is, I tear my eyes away from him to focus on dipping my brush into water, carefully manipulating the saturation of the pigment, and gradually, I move into the natural rhythm of painting that once felt so distant.

Luca occupies the time by fiddling with the loose threads of his shirt and playing with his phone. Sometime later, the last of the vibrant hues of yellow come to life on my sheet. I sit in that space, soaking in what it feels like to be whole again. This painting is so much more than a dreamy picture of the guy I'm falling in love with against one of the prettiest backdrops I've ever seen. It's a mirror of emotions reflecting back at me.

Luca moves behind me and rests his chin on my shoulder. 'You sure you want to go back to nannying? You should show your work to Clara.'

'Maybe.' I shrug.

'You're holding yourself back.'

'I want to make sure this isn't temporary. And maybe I'm not ready to call myself an artist yet.'

'But that's what you are.'

'I thought I was. I thought I was a lot of things. Now, I'm not so sure.'

'Your ability to paint like this, it's not temporary. You know that, right?'

'I'm just being cautious.'

'Let it go, Mia. Lean into life without letting the fear hold you back. It's what you deserve.'

'You think that's what I'm doing?'

'I know that's what you're doing. You're keeping yourself small, because you're afraid that what happened in the past might happen in your future. You need to trust a little more.'

I take some time to consider Luca's words.

He places his hand on my cheek, so I have to look at him. He guides my legs over his, and whispers, 'Painter girl, I think you're incredible.' He holds my face in his hands. 'There's so much light radiating from you now. There's no more room for dark pictures. I think you've moved beyond all of that.'

I nod, contemplating the likelihood of Luca knowing me better than I know myself.

'If you look at the work you've been doing since you arrived in Florence—what's it like?'

I take a deep breath because this is the instant I admit it to the world. And if I say it out loud, then it becomes the truth. And when it becomes the truth, then it might just mean I've healed one part of my broken self.

'I think it might be my best work ever.'

CHAPTER ELEVEN

On Monday afternoon, when I return to the Balduccis' after my morning shift, Massimo flings open the front door before I have the chance to knock. He glances at the bags of art supplies I've brought with me. 'Mia! Are you ready for our surprise?' he asks, wide-eyed with anticipation.

'Oh, am I ready for it? Are you ready for it?' I ask, scooping him up in my arms, tickling him before he escapes outside with his brother.

'Looks like you have two excited boys on your hands,' says Clara. 'They haven't stopped talking about you since this morning.'

'I'm so glad; it's nice to see them so happy,' I reply, pleased to hear about how eager they are.

Clara nods and quietly replies, 'Yes, it certainly is.' She says goodbye and I round up the boys.

'Okay, artists, have you got any smocks you can wear?'

'Yes! We'll go get them!' And they almost bowl each other over in a race to get inside.

I'm sharpening the last of our pencils when the boys come bounding towards me.

'All right, so this is what we're going to do. I want you to pick something to draw, anything you can see from where you're sitting.'

Alessandro chooses his soccer ball, and Massimo chooses the olive tree. I sit in between them both and gently place my hand over Alessandro's as I bring the tree to life with a series of pencil strokes. He sits still and silent while Massimo peers over my shoulder.

'Wow, Mia, you're like a real Botticelli,' he says.

I laugh and tickle him under his chin. 'Not quite, but thank you. Now it's time for the fun part—the painting.' I place the watercolours on the table with a dish of water. I show them how to use the paints and the boys quietly get to work, their tongues pointing out of their mouths in concentration. 'These ones are just for practice. The rest of our paintings are going to be for our art exhibition for your mum. How does that sound?'

Their faces light up and Massimo tells me it sounds great.

'Did Botticelli paint like this?' asks Alessandro.

'Well, not quite, you're painting in watercolour, but he used tempera for a lot of his paintings. Do you know what that is?'

They both shake their heads.

'It's a paint made using the yolk of an egg,' I say.

'You mean the yellow part?' asks Massimo.

'That's right! He would mix it with coloured powders called pigment. Many painters used it during the Renaissance. That was a busy time for artists. Your mum would know all about it. You should ask her sometime.'

I leave the twins outside while I set up the ironing board inside beside a window overlooking the garden so I can keep an eye on them.

Half an hour later Alessandro bursts through the door, a bundle of enthusiasm as he shows me his painting. I switch off the iron and meet him at the kitchen table, where I pull out a chair. 'Tell me about your picture. How does it make you feel?'

He shrugs. 'It's my family. That's Daddy playing soccer,' he says, pointing to a man with short dark hair, who is kicking a ball. I try to mask my reaction when I notice that the lady in the picture, who is no doubt Clara, has a downturned mouth.

'Mummy doesn't look very happy.' His innocent green eyes blink at me. I wrap my arm around his tiny waist, pulling him onto my lap.

'Why's that?'

'Because she's gone,' he replies, but I have little time to probe him further as Massimo bursts through the doors, triumphantly holding his painting.

'I love it! You did such a great job, Massimo. Botticelli would be extremely proud of you!'

The boys' laughter peals across the room. I hand them a couple of extra sheets of paper and encourage them to do some more painting while I head upstairs to put away their clothes. On opening their wardrobe, a pile of clothes comes tumbling down from the top shelf along with a rectangular pink box. As I pick up the loose lid and go to place it on the box, I notice a bundle of soft, pink items wrapped in tissue paper. Baby clothes. Pink blankets. A velveteen rattle with a bunny.

'Look, Mia! We're done!' says Alessandro, suddenly in the room with me and proudly holding up his work.

Massimo gasps. Alessandro looks at him, then at me, and then at the box. His eyes widen like saucers as his little mouth lets out a huff of breath.

'What's wrong?'

Massimo points to the box.

'It's okay, I'm just putting it back now. Is it a secret that your mum's having a baby?' I ask, smiling. 'That's wonderful, boys.'

Alessandro shakes his head. Massimo is biting his lower lip. I take a closer look at the items in the box. The clothes have been worn. And then I suddenly understand who is gone and who she has taken with her.

'Baby isn't here anymore?'

Alessandro nods, his eyes on the floor.

'It's our fault,' says Massimo.

'Oh, sweetheart, it's not your fault. Sometimes God takes our loved ones home sooner than we would like.' Beyond the pristine demeanour, the enormous house and the enviable career, here lies the reason behind Clara's sadness and the vagueness I recognise in her, the one that comes with living in your body but not being fully present.

I place the box on the top shelf before asking one more question.

'What was her name?'

'Isabella.'

Once Clara returns home in the evening, the boys race down the stairs to greet her, artwork in hand. She rests her briefcase on the kitchen table and lowers herself into a chair. Alessandro waves his painting in her face.

'Let's see what you have here,' she says. She holds it out in front of her and studies it carefully. As she comes to recognise herself in her son's painting, she flinches. Alessandro takes a magnet to place it in prime position on the fridge.

'Oh, it's too special for the fridge, darling. Why don't you let me have it and I'll take it to work with me?'

'And mine?' asks Massimo.

'Yours too, sweetheart,' she replies. Clara notices me standing on the staircase then, and appears somewhat embarrassed. 'Mia, how was your afternoon?'

'It was great. Can I help you with anything else before I go?'

She shakes her head. 'No, that will be all, thank you for all your effort. I can tell the boys are growing fond of you already. See you tomorrow.'

*

By the time I pass the *officina*, it's already closed. Disappointment washes over me at the thought of having to wait until tomorrow to see Luca. But minutes later, my phone rings, and it's him.

His smooth voice carries over the line. 'So you survived your afternoon shift at the Balduccis'?'

'I'm actually having a lot of fun with them. How was your afternoon?'

'I had to go to Siena to pick up some spare parts for the *officina*. I'll be leaving soon.'

This definitely means I'll have to wait until tomorrow to see him again. 'Oh,' I reply, unsuccessfully hiding my disappointment.

'Oh?'

'Oh, nothing.'

'I wanted to see you again tonight, *bella* Mia,' he says.

'Me too.' I sigh.

CHAPTER TWELVE

'Painter girl, I've got a surprise for you today,' says Luca. We're outside the *officina*, where almost every day for the past two weeks I've been meeting Luca during my afternoon break, unless he finishes early, in which case he waits for me outside the Balduccis' front gate. Today we both have a day off. I trail behind him as he pulls up the roller door of the *officina* and leads me into the garage.

'I thought this might make getting around a little easier for you,' he says, lifting a cotton sheet off a vintage bicycle. A bunch of pink roses spills from the wicker basket at the front of the bike.

'Oh my goodness! Really?' I reach for the flowers and bring them up to my face. The floral scent mixes with the smell of grease and petrol as the soft petals tickle my nose.

A smile stretches across his face. 'Yeah, those too.' He laughs. 'Hey, I thought we could go somewhere special today.'

'You know, you said that yesterday. And the day before that,' I tease, as my hands glide over the peach-coloured metal of my unexpected gift.

'The Val d'Orcia. You up for a ride?'

'Totally! Although I haven't ridden a bike in years.'

'Me either. Not this kind, anyway. Look at what you're doing to me,' he says.

Silvio pokes his head in and drops a woven basket at the door. 'Have fun!' he calls, before darting back to the bar.

'A picnic as well?'

'Just trying to step it up, painter girl.' He grabs the basket and places it in the boot of the car. Then he reaches for his bike and pauses before he lifts it onto the car's rack. 'You should blush like that more often. The colour suits you.'

He fixes our bikes onto the rack, and when he stops to wipe his brow, he catches me admiring him in a pensive gaze. The smoothest of smiles spreads across his face.

'What is it?' I ask.

'You're looking at me like that again.'

I raise my eyebrows. 'Like what?'

'Like you're falling for me just as hard as I'm falling for you.'

I brush my hands over the loose strands of my hair as I try to find the right words.

'It's okay. You don't need to say anything. Your eyes are doing all the talking, and they're making things very clear.' He opens the car door for me and waves his hand. '*Signorina*, once you've finished blushing, do let me know whether you'd like the roof open or closed,' he says with a smile so radiant my heart starts pounding against my chest.

'Open, please.'

We venture through Chianti past vineyards and sweeping hills that blur as we pass them by while the warm Tuscan sun works on giving us the kind of sun-kissed glow that stamps the memories of summer onto our skin. Here the landscape spans from south of Siena to Mount Amiata, and when it flattens out Luca parks the car on the side of the road and we ride our bikes through the scenic villages of our timeless surroundings. Eventually, we stop near a stream, parking our bikes and setting up a picnic spot under the shade of a leafy tree.

After lunch, and a little too much prosecco, I flick off my shoes and sit on the bank of the stream, picking wildflowers, while the cool water tickles my feet. Luca lies beside me, looking completely relaxed as usual. He must be rubbing off on me because I can't help feeling the same way.

'It's like time stands still whenever I'm with you. I love not having to be preoccupied with time,' I say, slipping my fingers through his.

'You don't have to be preoccupied with time, Mia,' he replies.

I start to pick the petals off the tiny purple flower in my hands. He rolls over so he's facing me and props himself up on his elbow. He lifts up his glasses and looks me in the eyes. 'I don't think you're as scared of dying as you think you are.'

I keep picking at the flower until all that's left is the stem. And then I start on another. Luca has an uncanny way of getting into my head. I sit up and try to wriggle away from him, not in the mood for this kind of confrontation.

'Why did you come here, Mia?'

My muscles tense as I look away uncomfortably. I don't want to answer him.

'I don't know,' I say eventually with a sigh. I look up at the sky and watch as a cloud resembling a dolphin morphs into a hummingbird.

'Why did you come here?' he asks again, his tone firm.

'I told you, I don't know,' I reply hotly. I swallow past the enormous lump that's formed in my throat.

'Close your eyes.' He takes my hand in his and places it on my chest. 'I know that this is difficult for you.'

'Then why can't you just let it go?'

He leans in close and whispers, 'Trust me,' as his warm lips brush my ear. Gradually, my irritation fades and my body softens at his closeness. 'I want you to see it for yourself.'

'See what for myself?' I ask, searching his eyes for answers.

'That you're not as broken as you think. It wouldn't have been easy for you to come here on your own after everything you've been through. But you did.'

I take a deep breath and think back to how hard I had to fight to get here, how I left my mum and dad after everything I'd put them through.

'There was no joy in my life, and I didn't know how to find it again. I thought that by coming here I could show myself that I could learn how to not be so scared of dying. I just knew that I wanted to feel happy and fulfilled again. I felt like a completely different person after the cancer. I felt… really, really empty.'

'Do you still feel that way?'

I shake my head. 'No, I don't. Since I got here, and met you and started painting again, I feel full. Fuller than I've ever felt before.'

'So there it is.'

'What?'

'You're not broken, Mia. In all of this, you have a choice. You can choose to embrace the life you are creating for yourself now. Or you can continue to use the fear of getting sick again as the thing that torments you day and night. If you put off your happiness for the day you get a hundred per cent survival rate, you'll never be truly free and happy.'

In many ways, Luca's right. I have been gripping tightly to my past. 'You make letting go of all that fear sound so easy.'

'Mia, if you didn't have to think about relapse, what would you be doing? How would you be living your life?'

'I'd learn to scuba dive. I'd study art and make new friends, and I wouldn't be scared that I would start studying and not be able to finish. I'd share my work without worrying about whether other people would see the sadness in my strokes.'

'What else?'

I bite my lip. 'That's it. What makes you think there's something else?'

'Stella told me you're still having nightmares.'

'Not as often as before.'

'What's scaring you?'

'I really don't want to talk about this anymore. Let's just drop it.'

'Why?'

I feel into that tender place for the words. 'Because I don't want to think about the fact that I could be responsible for hurting the people around me, Luca—the people who love me and care about me.'

'That's why it's hard for you to let them in?'

'I let you in! And to be perfectly honest with you, it petrifies me.'

'You don't need to worry about me. I'm not worried about you dying on me, Mia.'

I turn my body ever so slightly away from him. 'But I am,' I whisper, my eyes fighting back the tears. 'I don't want to hurt you. Six, twelve, eighteen months from now, when we are in so deep, I don't want you to watch me die.'

He takes hold of my shoulders and waits until I look up at him and our eyes lock. 'We are already so completely beyond deep.' He takes my hands in his and moves in closer. 'Listen to me, Mia. Nobody gets a guaranteed survival rate. Not me, not you, not anybody.'

'Nobody,' I repeat.

'Come here.' He pulls me into his arms. Leaning back against the tree so that I'm resting against him, he holds me, resting his head against mine, leaving me to contemplate things. Slowly, the truth seeps its way in. I've been spending all of this time focused on that one figure. Paralysed by it.

'I don't know what I expected. Maybe when they told me the figures, I wanted them to tell me it was all going to be okay. That there would be no chance of a recurrence. I wanted a guarantee. A guarantee to make me feel safe.'

'They're doctors, Mia. They don't have crystal balls. If that's what you were expecting, they'd never be able to tell you what you wanted to hear.' He slips his fingers through mine.

'How did you get to have such a beautiful mind?' I lovingly touch his face and wrap my legs around his. Placing my lips over his, I kiss him with all the tenderness within me, and when we finally pull apart, I'm left panting.

'Looks like you need to catch your breath, painter girl.'

'It seems to be a side effect I'm experiencing since I met you.'

'Not sorry.' He laughs softly then, making me want to kiss him all over again.

'Could we do it?'

'Do what?' he asks.

'Go scuba diving sometime?'

'Yeah, we should definitely do that someday.' He guides me to the ground. He's lying on top of me now and I wrap my arms around his neck, never wanting to let him go. I'm almost certain I've never felt so completely safe in my life.

'Luca?'

'Yes, *bella* Mia?'

'Is this what the beginning of love looks like?' I ask, losing myself in his eyes.

'I'm not sure. But it's definitely what it feels like.'

I anchor into my happy thoughts and lean into the feeling of blossoming love, where numbers mean nothing and life is every shade of absolute wonderful.

CHAPTER THIRTEEN

A week later, the art exhibition for Clara is finally ready to be revealed. The boys each have three paintings to display, which I've helped them mount in cardboard frames.

'Your mum will be so proud,' I say, stepping back to admire their work. I asked the boys to recall three of their fondest memories for their paintings. Massimo painted a Formula One scene, a beach scene and a Christmas scene, while Alessandro portrayed himself riding a bike, being tickled by his dad, and another cuddling a baby girl. I'm pleased that Clara has been depicted with a smile on her face in this one, but I'm nervous about her reaction to Alessandro's drawing.

She arrives home just before seven. The boys have covered the display with a black cloth and are standing beside it with excited smiles on their faces.

'What's this?' asks Clara, setting down her briefcase. She places her keys on the table and stands back to admire her sons' work.

'This is our art exhibition called "Things That Make Us Happy",' says Alessandro.

'One, two, three!' says Massimo, and they both pull down the cloth, revealing their frames, temporarily mounted on the entrance wall.

A smile spreads across Clara's face; she appears genuinely relaxed and engaged. She steps towards the first painting and says, 'Massimo, I bet this is yours. You've always loved Ferraris.' He nods enthusiastically, drinking in his mother's praise. 'And this one was done by Alessandro, because you're the one in the family who loves tickles,' she says, tickling him under the arms. She comments on the rest of the paintings and then pauses when she reaches the last one with Alessandro cuddling his late sister.

'Come here,' she says, kneeling down, pulling the twins closer to her. She rests her head on Alessandro's generous head of curls and then plants a kiss on each of their cheeks. She's visibly moved and I can't help feeling joyous about it, understanding the way that art has the potential to heal and connect one to emotion.

After what feels like a long time, Clara stands up and asks me almost nervously, 'Mia, would you like to stay for dinner?'

I find myself reacting with an unintentional look of surprise. Usually our greetings and salutations are cool and brief.

'Only if you don't have other plans,' she adds.

'No, not at all. I'd love to,' I reply, unable to hide my smile.

Clara prepares dinner while I help set the table. She doesn't mention the artwork until the boys are in bed when she invites me to stay for a cup of tea.

'Mia, what you've done with the boys, it's helping immensely. And not just in the way you might think.'

'Oh?'

'Let me explain.' She reaches for the teapot and holds the lid with one hand while pouring the steaming hot liquid into two cups. 'Sugar?'

'No, thanks.'

'The boys adore you. You've only been with us a few short weeks, but I'm already seeing a change in their behaviour. They seem much happier.'

'I'm pretty fond of them, too,' I reply.

'They miss their father. Things haven't really been the same since a tragedy that occurred in our family earlier this year. Bert started working a lot more then, as a means of escaping from the real problem.'

I nod. 'Clara, I should tell you something—'

Clara shakes her head. 'It's all right. I know you found Isabella's box. The boys told me. I've just been waiting for the right time to tell you about her.'

My body instantly tenses up. 'I'm sorry. I wanted to tell you I found it. It was completely accidental…'

'I know, Mia. It's fine,' she says, resting her hand on mine. 'I was just saying that Bert didn't cope very well with it all. Things between us have changed and we have some work to do.' She sighs. She pats her eyes dry with a handkerchief that she pulls from the pocket of her pants. 'Let me show you something.'

She leaves the room and returns a minute or so later with the pink-and-white-striped box, which she places on the table between us—Isabella's box. Her hands glide over the surface as though she's wiping away invisible traces of dust from it, and a dull ache inside me starts to amplify. She lifts off the lid and pulls the baby clothes from the box. 'Isabella was with us for nearly two years and has been gone for six months. I brought her home from the hospital in this outfit,' she says, smiling as she inhales. She lays it on the table in front of me and I want to touch it, to feel the softness of it, but I know that if I do, I'll break down. I sit there, frozen, staring at it, thinking about how Clara's daughter has been taken from her.

'I still can't believe she's gone, that I'll never hear the sound of her laughing again. She loved to laugh. She made us all laugh.' Clara closes her eyes and holds the outfit close to her, as if she's praying, or remembering. Whatever she's doing has thrown me, and I can barely keep myself composed.

'Was she sick?' I ask, gulping down my emotions.

'She had a congenital heart defect. We hoped that the surgeries might have corrected things, but we lost her after the third operation.'

Hearing Clara talk about Isabella like this is making me so uncomfortable that I'm fighting the intense desire to walk away, because seeing her grieving like this is almost too much for me to handle.

'I'm sorry to hear about everything you've been through. Losing a daughter...' My voice cracks. 'Must have been the hardest thing to...'

Clara looks at me through bloodshot eyes, her face twisting into a grimace. She blows her nose and reaches over, her fingers closing over my hands. She's shaking. I look at Isabella's box sitting between us and feel the staccato breath rise in my chest as I inhale.

'I'm sure that if Isabella was old enough, she would have told you that she'd want to see you happy. She wouldn't have wanted you to stop living because of her.'

She raises a hand to her mouth and takes a deep breath. 'Mia, those pictures showed me how much the boys need me, the best version of me, the mother they remember, not some hazy memory of a mother that once was. And for that, I'm extremely grateful.'

'You're going to be fine,' I say, almost breathing a sigh of relief.

'Yes, I am.' She smiles, and this time, she looks me straight in the eyes, and it does appear effortless.

She pours me another cup of tea and places the items back in Isabella's box. 'You know what, Mia, I think I'll take the day off tomorrow. It's about time we did something together as a family. How would you like to join me and the boys for a visit to the Uffizi?'

'I'd really love that.'

She lifts her cup of tea with a smile, clinks it on mine. 'To new beginnings.'

The first thing I do when I come home to the villa is call my mum.

'Mia! Is everything okay?'

'Everything's fine. I just wanted to... hear your voice. I wanted to make sure you and Dad are okay.'

'We're fine, honey. We miss you, but we're okay. He's taking me to play golf today. And you won't believe this, but I enrolled in cake-decorating classes.'

'That's great, Mum. You've been wanting to do that forever. But golf?'

'I'm doing the golf to appease your dad. I'm sure he'll be so impressed with my swing he'll be sure not to ask me to go again.' She laughs. A relaxed laugh, a genuine laugh, a laugh that's free from burden. I miss her laugh.

'Anyway, enough about us. Tell me about things. Your new job—are they treating you well?'

'I love it here.' I pause. 'I, uh… I met someone…'

Now it's Mum's turn to pause. 'You mean a… boy?'

'More like a man, Mum. His name is Luca.' I'm sure she can hear me smiling through the phone.

'You're happy,' she says, the relief in her voice evident. 'I'm happy, too, darling. I wish you were here, but I'm happy, too.'

I hesitate to speak, acutely aware of the silence between us as I ponder the thing on my mind that's tying my stomach into knots.

'Mia? Are you still there?'

'I'm here… Clara, the lady I work for… she lost a child. Her daughter wasn't even two years old. She seems so sad and broken… it made me think of you.'

'Oh, Mia.'

'There's something I need to ask you.'

'Yes?'

'If I got sick again and if things didn't go right and you and Dad were forced to… you know… live without me. Would you be okay?'

'Oh, Mia… don't tell me… Are you feeling unwell again?' she says, raising her voice in panic.

'No, not at all. It's nothing like that. I just need to know, that's all.' My voice is flat.

Mum sighs. 'I would never be okay without you. I'm your mother. You can piece together a broken vase, but you'll always be able to feel the cracks. The thing is, sweetheart, sometimes when we break, we learn to be okay with it because we have no other choice. Luckily for us, things worked out. So we all get to move on now, okay? That's what your dad and I are doing, and now it's your turn to do that, too.'

'Okay,' I whisper, hoping that I can.

'Now… tell me all about Luca.'

The following morning Clara and the boys meet me outside the Uffizi. It's early, but there's already a crowd of tourists snaking around the building in a significant queue. Tour guides carrying colourful umbrellas herd their groups into the line.

'Perhaps I can do something about this,' says Clara. She leaves the line and makes a phone call. A few moments later she's gesturing to us with enthusiasm, motioning us over to leave the queue and join her. We follow her to a security guard, who lets us straight through.

She raises her eyebrows at me. 'Perks of the job,' she says, smiling as we enter the gallery.

In this seemingly never-ending corridor of grey-and-white marble squares, my neck grows sore from trying to absorb the detail in the decorative motifs and almost caricature-like figures of men, artists, musicians and animals frescoed on the ceiling. They're so timeless I can almost smell the wet plaster. Shoulders brush against me as groups head straight for the numbered halls, oblivious to what is looking down on us from above.

'They're grotesques, which is an unfortunate name for the style, because they really are exquisite. The name has nothing to do with the depiction, but instead refers to the ancient Roman grottos in which they were rediscovered. If memory serves me right, these were created by a group of painters under the guidance of Alessandro Allori,' says Clara.

'How do you know all of this?' I ask, drawing my eyes away from the ceiling.

'Art school,' she replies. 'So much more interesting than an MBA,' she adds wryly. 'You'd love it.'

I don't have a chance to reply because Massimo interrupts, tugging at her sleeve. 'Where are the egg paintings, Mamma?'

I fall behind Clara and the twins as they forge ahead to the Botticelli Room, while the echo of each careful step through the eastern corridor lulls me to a time when apprentice artists toiled in the workshops of their masters before transforming into some of the most celebrated artists I admire today. As I step into the room dedicated to my favourite painter, I can almost hear the cracking of eggs, see the orange yolks being squeezed from their sacs to be blended with pigments ground from stones like lapis lazuli, cinnabar and malachite. Directly ahead of me is Botticelli's *Allegory of Spring*, where Clara is introducing the twins to Venus. Their voices become muted as I turn to my left to face a painting I've thought about often, one that sits at the very heart of the period of rebirth and rediscovery, the darling of the Renaissance: *The Birth of Venus*.

I draw a deep breath as my eyes hover over the dreamlike figures at the focal point of the painting, especially Venus herself. From sea foam she is brought to life, drifting to the shore. She appears almost weightless as she's about to step off the shell that has carried her to the shore. Standing there naked *contrapposto*, sensuous curves on display, tendrils of blonde hair illuminated with strokes of gold flowing around her body, she looks totally at peace. A figure wearing a floral embroidered dress awaits her arrival on the shore, ready to drape her in a billowing cloth, also embroidered with flowers. It's almost like Botticelli himself is whispering to me to take notice of what he's done here: the way his pink roses are fluttering towards Venus, so elegantly placed yet powerful enough to take my breath away. I take a step closer to the painting. Although I can't possibly understand everything he's telling me, I'm reminded of the most important things Botticelli has brought to this painting: a coming together of the driving forces of life—love and beauty, physical, divine and emotional.

'What do you see, Mia?' asks Clara.

'Everything is so beautiful I just want to leap into that world.'

'I think that's what he wanted you to feel,' she replies. 'Isn't that one of the reasons you paint?'

My eyes flick back to Venus and a smile spreads across my lips. Maybe Botticelli and I speak the same language after all.

Clara leaves me to explore the rest of the gallery at my own leisure. I meet up with her and the twins for lunch at a nearby restaurant, and I'm almost giddy from exploring hall after hall, painting after painting. Clara rests her shopping bags beside our table, all containing new clothes, shoes and swimming gear for the twins. She tells me that Ferragosto, or Assumption Day, a national public holiday, is coming up in a little over a month and this traditionally marks the beginning of the Italian holiday period, where flocks of families leave their hometowns for the beach to escape the unbearable heat, some of them taking the entire month off.

'I've organised a family holiday to Spain, a way for us all to reconnect. We'll be meeting Bert and as it happens, he's going to be requesting a transfer back to Florence soon. We're hoping he'll be back by Christmas.'

'That sounds promising,' I reply. It's nice seeing Clara like this; since our chat last night, she seems far more relaxed than usual. She invites me to go with them, but I tell her I'd prefer to stay here in Florence. Thankfully, she doesn't need me to explain why.

'It's pretty serious between you and Luca, then?'

'I guess so,' I say, as I smile into my plate of handmade ravioli.

'I noticed that you haven't stopped smiling since we entered the Uffizi,' she says. 'Stella tells me you've been doing a lot of painting lately. I really would love to see your work.'

I almost choke as my water goes down the wrong way.

'Is there something wrong, Mia?'

'No, not at all.' I shake my head. 'I'm just a bit nervous about sharing it, that's all. You deal with some really high-profile artists, and I just don't think my work would compare.'

'I'm not asking to see your work so I can compare it, Mia. I'm asking to see your work because I love art and I'm interested in you and what you do,' she says.

I set down my knife and fork to meet Clara's eyes. I glance over to the boys, who are playing beside the table with some toy cars. 'Clara, this is probably a good time for me to share something with you. Given you've been very honest with me, I feel like I should be truthful with you... about my past, that is.'

She nods and leans slightly forward. 'I'm listening.'

'I stopped painting after I was diagnosed with cancer—lymphoma. I'm in remission, but it's been a struggle learning how to paint again, learning how to trust in myself and in life again. It's taking a while for me to get a grasp on how my artwork fits into all of that.'

'Goodness, Mia, I had no idea. But what you're saying makes complete sense. I think you should share your work once you're ready, but I also think you should work towards the goal of being ready,' she says.

'I think I'm very close to being ready.'

Clara acknowledges what I've told her with a thoughtful nod. 'You're obviously doing a tremendous job of moving forward in your life, Mia. It's clear to me and anyone around you that painting makes you who you are, and in many ways it's a creative endeavour that helps you connect with yourself but also helps you to make sense of life, wouldn't you agree?'

I pause to think about her words. 'Yes, I think it does.'

'Have you given any more thought to enrolling in the Academy of Art here in Florence?'

'Not seriously,' I reply.

She takes a sip of wine. 'Well, I think you should enrol.'

'Maybe I should. I'll have a think about it.'

'I could help you with that,' she says, her mouth twisting into a smile.

I finish off my last raviolo and admire my empty plate, which means so much more to me than a good meal. It tells the story of how far I've come.

CHAPTER FOURTEEN

I spend the next month settling further into my sweet Tuscan life. Every day brings a new kind of awareness into my consciousness. My days start with a morning meditation on the swing outside, followed by a leisurely stroll to work, passing by Silvio's bar for a *caffè* with Luca. Silvio entertains me with local gossip, and they both indulge me with stories of the quirky nuances of living in a foreign country. Amongst the many things I have learned so far is that if a pregnant woman has a craving, she absolutely must satisfy it or else she should touch her behind, because the baby might end up with a birthmark and the best place for one to appear would be in someplace not visible to the public. Luca's also taught me the various meanings behind hand gestures, which I find amusing, though not nearly as much as the award-winning car-parking efforts I've witnessed in the piazza right under the noses of the traffic police known as the *vigili urbani*. I decide that these things should make it onto a list of why someone should visit Italy at least once in their lives.

During our work breaks and on our days off, Luca and I spend our time exploring the Tuscan countryside, stopping to sprawl ourselves under trees and amongst vineyards, sometimes talking, sometimes just sitting in the stillness. I'm trying to teach him how to meditate, but it always ends up in him goofing around and making me laugh. In the evenings we occasionally go out with Stella and Paolo, or we explore Florence by night. By now we have our favourite bars and meaningful spots in almost every corner of the city. Smiling comes easily, and my nightmares have become less frequent. I've only cried once in the last month, and I've painted. Boy, have I painted. I cannot imagine another day passing without painting. Life doesn't feel like a battle anymore. In fact, life could not be sweeter.

Here in Italy, inspiration for life and my artwork is all around me, in the simplest of things like a dinner-table setting or a bottle of Chianti and a bowl of grapes, or even an elderly couple who buys their bread in their best clothes every Sunday morning from the local *panificio*. Then there's the group of young boys that play soccer in the piazza, stopping only when they're called home by their screaming mothers from the apartment windows, because lunch is ready, the pasta will get cold and that will be the end of the world.

This morning I'm at the Balduccis' helping them pack. Naturally, the twins want to take far more than will fit in their suitcases. I remove Massimo's train set from his luggage. 'I'm sure you won't need this at the beach,' I say. 'Your mum and dad are going to have plenty of ways to keep you and your brother entertained. You love the water, remember? How about a snorkel and some flippers?' I grab the beach toys to show him. We finally reach a unanimous vote on what should go and what should stay.

Clara returns home after lunch as usual and tells me there's no need to return for my afternoon shift and I should enjoy the rest of the day. When I say goodbye to the boys, they each take hold of one of my legs and beg me to come with them. I kiss both their foreheads and give them a small package containing things to keep them entertained on the plane.

I turn to Clara before leaving and say, 'You know, I've been thinking about what you said. I'd like to show you my work when you get back.'

'That's great, Mia. Before I forget, I have something for you.' She unzips her briefcase and hands me a white envelope. 'We can talk about it when I return.'

The morning gives way to a soporific afternoon where I lie on the grass, basking in the sun, flicking through the prospectus Clara has obtained for me, seriously considering whether enrolling at the academy could be an option for me. I'm dissuaded somewhat by the fee schedule and turn my attention to one of Stella's recipe books instead. Tonight I've resolved to give handmade gnocchi a try.

When the sun slips away and the receding heat morphs into a pleasantly cool evening marked by the first hum of cicadas, I make my way into the kitchen, getting to work with peeling the potatoes, boiling them and turning them into the delicious little dumplings my *nonna* would have been proud of.

Luca calls me just as I'm rolling the last gnocchi on the kitchen table. He's been working in Siena for the day, helping Silvio's parents on their farm.

'Listen, Silvio's parents have asked me to stay for dinner. I can't say no—it's their way of saying thank you. But they'd like you to come too, and Silvio said he could give you a lift. He's closing the bar early tonight,' says Luca.

'So, I guess the gnocchi will have to wait until tomorrow.' I laugh, trying to keep the phone cradled between my ear and shoulder.

'I'll let Silvio know to pick you up from the villa.'

I've learned that I can't show up at someone's house empty-handed, but I can't find any unopened bottles of wine lying around in the cellar and it's too late for me to go out shopping. So instead of a bottle of wine, I take one of my paintings. This one happens to be of Silvio's bar.

'*Bella* Signorina Mia!' says Silvio, as he opens the door of his black Giulietta for me. He looks much younger out of his usual uniform. 'It normally takes me forty minutes to get to Siena, but Luca warned me not to speed with precious cargo, so we should arrive safe and sound at around seven o'clock,' he tells me with a wink. He's always been so sweet, and I wonder how someone so likeable could still be single. I decide that it simply must be a timing thing. Destiny, maybe.

We spend the trip singing to music at the top of our lungs and in between I try to teach Silvio English while he tries to correct my Italian accent. He tells me my Italian has improved considerably.

'For someone not looking for love, look at what you found in Italy,' he says as we get closer to Siena.

'Yeah, he's pretty special,' I say, as I stare out the window.

'He never stops talking about you. He'd do anything for you.'

'I know.' I lean back in my seat, reflecting on my life now compared to a few short months ago. Hearing Silvio's words sends a small pang of fear through me. We are in so deep. I push aside those fleeting thoughts that have the potential to torment me if I let them.

When we arrive at Silvio's parents' house, his mother, a stocky woman of short stature, is waving at the front gate, excited to see her son.

'*Ciao*, Mamma,' says Silvio as she kisses him through his open window. Italian sons have a reputation for being *mamma*'s boys, and I find it amusing seeing it in action. The Italian word for it is *mammone*. And Silvio, despite his age, is a big *mammone*.

'When are you going to bring a girl of your own home to me, Silvio?' she asks, her chubby arms raised to the heavens in exasperation. She's wearing a worn-out apron and a scarf around her head, looking as though she'd be ready to start dancing on a barrel full of grapes at any moment.

'Mia, this is my *mamma*. Everyone calls her Zia Flora.' He chuckles.

'Nice to meet you, Zia Flora,' I say, waving from my side of the car.

'*Buonasera*, Signorina Mia,' she says in her thick Tuscan accent. Her face is that of a woman in her early seventies, but the wrinkles sit on velvety-smooth skin and rosy cheeks. She checks the letterbox and then trails behind the car with the mail tucked into the front pocket of her apron, and a small dog by her side. Further up, Luca is leaning on the wooden fence, one hand in the pocket of his jeans. He looks so relaxed, and tonight I see something fresh in his smile. I'm so distracted by him that I don't notice the presence of Silvio's dad, who has approached the car door to open it for me, until I hear the click.

Looking at Silvio's dad is like looking at an older version of Silvio. He's as animated as his son, and he reaches for my hand like a gentleman, guiding me out of the car.

'*Ciao, sono* Beppe,' he introduces himself. 'Welcome to our home.'

He helps Silvio unpack the boot, and I walk over to Luca, who hasn't taken his eyes off me since we pulled up. He's still standing in the same position. He winks at me and takes my hands, guiding me towards him.

'I missed you today,' he whispers, his breath tickling my ear.

'Me too,' I whisper back.

His lips brush mine in a way that tells me he's not concerned with the public display of affection. As much as I'd love to play in this world of ours, I gently pull away.

'Guess what?' I say.

'What?'

'I'm going to show my work to Clara when she gets back.'

'Really? That's great,' he says, giving my hand a squeeze of encouragement.

'I know,' I say. 'It almost makes me feel like a real artist.'

Beppe shows Silvio the work they did today on the farm, briefing him on what else needs to be done in preparation for the *vendemmia*, the grape harvest, in September. His property is home to a large vineyard, and he has a good feeling about the wine this year.

We make our way into the farmhouse, and I present Zia Flora with my painting.

'This is for you,' I say.

She shrieks with joy and tells Beppe he must display it immediately in a prominent position.

'I think they like it.' I laugh, turning to Silvio.

In true Italian fashion, our dinner amongst friends lasts hours. After we clear the table, Zia Flora starts complaining about a toothache. She asks Beppe to get her some medicine and he taps her on the shoulder and signals for her to sit. He goes to the kitchen and returns with a clove of garlic, which he peels and then inserts into her ear.

'What is it?' she exclaims, touching the clove and pulling it out of her ear to take a look.

'A mighty clove of garlic,' he says proudly.

'Oh,' she says, shrugging her shoulders. She places the clove back where it was.

Beppe explains the unlimited uses of garlic to fight infection as well as some other important remedies. A glass of warm wine is called for a cold, and for the flu a mixture of milk, honey and garlic will do the trick. 'But it has to be raw honey, not the rubbish they sell in the supermarket,' he warns.

To my disbelief, half an hour later, Zia Flora declares that her tooth is no longer causing her pain. Silvio shakes his head and Beppe grins at me, saying a quiet, 'I told you so.' The word 'placebo' comes to mind, but I keep my mouth shut.

'We'll see you again for the *vendemmia*,' says Beppe as we leave.

'Does it involve stomping on grapes?'

'Of course, we can arrange that.' He laughs. 'You're family now.'

Zia Flora gives me a basketful of produce from the farm, which I place into the boot of Silvio's car.

'Where do you think you're going?' asks Luca, trailing behind me. He grabs me from behind and twirls me around. 'How does Siena by night sound?'

CHAPTER FIFTEEN

Stella heaves a large bag into Paolo's arms.

'Another one?' he says, rolling his eyes.

She pinches his cheek. 'Yes, *bello*, another one.'

Paolo's family has a holiday home in Sardinia, where he and Stella will be staying until the end of August. She hugs me affectionately before getting into the car. 'Hey, my share of the rent's on the kitchen table. Would you mind taking it to my uncle? I've left his address with the cash.'

'Yeah, sure,' I say. 'Have a great time! I'll see you both when you get back.'

I ride into Florence and, sure enough, Signor Fiorelli is sitting under the shade of a small umbrella affixed to his stand in the Piazza degli Uffizi.

'Signorina Mia!' he calls in his poetic voice. 'I haven't seen you in a while.'

'I've been busy settling in. I got a job. I'm working as a nanny for twin boys, for a family in Impruneta. Their mother's an art dealer, actually.'

'The Balducci family?'

'That's the one! How did you know?'

'Oh, I know Signora Clara very well,' he says, gesturing towards his paintings as if offering an explanation as to how they know each other. 'Over the years she's commissioned a few pieces of artwork from me.' Almost like an afterthought he asks, 'How is she?' and I know that he's referring to her loss.

'She's actually doing pretty well.'

'Tell me, has she seen your work?'

'Not yet, but soon.'

'Nervous about sharing?' he asks with a knowing look.

'Something like that,' I say.

'Aah, *bella* Mia. The artist's cure for self-doubt isn't success, nor is it approval from others. It's knowing in your heart that the creative process itself is enough to carry you through life's good times and not-so-good times. Your painting is an outermost expression of your inner self. So paint and share your art, knowing that your work is a gift, no matter what is reflected on the canvas. And do it because it is part of you, because when you don't do it, you aren't living the truest version of yourself,' he says.

I smile, contemplating his words.

'Mia, you seem preoccupied. Is there something else you want to say to me?' he asks.

'Uh, yes, there is, Signor Fiorelli. I have your rent money.'

He cocks his head to the side and frowns, his lower lip protruding from his mouth as if scanning his thoughts before asking, 'You live with my great-niece?'

'Yes. You have a very nice home.'

'Why didn't you say so?'

'I didn't know if I should. I saw your studio and Stella told me about—'

'Ah, my *amore* Amelia. Every time I went to paint I wanted to paint her. And so I resisted it, until such time that I understood that allowing the memories of her to come through my paintings was in fact the best thing I could have been doing.'

'And so you come here every day?'

'Every day, Mia, every day, since I realised that painting had the power to heal me.'

'If you don't mind, maybe one day I could keep you company? We could paint together?' I ask, hoping I don't sound too forward.

His face lights up. 'If you would like, I would love that.'

*

Luca calls me in the late afternoon, telling me he's closed the *officina* for the month and he'll be passing by in fifteen minutes. Like every other time, my heart skips a beat at the thought of seeing him again. Today we end up in Fiesole, a small, picturesque town located in the Florentine hills. He points out the Villa di Maiano before we drop in to the Fattoria di Maiano, an organic agricultural estate with its origins dating back to the fifteenth century. The friendly staff of the Lo Spaccio restaurant make sure our lunch is more than a delightful experience complemented with the local Chianti wine, to which I've become accustomed to drinking with my meals.

When in Rome... err, Florence.

After our late lunch we stroll through an olive grove before following a secluded path through some overgrown woods that eventually lead us to a clearing, revealing an almost hidden small lake, which is more like a large pond. There's nothing to be heard here except for the singing of birds and the sound of our own hushed whispers.

'Where are we? It's like we've stepped into a different world.'

'It's a secret lake. A client from the *officina* told me about it years ago, but I've never actually seen it,' he says.

I'm grateful for the drop in temperature after our long walk. Unlike a traditional lake, the small *laghetto* is surrounded by a rock wall on one side, where a quaint statue of the Madonna sits, carved into the stone. On the other side is an ancient tower with a small balcony, arched windows and a metal-studded main door. Luca and I sit with our legs over the edge of the *laghetto*, our feet swishing around in the emerald water.

He kisses the back of my hand. 'I like it when you're in your heart and not in your head.'

'What do you mean?'

'When you're not thinking about your stuff.'

'My baggage?'

'Your past.'

'You know what? I really feel like it's almost behind me, Luca. My heart is definitely leading the way right now.'

'How so?'

'You. Me. This. Us. You're the best thing that's happened to me since…'

'The cancer?'

'Since ever.'

The undercurrent of desire beneath the look he gives me is so strong I can't stand being even this far apart from him. I shift my body closer to his, my lips finding their way to his, but my smiling interrupts our kiss. I can't wipe this kind of smile off my face. Just like Luca, he shifts from dreamy and serious to playful in an instant; before I know it, he's splashing me. He stands up and takes off his T-shirt, revealing his tanned and fit body. Next, his shorts come off, exposing his boxers. Without hesitating, he makes a splash in the water.

Seconds later, his head surfaces and he calls out, 'What are you waiting for?' Swimming across to me, he takes my hand. 'It's not cold, I promise.' His irresistible smile makes it hard to say no. All my body wants to do is be near his. Half-submerged in the water, he reaches for the bottom of my dress and moves it up towards my thighs. I lift off my dress, revealing my favourite cream satin bra and matching underwear, exposing parts of my body he hasn't seen before.

Dear life, thank you for the right choice in underwear this morning.

We splash, we swim, we play, we kiss and kiss and kiss, etching treasured memories of young love in our minds that will last a lifetime in our hearts. When the skin on our fingers begins to shrivel and my teeth start to chatter, we find a spot to lie down, skin to skin, dripping wet, laughing uncontrollably just because we can. And as we let the warm Tuscan sun dry our bodies, he turns on his side to face me, head leaning on one elbow, and tells me he loves me. First in English and then, '*Ti amo.*'

Time stands still as the words sprinkle themselves over me and settle into that place inside of me reserved for him. My heart skips so many beats in a row that my hand reaches to my chest in an unsuccessful effort to still it. His hand traces the outline of my satin bra and he stops when he feels the insane beating of my love-soaked heart. How Luca has captured my heart and opened it in such a short period of time astonishes me. This is the kind of thing that happens to other people, not to me.

'So soon? Can what you're feeling be real?' I whisper, scrunching my eyes closed, hating myself for potentially ruining the moment.

'No girl has ever come close to making me feel the way I feel about you. Forget about measuring time, Mia. Love like this starts from when you feel it, not when you think you should feel it.'

'I think I should feel it in…'

His mouth forms an amused smile. 'I know that's not what you feel though.'

'I know you know that's not what I feel. And that's why I'm trying to tell you… that I love you too.'

His lips brush lightly against mine, our eyes closing, lips parting, surrendering ourselves to each other as he rolls my body closer to his and presses more firmly against me. Everything tingles. I'm not even sure I'm lying on the ground anymore because everything feels so light and dizzy, like I'm being carried away on a mattress of clouds as Luca's warm hands glide over all the curves and edges of my body.

'So now you really are *mia,*' he whispers breathlessly into my ear. My eyes flutter open, greeted by his beautiful smile hovering over me. I return the smile and then he says, 'So does this mean you'll come to Positano with me?'

'Wait, what? When are we going to Positano?'

'Can you wait until tomorrow morning?'

'Are you serious? I've been dreaming about visiting the Amalfi Coast!'

'Yeah, I noticed,' he says, tickling me under my chin.

I can't hold back my enthusiasm, but Luca suddenly presses his finger against my mouth, warning me to be quiet.

'Shh... I think someone's coming,' he says. He stands and pulls me up to my feet.

'I thought this was a secret place!' I can vaguely hear the sound of distant voices.

'It is, but it's also private property.' He laughs.

'No way!' I grab my dress and frantically begin pulling it over my head. 'Come on!' I say, willing him to hurry up. He's laughing at my urgency, taking his time as usual. I'm sure if we get caught he'll be able to sweet-talk his way out of it, but I don't care, I just want to get out of here. We grab our shoes and race through the bushes, back to the scooter, laughing most of the way.

I mount the scooter and hug him from behind. 'This has been such a good day.'

'*Amore mio*, it's not over yet.'

Back at the villa, after we freshen up and get changed, Luca grabs a bottle of wine from the cellar while I make up a platter of antipasto. We set up a cosy spot on the lawn near the swing. It's a balmy evening, the kind of evening that feels as though life has slowed down especially for us. I lie on my stomach, prop myself up on my elbows and read a book while Luca flicks through a car magazine. When the sun begins to set and the temperature drops, he takes my book and closes it, setting it down beside me. He guides me to stand, lifts me into his arms and carries me to the swing. My legs overlap his, and as the summer breeze tickles our skin, under a sky the colour of ripe peaches, we watch the rich orange sun set behind the green Tuscan hills. Completely loved up, we sit amongst the sound of silence, letting the gentle sway of the swing soothe our souls, until the first stars appear in the night sky.

'I think we should get a padlock, *bella mia*,' Luca casually whispers, gazing at the sky.

'What do you think the chances were of us meeting each other and it turning into what we have now?' I ask.

'I'd say probably close to zero. What do you think the chances are of seeing a falling star tonight?'

'Probably a little more than zero.'

'Look up,' he says.

I question him with my eyes and then he says, 'It's the night of San Lorenzo—the night of shooting stars. They're all yours to wish on—hundreds of them.'

'I don't have that many wishes though,' I murmur as I look up at the sky. Sure enough, there they are, silver streaks dotting themselves across the sky; glittering sparks of hope amongst a backdrop so vast it's never-ending. I sit there, mesmerised by how beautiful the sky looks tonight. 'I've never seen anything like this before.'

He pulls me across his lap so I'm facing him, and strokes my cheek.

'What will you wish for?' he asks, his voice low.

'Can't tell you.'

'But if you could?'

'To never be apart from you.'

'Don't ever let anyone tell you that wishes can't come true, painter girl.'

'What about you? What's your wish?'

He looks up at the sky and says, 'That we never stop feeling the way we feel about each other tonight.' Then he rests his forehead against mine and says, 'And for the record, I don't plan on going anywhere.'

'You mean tonight?'

'Tonight or ever.'

I couldn't have imagined tonight being any more special if I tried. I exhale a deep breath I've been holding onto.

My hands go to slip my shirt over my head.

'Not here, not yet,' he whispers. His hands travel under my top, sending slow currents of warmth through my body. 'Just let me kiss you.'

Suddenly everything feels like it's in slow motion, and I don't want any of it to speed up. I want to be locked in his arms like this forever.

Eventually the swinging comes to a gentle stop.

'Did you feel that?' I ask.

A smile spreads across his face. 'Your heart beating?'

'No—the raindrop.'

'It can't be raining.'

'Look,' I say, pointing to the drops of water on my arm. He takes my arm and kisses it slowly, all the way up to my neck, where his lips remain until the air turns humid. More raindrops start to fall on me, a light spray at first, followed by a few heavier droplets.

Luca must feel them too, because he pauses and looks up at the sky. 'Damn, it is raining,' he says, just as a flash of light flickers in the sky before a clap of thunder rolls in, bringing with it a light shower.

'I adore the smell of summer rain.'

'You do?' he asks in a shallow breath, bringing my face closer to his as water trickles over us.

'Mmm,' I murmur, his lips on mine, his hands framing my face.

Another thunderous boom echoes from the sky, bringing with it a downpour of droplets that hit the ground below us with force. Luca doesn't flinch or interrupt our kiss until another flash of lightning illuminates the sky.

'I should probably let you know that I'm not really a huge fan of lightning.'

He smiles lazily. 'Well then maybe we should take this inside.'

I hold onto him tightly as he scoops me up into his arms and carries me towards the villa, both of us now completely drenched from head to toe.

'Let me get you a towel,' I say.

I make my way into the en-suite bathroom and grab a towel for Luca, which I toss over to him. From the bathroom mirror I can see him sitting on the edge of the bed, where he pulls off his shirt, exposing his lean and muscular torso. As I stand there watching him, I realise just how special my feelings for Luca are. I'm all kinds of in love with this guy. The kind of love that covers all the bases, ticks off all the boxes. Physical, emotional and that rare, once-in-a-lifetime, soulful kind of love, where it feels like fate was knitted together long before you met. And when you do finally meet, you realise you've found the person you can never live without. You can't fathom how you survived even a day without that person—the one who makes you weak at the knees with every glance, smile or touch, who fills you up with so much of the good stuff that you forget what it ever felt like to be empty.

I emerge through the bathroom door into the shadows of my bedroom, lit up from the dim glow of the scented pillar candles on my nightstand. Luca's sitting on the bed, flicking through my art portfolio while he hums to some soft tunes playing in the background.

'I love this one,' he says, pointing to a painting of him sitting on the edge of the Ponte Vecchio.

My clothes are still wet, clinging to my body, and my skin has turned cold; there are goosebumps on my skin, but inside, I'm warmer and more alive than I've ever felt before. I move towards Luca so that I'm standing in front of him, close enough that I can feel the warmth of his body without him touching me. He holds my gaze with his as my hands travel down my shirt, pushing each button through its hole. The wet fabric feels heavy until I loosen it off my shoulders and let it drop to the floor beside me. Luca is watching me so intensely now that I'm finding it hard to even breathe. I inhale the top notes of vanilla, the heart notes of the summer rain, and finally, the base notes of his signature scent, the timeless fragrance that remains when the top notes evaporate away.

My hands find their way to the metal button of my jeans. I slide down the zipper and start rolling the wet fabric that has been clinging to me far too tightly and for far too long, down my waist, my thighs, and past my knees. I bend over and slip my jeans over my ankles. I take a step forward as my hands reach for the clasp behind my back.

Now I'm standing so close to Luca that I'm almost certain he can hear my heart beating. Seconds of stillness pass between us. His eyes are speaking a thousand words, but I only hear three of them. Before I can catch my breath, he reaches for my hand and stands up.

His hand travels around my waist, guiding my body closer to his, his touch warming me, breathing life into me. He rests his forehead against mine and I place my palms against his chest. My heart is racing, synchronising itself with his.

His eyes fixate on mine in a love-soaked gaze as he gently runs his hands through my hair, slowly tucking the loose strands that frame my face behind my ear. And then he brushes his lips across my cheek and whispers into my ear, 'You've never been more beautiful to me than you are right now.'

He plants a trail of slow kisses down my neck while his hand travels up my arm, his fingers slipping under the thin strap on my shoulder. He slides it down over one arm first and then the other before it falls away, and now there is truly nowhere to hide. My arms wrap themselves around him as he presses his body against mine, my body melting into his, surrendering completely as everything outside of us evaporates. He moves his hand behind my head and guides my face closer to his. I close my eyes and now I can feel the softness of his lips against mine. They're kissing me so tenderly it almost feels like I'm imagining it. He detaches briefly and in a voice so smooth and heavy, whispers, 'A lifetime of "I love yous" could not come close to what I'm feeling for you right now.'

I want to reply that I feel the same way, but as I return the kiss, I realise that I don't need to. He already knows.

CHAPTER SIXTEEN

While he makes some last-minute mechanical checks on the scooter the following morning, I call Mum and Dad to let them know I won't be in Florence for the rest of the month. Luca calls out to let me know it's time to go.

Dear Sarah, ti amo, bella mia.

She replies back straightaway. *Don't understand. Explain!*

It means I love you, my beautiful.

I love you too, kiddo. Wait! Did your lovely Italian guy tell you that?

Yes. He's incredible. Life is just perfect right now.

Told you things would turn around for you, Mia. Thrilled for you.

It's past midday by the time we leave Florence and her charming landscape, opting for the longer but more scenic route to the Amalfi Coast. I'm happily tucked behind Luca, observing the gentle hills and lush green valleys, welcoming the wind against my skin under the unforgiving rays of the sun. Two hours into our trip, Luca stops on a side road and reaches for a bottle of water. He takes a few sips and says, 'I was thinking, if it's all right with you... I haven't seen my sister and nephews since the funeral. I was thinking maybe we could stop by to say hello to them. They don't live far from here.'

I give his shoulders a squeeze. 'Of course. Let's do it.'

We reach Orvieto shortly after and park the scooter at the train station. Perched on a cliff of volcanic rock is upper Orvieto, and we can either walk to the hilltop town or take the funicular railway. Given the heat, we opt for the funicular, despite wanting to give our restless legs a stretch.

Luca shows me around the main piazza and the medieval *duomo*, stunning in its own right.

'Tell me about your sister,' I say as we stroll through a cobble-stoned street lined with ceramics shops. 'You don't talk about the accident much.'

'Rosetta? She's several years older than me. I have two nephews, Gianluca and Michele. They're six and four.'

'You haven't been back to see them since the funeral. Why?'

He shrugs. 'She wants things to go back to how they used to be, where I'd visit every month. I needed room to breathe, to get my head around what happened. Especially since…'

I question him with my eyes.

He shifts his weight from one leg to another and then clears his throat. 'I was in the car with them, Mia,' he says, a pained expression forming on his face.

'You were in the accident?'

He swallows hard. 'I was the only one who got out alive. Without a scratch. How is that fair?'

'I guess we just don't get to decide these things.'

We reach Rosetta's apartment, and Luca rings the doorbell. He takes a step back from the door, runs his hand through his hair and straightens the collar on his shirt.

'It'll be fine. She's your sister,' I say, giving his hand a squeeze. 'Does Rosetta's family speak English?'

Luca nods. 'You've nothing to worry about. The boys learn English at school and she tries to get them to practice at home whenever she can.'

'*Chi è?*' asks the voice on the intercom.

'Rosetta, *sono* Luca.'

'Luca?' The intercom goes silent, and a few moments later we hear the clapping of feet down the stairs. The door clicks open and Rosetta flings herself at her brother, kissing his cheeks, stepping back and hugging him again. Her sleek brown hair falls around her shoulders. She has his eyes. Brown, intense, perfectly rounded.

Once she calms down, she notices my presence and smiles.

'Rosetta, this is Mia. She's from Australia.'

She kisses me on both cheeks. 'Please, come in, the boys will be home any minute. They're out playing soccer with Francesco.'

Rosetta fumbles around in the kitchen, pulling out a tray and biscuits. I find it amusing that every Italian kitchen has a drawer for special food, not to be touched by anyone, only to be used for visitors. The tray is, of course, a mandatory part of the formalities.

'*Caffè?*' asks Rosetta.

'*Grazie,*' I say, making sure I don't offend.

Francesco and the boys arrive home as we're finishing our espressos. Once the boys recognise their uncle, they hurl themselves at him. Luca lifts them into the air one by one. Francesco shakes Luca's hand, gives him two kisses on the cheek and pats him on the back, telling him how great it is to see him. Luca makes his introductions again and the boys ask me lots of questions about life in Australia, like whether I own a pet koala and whether kangaroos roam suburban streets. I can't help noticing the disappointment in their eyes when they discover my answer to both questions is no. The conversation turns to some heavier stuff between Luca and Rosetta about how life has been since the funeral, so when the boys ask me if I'd like to play video games with them, I leave the kitchen to join them, glad to give Luca and his sister the space they need to talk about things.

'Are you and Luca getting married?' asks Michele.

'Idiot! You don't ask people those things. It's called personal,' says Gianluca.

'Are you?' asks Michele intently.

'Maybe one day.'

'How old are you?'

'Almost twenty-three.'

'Wow, that's old.'

'I bet I can still beat you at this game,' I reply.

Sometime later, after I've lost every game against the boys, Rosetta calls me into the kitchen for another coffee. Traces of smudged mascara lie under her glassy eyes and when I search Luca for answers he nods, letting me know that everything's okay.

'Zio Luca, Mia said you're gonna get married.'

Shocked, I almost drop my coffee cup. I shake my head, wishing the ground would swallow me right here, right now.

Luca starts laughing. 'Oh, did she? Well, I already know that one day I'm going to marry that girl, smarty pants,' he says, poking him in the stomach and throwing him over his knee to tickle him.

Rosetta smiles into her coffee cup. Francesco raises his eyebrows. I sit there, feeling the heat in my cheeks fire up.

Luca looks at me and winks. In an effort to mask my embarrassment, I grip my coffee cup with an unnatural tightness and I don't loosen it until Rosetta lifts the cup from my hands.

'Luca was telling me you're an artist.'

'I like to paint mostly.'

'You should see her work, Rosetta. This girl is amazing. She could turn anything into a work of art. Us sitting around here, for example. She could go home and paint every single detail of it with such perfection and vividness that you'd think it was a living, breathing thing.'

Rosetta smiles at my embarrassment. 'Sounds like someone's smitten,' she whispers to me. 'Come, let's chat.'

I follow her into the kitchen, where she places the tray of coffee cups beside the sink. She leans against the sink, drops her head and takes a deep breath.

'I've been worried about him, Mia.'

I frown as I try to work out what she means.

'I didn't realise how he'd been feeling about being the only one to survive the accident. He told me that he was never able to really understand why he was the lucky one until he met you.'

'Really?'

'Yes. I'm so glad you both stopped by.' She looks up at the clock. 'You know, it's getting late. You two should stay for dinner and head off in the morning.'

'That sounds great. Really great.'

She reaches for her phone. 'Let me make a few phone calls. We can't have anyone missing out or we'll never hear the end of it.'

Luca enters the kitchen and wraps his arms around me from behind. 'You know who she's calling, right?'

'Uh, no?'

'The whole family.'

'You mean, like extended family?'

He laughs. 'This place will be full within a couple of hours. Come with me. I want to show you something,' he says, leading me into the other room. He takes a photo album and sits down next to me on the sofa. 'That's her.'

'Your mother. She's beautiful. You have her eyes,' I say, looking up at him. 'And this must be your dad.'

He nods. 'I wish you could have known them.'

'Me too.'

'I should have come to see Rosetta sooner. She needed me as much as I needed her.'

'You're here now,' I say, squeezing his hand. I can't help thinking about my own parents and how I still haven't told them how much I miss them, how much they mean to me, how much I wish I had handled things better. I make a mental note to call them as soon as we return to Florence.

Luca rubs his cheeks and inhales. 'After the funeral, I was so angry that something like this could have happened to our family. My parents were here, and then suddenly… they weren't, and I became a different person overnight. I couldn't find a single reason to smile. It was like I lost interest in everything. Stella and Paolo tried so hard, setting me up on dates, insisting I go out with them, but I just wanted to be left alone. On my days off, I'd get on my scooter and ride, not knowing or even caring where I'd end up. I'd sleep on a beach in Livorno, or sit on the steps of a church in Assisi, and contemplate what it all meant—what the reason was for everything. Why we live, why we die, why bad things happen to good people. For so long, I was desperate for answers, an explanation, or at the very least, some kind of reassurance that losing both my parents happened for one good reason.'

'And? What changed?'

'One day, I somehow ended up in the Sistine Chapel. There's a fresco on the ceiling there, painted by Michelangelo. Two hands, fingers almost touching…'

'*The Creation of Adam*,' I whisper, thinking back to the painting I saw in my mind's eye during my meditation before leaving for Italy. 'God reaching out to Adam.'

'That's the one. There was something about that painting that showed me I could either keep spiralling downwards, or I could move forward, towards life again. I suppose I got tired of pushing and fighting something I knew I'd never be able to change. I'd been moving away from life, from the pain, from the confusion, from all the things I wanted to understand but failed to. And shortly after I stopped searching for answers, I met you. When you told me you were an artist, I couldn't help but think about that fresco. You made me feel alive again, Mia.'

'I'm so sorry you lost them. And that you've been hurting like this.'

'I'm fine. Honestly. You've made life better.'

Soon the kitchen is buzzing. I'm peeling potatoes and Rosetta is pouring jars of tomato sauce into an enormous pot. Francesco enters the room and starts extending the kitchen table, while Luca helps by bringing in some extra chairs.

The doorbell rings. Michele opens the door to greet the guest.

'Zia Angela!' he says.

'That's my aunt from the apartment downstairs. My mother's sister. I guarantee she'll have a cherry ricotta tart with her,' says Luca.

Sure enough, when she enters the kitchen, she's carrying a basket in one hand and an unbaked tart in the other. She shoves the goods into Francesco's arms and slides across the room to Luca, flinging her thick arms around him. She then proceeds to drown him in a sea of affectionate kisses. Luca winks at me from her loving embrace.

'So good to see you, Zia,' he tells her in his hometown's dialect. I have to work a little harder to understand them. Luca's aunt pinches his cheek before flinging her arms around him once more.

'And who is this beauty?' she asks in Italian, glancing at me and then back to Luca.

'I'm Mia,' I say, extending my arm. She ignores it and instead gives me a dose of her affectionate treatment, as if I'm part of the family, too. There is a floral scent to her, but also a floury one, as evidenced by the apron she is wearing.

She retrieves her tart and says, 'Just how you like it, Luca!'

He reaches for a plump cherry and she slaps his hand away, heading straight for the oven, where she slides it in with gusto. She then moves towards the kitchen sink, where she washes her hands and begins unpacking bags of flour and loose eggs from the basket she's brought with her.

'Rosetta! Pass me the sugar, please! And the vanilla!' she orders. 'Mia, you can crack the eggs. Eight of them. That bowl over there.'

I glance at Luca, whose face is lit up with amusement. 'Got it,' I say, raising my eyebrows.

Francesco hands Luca an olive pitter and they sit at the table filling bowls of green olives for antipasto.

'Good harvest last year?' asks Luca.

'Average. We missed you,' replies Francesco, pressing down on the pitter.

Luca pops an olive in his mouth and nods my way, explaining, 'It was a tough year. It hailed.'

Someone asks about the soccer then and the kitchen fills with a heated back-and-forth discussion about the scores. Luca's right. Within a few hours, cousins, aunts and uncles armed with dishes of the warm and cold variety, both sweet and savoury, fill the modest apartment. The feast ensues, and I think about how much love is infused in those dishes and how food can bring an entire family together. I'm told to try everything, and just when I think I can't fit anything else in, Luca grabs a fork and passes me a slice of his aunt's tart.

'You need to try this,' he says.

My mouth fills with the tart flavour of the ruby-red jewels, offset by the delicateness and smooth texture of the ricotta.

'It's so good!' I say, smiling into his eyes.

For coffee and after-dinner drinks, we move into the lounge, which is filled with a cacophony of music, laughter and lively conversation. There is the telling of jokes I cannot comprehend, but I'm not perturbed by this in the slightest. The hand gestures offer enough amusement for me. Luca's uncle picks up an accordion and entertains us with his performance. A few voices, dripping with the sound of one drink too many, chime in with lyrics I can't understand, and then Luca's *nonno*, who is elderly, takes me by the hand and leads me to the centre of the room, where he twirls me around and begins dancing, leading the way so expertly that I have little time to think about what I'm doing. All I know is that this is fun, so when he looks at me with a smile on his face, I find myself grinning back at him. Applause follows, and he takes a bow and kisses my hand before leading me back to my chair. Breathless, I sit down and look for Luca. There he is, on the other side of the room, smiling at me in admiration. This is his family in all their glory, and in this space of joy and connection with each other, I think to myself that we must come back and do this again sometime.

The next morning, after a tearful goodbye in Orvieto with promises to return sooner rather than later, we take the scenic route along the coast, stopping frequently in the various seaside towns like Sperlonga, with its whitewashed houses and alleys and clear waters brimming with tourists escaping the sweltering Rome heat. We reach Positano just as the sun is setting behind the Lattari Mountains. The coastline is surrounded by magnificent cliffs, dripping with magenta bougainvillea, and it looks as though someone has picked up the pastel-coloured buildings and stuck them on the side of each limestone cliff.

We find a spot on a private stretch of beach, where we watch the fishing boats light up the sea before their weary owners retire them for the evening. The scent of tanning oil and sticky bodies lingers in the air. The light breeze settles on my bare skin, reviving childhood memories of how I used to love licking the salt off my skin after swimming in the sea. Those were the carefree summers of endless ice creams and the absence of any kind of preoccupation other than urgency to reach the beachfront from our coastal abode each morning.

I lick my lips and the back of my wrist for a taste of childhood innocence. Luca flashes me a look of curiosity.

'I want to be in there,' I say, staring into the sea. I flick off my sandals. 'Race you in.'

Luca tears off his shoes and T-shirt at lightning speed, catches up to me and grabs me around the waist, before pulling me into the water with him. I resurface with a gasp and fling my arms around his neck, searching for his lips, my eyelids still heavy with water.

He whispers into my ear, 'If this is what the sea air does to you, I like it.'

'I love our salty water kisses.'

'Really?'

'Mmm.'

'This feels so good. I just want moment after moment like this with you.'

'By tomorrow morning all of this will be a memory. But you can keep a memory safe, you know. You carve a space and you tuck it in and you pray you'll never forget it. Or you could paint one, like I do, but in your mind. Because one day, days or years from now, you might be sitting on a beach somewhere and you might want to recall this exact time in your life—just to feel this way all over again.'

'I never want to forget the way you kissed me just then,' he says.

'Should I do it again? Repeat the moment? Make a new one?'

'What are you doing to me?'

'Just making you breathless.'

As we emerge from the water, bodies shivering and stomachs growling, Luca looks me up and down and says, 'I was going to ask whether you wanted to join me for a candlelit dinner, you know.'

'Oh, really? And what made you change your mind?'

'Mainly the fact that you're wearing a dress as a bathing suit.'

I pretend to sound shocked. 'Oh, so I am. How about pizza? On the beach?'

*

I sit on the beach wringing the water out of my cotton dress and Luca returns a while later with a towel, a couple of pizzas and a bottle of wine. Satiated and comfortably warm, I flop onto my back and close my eyes.

'It's hard to imagine how busy life used to be back home. Here, it's like time has slowed down, especially for us, so we can savour every second with each other.'

'Listen,' says Luca.

I open my eyes and turn to my side, resting my head on my hand. 'What am I listening to?'

He raises a finger to his mouth. 'Shh.'

Fluttering into my awareness comes the sound of a live band playing in the distance, along with the voices of men calling out to each other in a dialect that is foreign to me. Then comes the faint clattering of plates and cutlery from a nearby restaurant, all against the backdrop of the gentle waves that crash so effortlessly, they would remain unheard if not consciously listened to.

'That's life happening around us,' he says. 'And this,' he guides my body closer to his, 'is us making the most of life.'

'I love this life,' I whisper, catching a glimpse of the sky full of stars that feel like they're dotted there just for us.

'I love us.'

He stands up, brushes the sand from his pants and extends a hand to help me up.

'Luca?'

'Yes, *amore mio*.'

'I never want to go back home. Ever.'

'I've been waiting for the day you'd say that, painter girl. Because I didn't really want to have to move all the way to Melbourne.'

CHAPTER SEVENTEEN

The burning in my thighs as I roll out of bed this morning is a reminder of the hundreds of steps we took last night to reach our apartment. Perched on a cliff with postcard views to the sea, the only way to reach our home from the shore is to travel up a winding staircase of seemingly endless stone steps.

Luca is nowhere to be seen. Maybe he's gone for an early-morning swim. The Mediterranean sun is already filtering through the bifold door of our bedroom, which leads to a balcony where there's just enough room for a small stone table and two wrought-iron chairs. A number of terracotta pots are housing lemons the size of grapefruits, and there's a heady scent of sea breeze and tang that wraps itself around me, gently awakening my senses after a deep night's sleep.

'I should have told you that we've got stellar views. But they come at a price. You feeling it this morning?' says Luca from somewhere behind me.

'Completely, but look at this view. The steps are totally worth it.'

'I brought you a surprise.'

I turn around and it's impossible to not be distracted by his physical presence. He's immaculately dressed, as though he's been out and about already.

'What are you looking at?' he asks, a lazy grin spreading across his face.

'Nothing special,' I reply, my mouth bending up into a smile.

'Wait until you try this.' He unwraps the package he's holding. He tells me it's a local dessert called *delizia al limone*, a spongy cream custard, and it's as delightful as its name implies.

'This is so good. Wait! Did you just spoon-feed me?'

He laughs.

'I can't believe you just did that!'

'*Sono italiano*,' he says, raising his eyebrows. 'It's the romance gene. It's hard to switch off. Especially around you.'

'You sure this can pass for breakfast?'

'The Amalfi Coast is home to the best lemons in the world. They grow in every terraced garden. We're just supporting the local trade.'

'Could we visit a lemon grove today?'

'You really want to paint today?'

'How did you…? I didn't say that.'

'But you were thinking it, right?'

'Yes.'

'Read your mind. Let's go.'

After I get ready, we make our way up steps and through alleys until we finally reach an expansive lemon grove. The sturdy branches of mature trees elegantly hold the weight of fruits the colour of the sun, and thick drops of water roll off the plentiful green leaves, the residue of an early-morning spray. I snap off a leaf and crunch it between my fingers, and the citrus aroma brings me closer to what will become my subject matter. It takes me a while to find the right place to sit and work, but once I settle in, the world around me contracts and it's just me, my paints and my brushes. My eyes scan the area in front of me, and as soon as I take a step back from my easel to contemplate the scene, Luca leaves me to browse the local artisan store that lies in my direct line of sight beyond the trees closest to me. I start by sketching an outline of a basket from which oversized lemons spill. Then I move to the rows of glass bottles with their cork tops and vintage labels that read: *Limoncello di Positano*. Inside each one is a slice of the Amalfi Coast in citrus liquid form.

Somehow Luca calculates exactly the right amount of time for me to have finished the main components of my work in progress.

'Perfect timing,' I murmur.

He guides a paper straw into my mouth, urging me to take a sip of the zesty, sugary, bubbly liquid. I shift across, making room for him. 'Sit here.'

'No, keep going,' he says. 'I'll watch.'

'I don't want you to watch today,' I say, cleaning my brush with water. 'I want you to try.'

'This is your thing. I can't do this. I haven't painted since I was around ten years old. I'll ruin it.'

I slide the brush into his hand and move behind him, resting my hand over his, guiding it into the yellow paint and onto the paper.

His hands tense up and he shakes his head.

'It's okay. You won't mess it up. You just need to loosen up a bit. Like this,' I say, showing him how to let the brushstrokes flow. 'And here, if you do this, you get depth.'

He watches with interest and nods in silence before gradually loosening his grip, and then I let go completely, watching him as he takes to this new experience.

'This is why you paint and I turn screws,' he says, retiring the brush into the muddy water. 'But I like the world you play in, painter girl.'

With the sun high in the sky, we start the hike back to the apartment. Overhead, the emerald coastline glistens, beckoning us closer to it. Perspiration is dripping from my temples, which I wipe away with my forearm.

'This heat is off the charts,' says Luca, lifting his T-shirt to wipe his brow.

'Could we take a rest?'

We find a spot in the shade under a lemon tree, where the coastline dotted with sunbathing bodies, colourful umbrellas and glistening blue-green waters lies beneath us.

Luca passes me a bottle of water. 'Make sure you drink. We should have left earlier. This sun's ferocious,' he says, pouring a bottle of water over his head.

'But don't you think it's worth it? I mean, look at the view from here. Look at how good life is right now.'

He smiles. 'You've come so far.'

I nod thoughtfully. 'Yes, I think I have.'

He hesitates slightly before speaking. 'What was it like? The chemo, I mean.'

'You don't want to know.'

'No—I do want to know. I know it's behind you, but I want to know what you went through.'

I lean my back against the tree before taking a deep and purposeful breath. I don't want to ruin our holiday with memories I've worked so hard to leave behind. He deserves to know though, so I open the door and let him in and hope we will never have to discuss it again, because I am truly ready for that door to close.

I was scheduled for my first chemo session at eight in the morning. I sat on the edge of the hospital bed, picking at a loose thread on a thermal blanket. My mum paced up and down the room, poking her head out the door every five minutes. My dad sat in a chair and stared at the floor, not looking at anyone. It smelled kind of like the dentist but worse. With every inhale, I felt my stomach growing queasier.

A nurse entered the room and started checking my vitals: blood pressure, pulse, temperature. She recorded everything on a green clipboard and left the room, her rubber shoes squeaking against the grey linoleum floor. When she returned, she was wheeling in a trolley that rattled so much I thought she'd lose some of the cargo: tubes and dishes, boxes, wipes and needles, all neatly arranged on the top tray. She pulled at the fingers of her latex gloves before stretching them over her hands and tearing open a packet of sterile wipes. She started wiping parts of my body with them while I sat there imagining what might happen to my parents if I didn't make it. Would my mum walk into my bedroom and curl up on my bed, calling out to heaven for me to come back? Would my dad lose his grip on the steering wheel of his car on the way to work one morning, blinded by the tears?

'Okay, Mia, I want you to take a deep breath. Think of something that makes you happy,' said the nurse. I tried to breathe out the fumes of alcohol before leaning back into the pillow, my mind scrambling for something to hold onto before she punctured me, but nothing surfaced. I fought for a breath and then she pressed the needle into my arm, pushing through the thin layers of skin. She held a tube against it, my blood filling it up like a leaky tap. She smiled at me. 'You didn't even flinch. I'll be back soon, sweetheart.' There was a metallic sound from the vial hitting the kidney-shaped dish and then she turned to my mum and dad. 'You should grab a coffee. Just head down the hall and turn right,' she said.

'Um, when will we see Doctor Henderson?' asked my mum, glancing over at me.

'He'll come by soon,' she replied.

My mum and dad didn't say a word while we waited for Doctor Henderson.

When I couldn't bear the sound of the ticking clock any longer, I broke. 'Can you please just stop it?' My voice was louder than I intended it to be.

My dad blinked away his surprise before clearing his throat. 'What's gotten into you, Mia?'

'Look at the two of you! I'm not dead yet! How am I supposed to believe this is going to be okay if you don't believe it's going to be okay?'

'We're just worried about you,' said Dad.

'What about me, Dad? How do you think *I* feel? When that nurse comes back, she's going to pump me with poison, and in a week or two, I'm going to lose my hair!'

I could feel my mum's hand rubbing my back, but I shrugged her away. 'And it might work or it might not.' My voice turned into a whisper. 'I just don't know how to make this okay for you if it doesn't work like it's supposed to.'

My dad rubbed the stubble on his chin. 'You don't have to worry about us, Mia. It's our job to worry about you.'

'But what if this doesn't work?!' I asked, hysteria creeping into my voice.

'It's not going to get to that. Doctor Henderson said—'

'What did I say?' asked Doctor Henderson, suddenly appearing through the curtain. He offered a warm smile; I wanted to reciprocate but couldn't.

'Her chances, Doctor,' said Mum. She glanced at me nervously. 'You told us that—'

'Her chances are good. You just need to focus on here,' he said, pointing to his head. 'Now, we're good to go for today. Do you have any questions?'

Will I live or will I die?

I shook my head just as Mum nodded. She followed him out of the room and my dad made his way to sit down beside me on the edge of the bed.

'Remember when you were eight and you fell from the monkey bars at school? You begged the teachers not to call me and your mum because you didn't want to worry us, but they did because you almost passed out from the pain and wouldn't tell them where it hurt.'

I nodded. 'I remember. My arm was fractured.'

'You never complained about it hurting, so we didn't find out until three days later. I'm sorry that I never told you how brave I thought you were, pumpkin.'

'But I already knew that you did,' I whispered.

'Well, I want you to remember that you still are.'

He pinched the bridge of his nose to stop himself crying just as Mum re-entered the room. The nurse wheeled in a drip stand with a pump seconds later.

'I'm sorry, but the doctors only allow one parent to stay,' she said. She loosened the plastic tubes and hooked a bag of saline at the top of the stand. She was moving so fast I could barely keep up with what she was doing.

My dad looked at the drip for a second or two before standing up. 'You stay, Julie. I'll go get some coffee.' He looked almost relieved.

Mum glanced at him and bit her lip as they shared an exchange: one look, a nod, no words. She held my free hand while the nurse propped my arm on a cushion, under which sat a heated pad. The clear tubes snaked up and around the pump and then into me. The nurse pumped me with the saline, and then I knew I was almost ready to marinate in the liquid contained in her small zip-lock bag.

'How are you feeling, sweetie?' she asked, checking the tubes. 'Are you comfortable?'

My eyes travelled from the machine to the bag to the tubes to the needle in my arm and then back to her. 'Uh, yeah, I think so,' I replied, biting my lip.

She squeezed my other arm and smiled.

The drugs were now trickling through the bag and into my body, to the background noise of a pump, whirring and sighing and stuttering, slowly separating me from the life I once knew. I closed my eyes, trying not to think about the months ahead, but when I did, a part of me faded away, as if a part of my spirit became diluted when it let the fear seep in. My palm found its way to my heart. It was beating differently now, like I had to remind it to keep pumping. I begged my body to let the drugs do their thing, and when I opened my eyes, the nurse was gone and my mum was sitting on the side of the bed, watching me. She smiled.

'Hey there,' she said.

'I don't want to be here,' I said. 'I don't want this to be happening. I just want to go home. I really, really just want to go home.' The muscles in my face contracted and my mouth contorted into an ugly shape while I tried to hold everything back. 'I can't do this, Mum. I don't want to do this.' I pulled my arm away from the drip stand, and my mum lurched from the bed, catching it just in time. She clasped her hand around my arm, pulling it down and back beside me. She moved closer to me and framed my face with her hands, begging me with her eyes to relax. She ran the back of her fingers across my cheek and through my hair, and then I let my head fall back onto the pillows behind me. She stood up and walked to the other side of the bed and nudged me to make room for her. She reached over me for the TV remote and switched it on to a reality show.

'I hate this show,' she said.

'Yeah, me too. It sucks.'

She changed the channel and I rested my head against her chest. She was soft and warm and I could hear her heart beating. Her lips rested on the top of my head while her hand stroked the bare skin on my arm. Her fingers travelled down to my free hand and she intertwined her fingers through mine. And every few minutes she'd press her lips more firmly against the top of my head, playing with my fingers, almost like the way you'd play with the fingers of a baby, waiting for them to grip your finger back. We sat there, playing that game until the whirring of the machine stopped. And all that time, I couldn't help wondering whether she'd have to remind her own heart to keep beating if this whole chemo thing turned out to be a complete failure.

I look up at Luca, who is trying hard to mask the pool of tears fighting to escape. He turns his back to me and faces the horizon, discreetly wiping away the traces of empathy before turning back to face me.

'*Amore mio*, come here,' he says, pulling me into his arms. At his touch, a flash of panic surges through me and all I can think of is that I never want him to see me go through what I have just described. This thought brings with it a wave of nausea, and I have a hard time discerning if it's a sign urging me to stop and listen or simply a physical reaction to recalling what is finally becoming a distant memory.

CHAPTER EIGHTEEN

The last slivers of after-sun lotion stubbornly slide out of the bottle, forming a pretty flower-like shape on my arm that I admire with curiosity before rubbing it into my thirsty skin, which now smells of coconut and papaya.

'I've made some reservations for tonight at a beachfront diner,' says Luca.

I take a long sip of my lemonade, which I've been drinking copious amounts of since it became my beverage of choice last week.

'You do know I'd be happy eating off paper plates with plastic forks as long as I'm with you, right?'

He rolls his eyes without wiping away the smile that is doing the most delightful things to his face. 'I think you better leave the romance to me, Australiana.'

Laughter spills out of me. 'It is your specialty.'

'I should let you know that we have to catch dinner ourselves. From a boat.'

'So that's the catch?'

He reaches over and tickles me. 'Oh no, you're the catch. And a slippery one at that.' He slips a slice of red-wine-infused peach into his mouth and licks his lips.

'Remind me again why you do that? Your drunken peaches,' I say.

He shrugs. 'Tradition. Here, try.'

I take a bite. 'It's good.'

Luca takes a slice of peach and guides it into my mouth. 'Take mine. I'll get another.'

'No, I should start getting ready. Don't want to miss the boat.'

'We've got time,' he says, uncrossing his legs and leaning over for what turns out to be a fruity alcoholic kiss that has me questioning whether it's him or the wine making me giddy. He glances up at the clock. 'Actually, enough time to get undressed and dressed again.'

He nestles his face into the space between my neck and shoulder, and I whisper, 'It wouldn't be so bad even if we did miss the boat.'

Ours is one of many boats dotted across the stretch of water, all competing for something to bring home for dinner. There's a deliciously salty breeze sweeping through the air, and the sky is glowing orange and pink, affording us more minutes of sunlight before we need to head back. Luca reels in our second fish and it makes its way into the bucket with a splash.

'Hey, I've been thinking about what you said. How do you feel about learning to scuba dive tomorrow?'

'Really?'

'We can get certified, then see if we like it enough to keep doing it.'

'I'd love that.'

He laughs and pulls me closer. 'Looks like we're crossing that one off your bucket list.'

We make our way out of the boat, where we're greeted by a man who escorts us to a table on the beach. There's soft music playing in the background, and while he cleans and cooks our fish for us on a nearby grill, daylight fades completely. For light we rely on the gentle glow from the candles on the table and around us.

'I think we should make this a yearly thing. Thoughts?'

There's something permanent about these words that unsettles me and has been bothering me ever since my revelation on our hike back to the apartment from the lemon grove last week. I can't seem to shake the vision of Luca wiping away his tears.

He gives me a questioning look. 'Mia?'

The wine splashes down my throat so quickly that I can't hold back a cough. 'Sorry, I was distracted.'

'I don't think you were. What's wrong?'

Just when I thought our relationship couldn't go any deeper, these past weeks have given the two of us access to each other's souls. While it's clear that I can't hide my concerns from Luca any longer, it doesn't stop me from trying to.

I reach for the wine and his hand closes over mine.

'Mia, don't you think we're at the stage where you can be open with me? Are you okay?' he asks with an element of scepticism in his voice.

'I think so. I'm fine. It's all fine.'

'Are we okay?'

'Yes. We're okay.'

Or at least I think we are.

The waiter brings out our grilled fish, and I try my hardest not to poke around it with my fork. Despite its mouth-watering flavours, I force down every bite, along with my emotions, so that the evening he's gone to so much effort to organise isn't ruined.

'I've got something for you,' he says between our last course and dessert. 'Well, actually, it's for the both of us.' He reaches into his pocket, produces a small box and slides it into the middle of the table. He watches me intently as I pull the ribbon.

'I think I know what this is,' I say, a smile spreading across my face. The box is heavy and exactly the right size for the item I think it contains. 'You did it. You got us one!' I say, turning

it over to read the message engraved on the padlock: *Luca &*
(bella) Mia. I trace my fingers over our engraved names, and in
an instant my elation…

'That's my way of saying that you're my forever, Mia.'

… turns into fear.

That night I toss and turn until the first rays of sunlight trickle
through the window to our bedroom, bathing us with dappled
light, casting tiny rainbows on the ceiling.

'Up for a swim, painter girl?' asks Luca.

'I just want to sleep for a little longer.'

'You tired this morning?' he asks, brushing his hand across
my cheek.

I nod and close my eyes. 'Just half an hour.'

When I do reluctantly pull myself out of bed, it's too late to
get a spot on one of the main beaches.

'Doesn't matter, we have that,' says Luca, pointing to an inlet
where a small rock pool and lagoon that lie below us are tucked
away between the cliffs. The aquamarine water lazily beckons us
with its seductive appeal.

'I thought you said it was a private lagoon?'

'I did. It's our private lagoon.'

'You're full of surprises, aren't you? Let me grab my towel.'

The only terrible thing about stepping down the hundreds of
steps leading down to the lagoon is knowing that we'll need to
walk back up them later on. We reach the rock pool, dropping
our towels and beach bags in the sun, heading straight into the
water, which is as warm as a freshly run bath. Once we've cooled
off, we find a cosy spot to lie under the sun.

'Mia, I need to ask you something.'

'Oh? What's that?'

'Last night, you seemed a little quiet. Are you homesick? I know you said you didn't want to leave, but I understand if you're homesick.'

'Oh, no,' I say, shaking my head. 'It's nothing like that. I mean, I miss my parents, but things with them have been a little easier recently.'

'Then what is it? Because I know you didn't sleep last night.'

I hold onto my breath before exhaling deeply. There's nowhere to turn, nowhere to look away when he pierces my eyes with his intense stare. He waits for me to respond.

'You cried the other day.'

'What do you mean?' He furrows his brow.

'At the lemon grove, when I told you about—'

'That's what this is about?' His eyes widen in surprise.

'It's fine, I mean, it's okay that you did, it's just that it made me worry that if it happens again—if I get sick again—it's not fair for me to condemn you to a life where you might be the one watching me go through that kind of stuff again, Luca. If you got upset just listening to me tell you about it, and you weren't even there, what are you going to be like if you see it unfold before your eyes?'

'Of course I got upset! How did you expect me to react?'

'What happens if you lose me? You've already had to deal with losing your parents so suddenly. I don't know if I can do that to you. I don't know if it's *right* to let that happen to you.'

He sits up now and his hands begin speaking in rhythm with his words. 'You've been sitting on these worries for how long now?'

'A week? Don't be upset. Please.'

He glides his hand over his forehead. 'Mia, I am upset. Not because you're thinking what you're thinking, but because you didn't talk to me about it. You can't keep that kind of stuff inside you. We're a couple. You need to trust me.'

'I do trust you.'

'Then you need to trust that I know what I'm doing. I know you're in remission. I know what you've been through, and I know what could or could not occur in your future. We already spoke about this, and I thought you had gotten past it.'

'Well, I thought I had, too. I don't know what to say. I'm sorry for feeling the way that I do.'

'I'm not going to sit here and pretend that I wouldn't be devastated if you got sick again, or that I wouldn't be worried. But I can tell you this: I'm not going anywhere. I'm certain that I would rather live my life knowing I made every single day count with you than be apart from you, knowing that you were living your life someplace else without me.'

I draw my knees up to my chest and fight back the tears.

He stands up and makes his way to the rock pool. 'Don't let your fears come between us, Mia. What we have is too special.'

CHAPTER NINETEEN

After spending the last few days travelling to the dive centre in Sorrento and learning the basics, today is the day we're making our first boat dive. We follow the coastline to Sorrento, where Nico, our instructor, greets us at the pier. On one side, a row of colourful fishing boats sits patiently in the blue-green waters, gently swaying to the rhythm of the sea. On the other side, Nico unties a rope and motions for us to follow him onto the dive boat.

'I can't believe we're actually doing this,' I say, before stepping onto the boat.

When we reach the dive point, Nico stops the boat, and I get my gear ready. 'All right, are we set to go?' he asks, flashing a grin. 'As we descend, I want you to use your lungs and your buoyancy compensator. I'll ask you to stop so you can get the hang of what neutral buoyancy feels like.'

'Great,' I say. Luca flashes a thumbs-up sign.

Nico helps check our equipment before getting himself ready. 'Let's do this, *ragazzi*. Remember, I want you to check your depth gauges and let me know once you're at our agreed depth. Please use your hand signals. I'll be right beside you both the whole time.'

Luca squeezes my hand. We exhale on the surface and begin our descent. I'm controlling my breathing with ease, and enjoying the serene, almost motionless underwater world we've entered. Fish glide between and around us, and I watch them with sheer awe. I acknowledge Nico's hand signals and we stop before descending further. I check on my breathing and Nico gives us the go-ahead to keep descending. As seahorses drift around us, and rich red sea fans come into our line of sight, I savour each minute we spend in this underwater world as nature and I become one. As octopuses and sea animals go about their day, oblivious to our presence, I become a weightless observer of a world I had never before witnessed. After what feels like the blink of an eye, Nico signals for us to make our ascent and I reluctantly follow his instructions. Luca reaches for my hand just before we resurface and I give it a squeeze.

'Great job, *ragazzi*! Whenever you like, come back and you can do your first open-water dive.'

'We did it,' I whisper to Luca.

'That was one of the most beautiful things I have ever seen,' he replies.

I don't answer him.

'Mia?'

'Shh—I'm trying to remember it.'

When we get back to Positano, we hire a boat for the rest of the day.

'We've got one week left together here, painter girl. How are we going to make the most of it?' asks Luca, reeling in a fish. 'Sea bream,' he says, admiring his catch, before he unhooks it and releases its slippery body back into the water.

'I think we're doing a pretty good job of making the most of every day,' I reply, trying to keep my hand poised. Painting on a boat in the full sun was a terrible idea. There's a thrumming in my head that no amount of rubbing my temples seems to be relieving. 'Horse riding along the beach, romantic seafood dinners, late nights and lazy mornings. Oh, and did I mention I've developed a love for scuba diving now that I'm on my way to becoming a certified diver?'

'Told you, painter girl, we've got this,' he says. He tilts his sunglasses down and pierces my eyes with his. 'Right?'

'Right.'

He winks at me and moves to the back of the boat. Now his legs are happily immersed in the water, and the sun's rays bounce off his deeply tanned skin. I lift my sundress up, over my head, and jump off the back of the boat with a splash, the water offering temporary respite from the heat.

'Come in,' I say, pulling him into the water, where I shower him with a dozen kisses that morph into one long clumsy one as we both struggle to keep ourselves afloat. Luca disappears beneath the surface and pulls me under, tickling me. I resurface, draw my first breath, and a wave of laughter escapes me. He's laughing too, and when our laughter draws to an end, I realise with urgency that this experience will someday become a memory just like all the others.

'Promise me you'll never forget today.'

He grins at me. 'Promise.'

Later, we return to the shore and have a bite to eat at a nearby restaurant before starting our stroll back to the apartment. Making my way up the steps is turning out to be more strenuous than usual, and I pause for a few minutes, leaning against a stone wall, to wipe the perspiration from my forehead. 'You know what? This has been a really long day, and I think I've had too much sun.'

Luca places his hand on my forehead.

'What are you doing?'

'Just checking to see if you have a temperature. You seem okay.'

'Let's just rest for a bit. I'm feeling a little dizzy.'

Luca's eyes narrow. 'It might be heat exhaustion.' He screws off the lid from a bottle of water and waits for me to finish drinking. 'Let's go slow,' he says, placing his arm around my waist so I can lean on him.

We eventually make it back to the apartment, where I head straight for bed. As soon as my head sinks onto the pillow I'm out, waking only when Luca comes in to check on me.

'Feeling any better?' he asks, his palm resting on my forehead.

'Mind if we stay in tonight?' I ask, pulling the covers up to my chin. 'I think I might be coming down with something.'

'No problem.'

As my fingers travel to the spots behind my ears, to my armpits and to my groin, I hope with every inch of my being that he's right.

The following morning, I join Luca on the balcony, where he's flicking through the sports pages of the newspaper.

'How are you feeling?' he asks, pouring me a juice.

'I think I'm getting a sore throat, but I'm okay,' I reply, hoping I'll feel better after a shower.

Luca looks at me intently, trying to discern whether I'm well enough for today, a full day of diving.

'Really, I'm fine.' My back is still aching. I can barely find the energy to move, but I know today's important so I paste on a happy face and wash a couple of headache tablets down with my juice, hoping Luca doesn't notice me wincing in pain.

'Maybe we should stay in today. You look a little pale. We can reschedule.' He reaches for his phone.

'No way! I'll be fine.'

I mustn't appear too unwell because he folds his newspaper, kisses me on the forehead and says, 'Come on, then. Let's go make some beautiful memories.'

We reach Sorrento within the hour, and Nico greets us with enthusiasm, shaking Luca's hand and patting him on the back. 'You ready, Mia?'

'Can't wait,' I reply. Despite the painkillers, my body still aches and the air-conditioned dive centre isn't helping. Without drawing attention to myself, I run my fingers behind my ears and down my jawline. A veil of panic starts to slip over me as my fingers move over the two bumps, but Nico distracts me by calling for us to get our gear ready. He runs us through everything we need to know for this particular dive and I nod where I'm supposed to, trying my best to concentrate on his words instead of my body.

Nico escorts us to the dive point by boat and I spend the ride holding on tightly to Luca's hand.

'You nervous?' he asks, squeezing my hand.

'Yeah, a little,' I reply, pushing everything down into the pit of my stomach. *Just get through the dive, Mia.*

'You know what to do. You'll be fine.'

We stop when we reach a small rock in a protected marine area on which sits a bronze statue of the Madonna. Nico anchors the boat and instructs us to get ready. 'All right, *ragazzi*, this is it,' he says.

I fit my gear into place and focus on controlling my breathing, then Luca and I position ourselves on the edge of the boat. We make our hand signals and roll backwards into the water. The water closes over me and my attention focuses on descending slowly and steadily. Minutes in, Nico flashes me the 'okay' sign and I sign it back to him. Luca grabs hold of my hand then, but his touch somehow ignites a rush of anxiety in me. My chest tightens. I'm inhaling and exhaling way too fast, wasting precious oxygen as I struggle to control my breathing. I'm trying to think of what I need to do to signal to him that I need to ascend, that I need to get out of here, right now. I tug my hand away, breaking free from his grasp, kicking my flippers in a flurry of panic.

Air, I need air.

Safety feels so far away. Luca's hand wraps around my forearm tightly, and I try to twist away but his grasp is firm. He signals with two fingers for me to look at him. And then he motions with his palm flat. What does that even mean? What is he saying?

I don't remember how to tell him there's a problem. That I need to get out of here. Now.

Let me out of here right now.

He grips my arm tighter and signals again.

Slow down. I need to slow down. He's telling me to calm down. Now he's pointing to his head.

Think. Think, Mia.

Luca's signals distract me enough from my panicked breathing and I manage to slow down the ascent. We reach the surface, where Luca lets go of my arm and rips off his mask.

'Mia, what were you thinking? You could have killed yourself!'

'*Ragazzi*, what happened? Is everything okay?' calls Nico.

I make my way to the boat and climb up the ladder.

'I don't know. She panicked,' says Luca, pulling himself up onto the boat after Nico.

'Are you feeling all right?' asks Nico, checking me over. 'Dizzy?'

I shake my head. 'I'm fine.'

Nico and Luca talk amongst themselves as they discuss what transpired below the surface. I slide my gear off and curl up in the back corner of the boat with a towel around my shoulders.

'Mia, don't let today put you off. We'll go over what I've taught you and we'll try again, together, another time,' says Nico. 'It's very important that you don't panic in a situation like this, okay?'

I nod. 'Sure.'

Luca slips out of his gear and sits down next to me. 'What just happened down there?'

'Like you said, I panicked.'

'But why?'

'Maybe because I'm not feeling well.'

'You told me you were feeling okay. You shouldn't have done the dive if you weren't feeling up to it. What are you feeling?' he asks with an air of frustration.

'I don't want to talk about it. Please. I'm embarrassed enough as it is.'

He reaches for my hand, but I pull away and fumble through my backpack for another painkiller, even though I doubt it can take away the kind of pain I'm feeling right now.

I don't know how I manage to haul my body up the stone steps to the apartment. Luca pushes open the front door and holds it wide for me.

'I'm sorry I ruined today,' I say.

'Don't worry about it, you just need to rest.'

'I am worried about it, Luca,' I reply, more forcefully than I intended.

'Tell me what you're feeling.' He tosses the keys on the table and sets our bag down.

'No energy. Chills. Achy. Sore throat.' I fiddle with the belt of my dress, the belt that tells me my waist has got smaller since I last wore it.

'Okay, so we'll call a doctor.' He reaches into his pocket for his phone.

'No, I don't need a doctor, Luca.'

'But you're sick.'

'I don't want to see a doctor.' This is the truth, but my words spill out too harshly.

'Fine.'

'I'm going to lie down,' I say, heading for the bedroom. I don't bother changing before I slip under the covers. Luca curls up behind me, nestling his chin between my neck and shoulder.

'Hey,' I say, my voice flat, not bothering to open my eyes. 'You were right. I shouldn't have done the dive.'

'It's over now; stop thinking about it.'

'But I'm scared, Luca.'

He props himself up on his elbow and looks at me. 'That's why you panicked in the water, isn't it?'

'Yes.' I roll over to face him. 'My glands are swollen.'

'You're worried you're sick again, as in… Why didn't you tell me?'

'Maybe calling a doctor would be a good idea.'

'Listen to me. You're probably just fighting off some kind of virus or infection and it's likely to be nothing and then he can reassure you,' he says, his tone firm. He reaches under my ears and runs his fingers over the two swollen nodes. 'Mia, look at me.'

I avoid his gaze.

'Swollen glands don't necessarily mean…'

I close my eyes then, because I don't want to hear him finish his sentence.

He gets up and opens the bifold doors that lead to the balcony. He sits down and takes out his phone. I'm sure he's calling a doctor. When he ends the call, his knees shake at the table as he twirls an empty coffee cup in circles.

'I just realised I don't even know when your birthday is.'

'February,' I croak.

He flips around to face me. 'Date?' he asks.

'The second.'

He turns back around and keeps twirling his cup.

Doctor Rossi arrives hours later, apologising profusely for the delay. Luca tells him that if we need him again, he'll pay him 200 euros if he gets here within half an hour of his phone call. I stare at Luca, shocked at his proposal, which the doctor has shaken hands on, but he averts his gaze.

'I want you to check everything,' says Luca, hovering over the doctor's shoulder.

Doctor Rossi feels my glands, goes through my entire list of symptoms and takes a comprehensive history.

'You definitely have an infection, but come and see me the day after tomorrow at the hospital for a full check-up. We'll run some tests. I'll be sure to clear my schedule,' he says. 'In the meantime, here's a script for some antibiotics and my direct number in case you need to call me.'

'*Grazie, dottore*,' says Luca. He sees Doctor Rossi to the door and returns to the bedroom a few minutes later, then grabs his wallet and keys from the chest of drawers.

'How could you do that?'

He flips around and looks at me strangely. 'You can barely sit up, Mia! You heard what he said, you need antibiotics.'

'I don't mean calling him. I mean making a deal with him like that.'

'What you just saw is nothing compared to what goes on in this country,' he dismisses. There's no use in getting him to see it my way. He's adamant that he's done the right thing. 'Nobody in this world is more important to me than you are. And I will do whatever it takes to look after you. Whether you're sick or not.' He folds the script and tucks it in the pocket of his jeans.

My mind shifts into overdrive, playing all the different kinds of scenarios in my head, all dependent on the results of Doctor Rossi's tests.

'What if the cancer's back?' I whisper.

He rubs the stubble on his chin. 'It can't be back.' Then he runs his hand through his hair and says, 'I'm going to the pharmacy to pick up your medicine.'

'I don't want to have the tests.'

'You have to have the tests, Mia. The results are going to confirm that everything's fine.'

'But what if they don't?'

He walks out the door, leaving me without an answer.

*

At the hospital, Doctor Rossi leads us into a room and takes some blood. 'I'll see what tests I can manage to do this morning, and then you can come back again tomorrow for more,' he says.

'She's not going anywhere until you run whatever tests you need to run,' says Luca.

Doctor Rossi puts me through all the tests and asks for permission to call my oncologist back home for some background information. I agree, but the thought of having to tell my parents about this unsettles me. I don't want to worry them unnecessarily.

By late afternoon we're given the okay to go home.

'It'll take some time for the results, but I'll call you as soon as I have news,' says Doctor Rossi.

I can't quite decide whether or not I want to hear from him.

CHAPTER TWENTY

Today is supposed to be our last day in Positano, but it's not, because Luca has insisted I'm not well enough to go home yet, even though the antibiotics have kicked in and I can get out of bed in the morning without feeling like I've been hit by a semi-trailer. The coffee machine's broken, and Luca has spread out dismantled parts and screws all over the outside table.

'If I could just get this part here to work,' he murmurs, turning a piece of plastic around between his thumb and forefinger. I know he's enjoying himself even if he acts like repairing this machine is a chore. Pulling things apart and putting them back together is Luca's style of meditation, his unique way of unplugging and resetting. I stand there for a while, watching him, until he looks up at me and smiles. He flashes me a wink and I have to turn away because every time he looks at me this way, my body reacts accordingly, and this time when I feel the flutters, they're diluted with emotions I can't seem to shake yet know I need to work through.

'I think I might go for a walk,' I say, grabbing my cap and sunglasses.

'Are you sure you're up to it?'

'I need the fresh air,' I reply.

'Okay, well, wait up, I'll just be a second,' he says. 'This can wait.'

'No, keep doing what you're doing. I won't be long.'

His eyes linger on me as I leave the room. I carry the weight on my shoulders out of the apartment and to the starting point of one of the hiking tracks that connects various towns along the coast.

A grey sky looms above while I set off down a jagged path lined with overgrown bushes and wildflowers. I pick a sprig of wild rosemary and slowly tear away each needle-like leaf until I'm left with a woody, brittle stem. Any day now Doctor Rossi is going to call. If he tells me what I don't want to hear, I need to be prepared for what that means, not only for myself but for Luca. I haul my body uphill, pushing for answers, feelings, direction. I push past the fatigue, focusing on the luminous stretch of turquoise along the jagged coastline until I can't feel the pain in my legs anymore. I reach the summit, panting for breath, feeling no lighter than I did before, no closer to deciding what to do. All I know is that I need to make a decision before Doctor Rossi calls.

A carelessly erected wooden fence offers little protection from the steep drop to the sea. The clouds break and as I stand there under the summer shower, with nothing to protect me from the rain, my heart argues with my head.

'Hey, you were gone all day, I was worried about you,' says Luca, opening the door to the apartment. He almost takes a step back when he sees me. I must look as dishevelled as I feel.

I give him a quick peck on the cheek and head for the kitchen to pour myself a glass of water.

'Why were you worried about me?'

'Because you were gone all day. You said you were going to be back soon.'

'You don't need to worry about me.'

'The coffee machine works. It took me all day to fix,' he says. He approaches the counter and goes to grab a cup. 'Want a coffee?'

'No, thanks.'

'Do you feel like going out for dinner tonight? We could try the—'

'Um, I'm a little tired, actually. I think it's going to be another early night,' I say, heading towards the bathroom. 'I shouldn't have stayed out all day.'

'Then why did you? What's going on with you, Mia?' he asks, following me into the bathroom.

'Nothing, I'm just going to take a bath. I went hiking today. I'm filthy.' I bend over, push the plug in and turn on the tap.

'You know that's not what I mean. You didn't even take your phone with you.'

'Well, I'm sorry about that, but I forgot it.'

'No, you didn't.'

'Yes, I did.'

'Mia, don't do this.'

'You're right, we shouldn't be arguing over a stupid phone.' I reach for the bath salts and toss a handful into the tub. They fall against the surface like a spray of bullets.

Luca looks at the bag of salts and then at me. 'That's not what we're doing.'

'The water's running, Luca, and I'm aching. My legs are aching.'

He turns around and closes the door behind him. I bang my palm against my forehead. I don't want things to be this way. I don't want it to be like this. I turn back to the door and poke my head out.

'Did Doctor Rossi call while I was out?'

'No, he didn't.'

'What do you feel like doing today?' asks Luca the following morning. He pushes the button on the coffee machine and clicks his tongue with satisfaction. 'Works better than it did before,' he says. He hands me a short *macchiato*, grinning.

'No, thanks,' I reply.

He tilts his head and looks at me curiously.

'What?' I say, shrugging my shoulders.

'I know you're worried, but waiting for that phone call is making you act a little crazy, painter girl. Have you called your parents yet?'

'I think we should go down to the beach,' I reply, dismissing his question.

'That's not what I asked.'

The thought of having to call my parents to let them know I'm waiting on test results is unbearable. My parents would be beside themselves at the slightest hint of me being sick again.

'They would want to know what's going on with you, Mia. And you might even feel better if you spoke to them.'

'No, Luca,' I reply firmly. I'm trying to ignore the nauseating feeling in my stomach. 'Let's go.'

'But you haven't had breakfast yet.'

'I'm not hungry.'

I head to the bedroom and start stuffing beach gear into my bag. When all the usual things don't fit, I turn it upside down and shake all the contents out onto the bed.

Luca leans against the door frame of the bedroom and takes a bite of his croissant. The way he stands there casually, like there's nothing wrong, like this is just another day, irritates me. Luca never irritates me.

'You barely touched your dinner last night, I'm pretty sure you skipped lunch yesterday and—'

'Please, Luca, just drop it. I don't feel like breakfast, and I don't feel like analysing it. Let's go before we miss out on a spot on the beach.'

'We don't need to rush. We have our own private lagoon. We can go there instead if we need to.'

'I don't want to go to the lagoon today. I want to go to the main beach,' I say. As I reach for the bottle of sunscreen, I force myself to slow down, calm down, breathe. I pick up our belongings and place them in the bag: our water bottles, our hats, my book, his magazines. These items had no significance yesterday, but as I tuck them away, they fit into my bag perfectly, suddenly meaning everything to me.

Luca takes the last bite of his croissant and, with his mouth full, says, 'Fine. Let's go.'

'I'm sorry,' I say, feeling helpless.

He takes the bag from me and kisses me on the head. 'Come on, *andiamo*.' He goes to grab our phones from the chest of drawers.

I grab his wrist and pull it back. 'No phones today. Just us,' I say.

'But what if…' He stops himself. 'Okay. Just us.'

Just for a little while longer.

When we arrive, I watch Luca at the beach bar organising the payment for our sun loungers. A girl, probably a few years older than me, approaches him and hands him two rolled-up towels. She flicks her hair away from her face, and from the way she's standing, I can tell she's flirting with him. Luca smiles back politely, tucks his wallet in his pocket and looks straight past her, to me. She stops talking and glances over her shoulder, looking me up and down, before heading back behind the bar. As Luca walks towards me, a shattering sense of guilt crashes against me. If Doctor Rossi calls with news we don't want to hear, I know that Luca will be equally crushed. A relapse will mean having to return home to Melbourne for treatment. No matter how I look at it, I can't find a way for Luca to fit into that life without hurting him. While I have some control over a few things in my life, the only thing I know I can control with certainty is how deeply I hurt him. Even if Doctor Rossi tells me everything's okay, another doctor might call tomorrow telling me it's not. Saying goodbye while things are like this surely has to be the less painful option for Luca.

He opens the umbrella and moves his sun lounger closer to mine so that they're touching. He takes off his shirt, lies down beside me and turns to his side. He leans across and lifts my sunglasses off my face and then his hand glides over my stomach, gently resting it there. He drinks me in like he always does before kissing me, the slow blink of his eyes capturing my attention, before his lips connect with mine, first slowly and then more deeply. This kiss breaks me apart in a way none of the others have, maybe because I'm not fully part of it or maybe because I'm so focused on not forgetting it.

'I feel like I haven't kissed you in years,' he whispers. He leans back into his lounge. His hand searches for mine, and I find myself staring at the way my hand fits perfectly in his.

'You know, painter girl, I've been thinking—I've kind of gotten used to waking up beside you every morning,' he says.

My heart skips a series of beats before my entire body freezes. 'Yeah, me too,' I reply, my voice barely louder than a whisper. Sleeping alone will take some getting used to. One of the best feelings I've ever experienced has been knowing he's been there beside me all night, night after night. I hide behind my sunglasses and sink deeper into the mattress of my lounger.

'I don't ever want to know the feeling of waking up with an empty space beside me again… So I'm thinking we need to figure out how to fix that when we get home,' he says casually, looking out at the waves lapping gently against the shore.

I squeeze his hand so I don't have to respond. Just for a little while longer.

*

The first thing I do the following morning is check my phone, as if there might have been a chance that Doctor Rossi called during the night without me hearing my phone ring.

'Good morning, *bella mia*,' says Luca, rolling over to face me.

He reaches for the top drawer of his bedside table. 'I know you said your birthday isn't until February, but I got something for you,' he says, handing me a gift box. Inside is a charm for my bracelet, a silver art palette, studded with coloured crystals.

'I thought it might cheer you up,' he says.

I concentrate on fastening the clasp, hands trembling, heart racing. 'It's perfect, thank you.' I give him a peck on the cheek and then get up, hoping I can make it to the bathroom before I crumble.

'Hey, where are you going?'

I take a deep breath and glance over my shoulder at him. 'Shower,' I reply, avoiding eye contact. I know that one smile could be all it takes to change my mind. I sit on the cool bathroom tiles, knees pulled against my chest, listening to the running water as steam fogs the room. And all the while, I am trying to draw the strength to do what it is I need to do, don't want to do, have to do.

Luca showers after me while I prepare breakfast.

'Hey, should we go to Capri today?' he asks when he emerges, running his hands through his wet hair.

'Um, I don't know.'

'Okay, well, you decide. We'll do whatever you want to do.' He finishes fastening the buttons on his shirt and sits down to join me.

'Let me just think about it for a minute.'

His eyes narrow and I can feel him looking at me as he takes a sip of his coffee. I force down the rest of my breakfast. When I'm done, I immediately start clearing the table, not caring that Luca has yet to take the last sip of his orange juice.

'Hey, what's the hurry?' he asks, following me into the kitchen.

I start packing the dishwasher so I don't have to look at him.

'What's going on in that beautiful mind of yours, Mia? Talk to me, tell me what's happening.' He moves closer to me and tries to hug me. I push him away. I take a deep breath. There will never be the right time for what I'm about to say.

'Mia?'

A glass slips from my fingers and smacks against the tiles, and now I'm a trembling mess, surrounded by shards of glass and spilled orange juice. No matter where I step, I'll step on broken glass. I stand there in the middle of the kitchen, frozen, not sure where to move, and when I look up at Luca, he's staring at the floor, too. We look at each other and I go to speak but can't. I'm mute.

'I need some fresh air,' he says.

There is a dull ache in the silence between us that lingers long after he leaves the room. He walks out of the apartment, slamming the door behind him, leaving the vibrations of his tension release to reverberate throughout my entire body.

Luca returns an hour later with a bunch of flowers, carrying himself the way he usually does, cool and collected.

'I'm sorry, I just don't know how to make this easier for you,' he says, handing me the flowers. 'I know that waiting for that phone call is hard, but you have got to trust that things will be okay.'

'Luca, stop. I'm the one who needs to apologise. You did everything right.' I clear my throat and take a deep breath. 'Look, I know it's been an emotional few days and I haven't been myself.'

He nods.

'This isn't what life is like for everybody though. I mean, what I'm trying to say… is that this isn't a good idea.'

He inhales deeply and stares at me intently. 'What, exactly, isn't a good idea?' he asks, his eyes searching mine.

'This. Us.'

He starts shaking his head. 'Don't let this freak you out, Mia.'

'But I can see how worried you are! You keep saying the test results are going to come back clear, but I see the way you jump when the phone rings, the way you looked at me when I told you my glands were swollen. I know that deep down you're as worried as I am. And I can't do this to you.'

'What are you talking about? What exactly do you think you're doing to me?'

'It's not fair to you. Trust me, it will be so much easier for you to say goodbye to me now.'

He runs his hands through his hair. 'I honestly can't believe I'm hearing this. This is crazy, Mia. What you're thinking is crazy. Your test results—when they come back clear? What then?'

'If this is a scare, there might be others after this one. And if this or the others confirm a recurrence, I'm not prepared to let you see me wilt away before your eyes. It's better if we stop this now, before it gets more serious.' I bite my lip in a futile effort to stop the quivering.

'How much more serious can it get? This isn't a practice run for me.'

'It's what I want.'

'This is not what you want. And it's not the solution to your problem.'

'My problem?'

'Your fear. Everything you've been running from. You're not scared of dying, Mia—you're scared of hurting the people around you who you love the most. But you have got to get your head around the fact that I can handle this. You need to trust me. You don't need to worry about me.'

'But I'm doing this for you! *Because* I love you.'

'This is unbelievable,' he says, throwing his arms up in the air. He moves towards me and takes the flowers from me, setting them on the bench. He tries to touch me; I pull away.

'Sorry,' I blurt. 'I can't do this.' Hot tears fill my eyes and an overwhelming sense of guilt washes over me, causing all kinds of profanities to be directed at myself, all of them confined to my head.

'Stop,' he says, pulling my hand towards his chest. 'Feel,' he instructs.

'This, Mia, *this* is how I feel about you,' he whispers. His heart is racing; his skin is flushed and warm.

I lower my gaze. 'I'm sorry. I thought I could, I honestly did… but I can't…' My voice is fractured.

'You're thinking about killing something that doesn't need to die,' he says.

'I've already thought about it. It's easier this way.'

'Easier than what? Easier for who? You can make all the excuses you like. But you know this isn't what you want.'

'Stop.'

'Stop?' He raises his voice and I flinch because his voice is filled with so much hurt it's almost unbearable for me to listen to it. 'You tell me why you want me to stop. Why don't you want to hear this?'

'Please,' I whisper.

'What? You want me to tell you that you don't matter? Make it easy for you?'

'No. Of course not.'

'Then what? Because I'm too old for games. I've played them all before, and I stopped playing them the day I met you.'

The words roll out slowly, because I know how hopeless they sound. 'I'm not playing games.'

'Then you need to have a conversation with that voice in your head that's telling you to do this. Because I have made it pretty clear that I love you and I'm prepared to be with you, by your side, *if* you get sick. Which you won't. But *if* you do, I'm there. *Capisci?*'

'No,' I reply, my voice void of emotion.

'Then we have a problem. When I wake up in the morning, I see your face. When I go to sleep at night, I see your face. All that matters to me is your happiness. I'd do anything for you. But I'll warn you now, I will not let you go without a fight. Don't expect me not to fight for you.' He pauses and then lowers his voice. 'I'm prepared to lose you, Mia, but not like this.'

'But I'm not prepared for you to lose me any other way.'

It takes every ounce of willpower I have to turn around. I know that if I don't move now I might slip back into his arms forever. By some miracle I'm able to move my body forward. I slowly close the front door behind me and head down the steps, chest pounding, legs trembling, heart breaking. Two hours pass while I sit on the pebble beach, staring into space, unable to shed a tear, my heart closed, just like old times. When I eventually head back up the steps to the apartment to gather my belongings, there's a note on the table for me:

I've gone looking for you. Stay here and wait for me so we can talk. Luca xo

I scribble a note on the back of his:

I'm going back home because I know that if I stay, you'll never let me go.

I purposefully leave my phone at the apartment because I know that it will take little more than the sound of Luca's voice to get me to change my mind. I take the bus to Sorrento, and two train changes later, I'm back in Florence. Arriving back to the villa, I'm relieved to find that Stella isn't home. The landline starts ringing. I let it ring out three times until I can't ignore it any longer. It's Luca.

'I wanted to make sure you got home okay,' he says, his voice flat.

'Yes, I did,' I reply, trying to keep my voice even.

'Are you okay?'

'Yes.'

'Do you need me?'

Yes. I need you. I don't know how I'll live without you.

'No. I'm okay.'

He clears his throat. 'Doctor Rossi called. You're clear, Mia. It was just an infection.'

My hand grips the phone tighter. 'That can't be right. Are you absolutely sure?'

'He even got your oncologist back home to check things over.'

I cover my mouth with my hand and stare at the phone in disbelief. I'm stunned. Shocked. Relieved. Not relieved.

'Mia?'

Nothing.

'I'm leaving now. Everything's fine. We'll talk when I get there.'

Nothing.

'I love you, Mia.'

I love you too.

He hangs up, and then there is silence.

I drop to my knees and stay there until I can no longer feel the sensation in my legs. And all I can think of is that nothing can heal us, or hurt us, quite like love can.

CHAPTER TWENTY-ONE

When Stella arrives home at nine o'clock that evening and checks on me, I pretend I'm asleep. She walks upstairs and a few minutes later I hear her stomping back down again. She barges into my room and rips the covers off me.

'Leave me alone, Stella,' I groan. I try to pull the covers over my face, but she won't have any of it.

'Get your ass into the kitchen,' she says, switching the light on as she leaves the room.

I scrunch my eyes closed at the sudden influx of light and obey like a child, using every ounce of strength to pull myself out of bed to face Stella's wrath.

She pulls out a heavy wooden chair, scraping it viciously against the terracotta tiles. 'Eat,' she says, shoving a sandwich in front of me. She opens a bottle of wine and pours me a glass. 'Whatever you need to get out of your system, get it out now.'

I slide away the wine glass and she firmly places it back down in front of me, like a mother of a small child who isn't complying at mealtime. I know there's no point fighting Stella. Her relentless nature would win every time. She's determined to pull me out of this hole, and I suddenly hate her for it.

'I can't talk about it, Stella,' I tell her as adamantly as possible. 'It's also none of your business,' I add, hoping this will be the end of our conversation.

'Can't talk about what?' she asks. 'Luca sounded pretty upset when Paolo spoke to him earlier today. Whatever you did, you've done a great job of messing up something great,' she says, crossing her arms, waiting for my reaction.

My stomach is churning and my head is spinning. I know I should eat, but I have no appetite.

'It's nobody's business,' I say coldly.

'Your relationship with him is nobody's business. But you? You're my business,' she says, like a tigress ensuring the wellbeing of her cub.

'I'm not your problem,' I mutter, with an ugly bitterness in my voice.

'Friends. Friends, Mia. You know, *amicizia*. You're practically family,' she says. 'The people who care about you? We worry. It's okay for us to worry. I've only heard about what happened via Paolo, but if you think anyone believes for a second that you're not in love with him or that he doesn't mean the world to you, then the only person you're kidding is yourself. And you can bet your ass that you're making the mistake of a lifetime because what you and he have is unlike anything I've ever seen before.' She reaches for her wine glass and takes a gulp.

The tears slowly begin to roll. I cry for what could have been a relapse and for what I'm doing now. I can't make heads or tails of this distorted reality contaminated by fear. Throwing everything that's good in my life down the drain surely cannot be the way forward.

'Let it out,' she says. 'All of it. As long as it takes.'

When I don't have any tears left or energy to expend, Stella reaches for a box of tissues and pours me a shot of strong liqueur. 'You have to eat though. Just a little bit,' she says.

I don't have the energy to argue with her so I take a bite of my sandwich. She waits until I finish and then hands me the shot.

'Now we talk,' she commands.

'I got so scared. I didn't want to hurt him. You should have seen him. He was worried. He tried to hide it, but those doubts about whether I was sick or not—I saw the fear in his eyes.'

'You need to let him love you.'

We're interrupted by Stella's phone ringing. It's been buzzing continually with text messages. I know it's Paolo because of the ringtone.

'Hold on. I'll tell him I'm busy.'

'*Pronto, amore*, I can't really chat now. I'll call you back tomorrow.'

Paolo's voice is unusually loud, but I'm not close enough to hear what he's saying.

'What?' she gasps, her hand covering her mouth. The colour drains from her face as her voice wavers. 'What do you mean? Which hospital?'

She darts out of the kitchen and grabs her jacket from the sofa.

'What's wrong?' I ask, following her as she races around the house, trying to find her keys.

'There's been an accident. I have to go,' she says.

'What kind of accident? Who's hurt?'

'You don't know her,' she says, sounding desperate.

'Let me call you a cab, you can't ride in this state.'

'Stay here until I call you,' she says.

I grab her phone and follow her. 'Wait! Your phone!' She's already out the front door and by the time I call out again, she's whizzing past me on her scooter.

I wrap myself in a blanket and sit on the swing outside, taking the time to reflect on everything Luca helped me to see, and how because of him, I've been able to truly embrace my life. I know this isn't the answer. It's almost ten o'clock, and he still hasn't come past the villa. Maybe he's changed his mind. I try calling him using the landline, but there's no answer. I curl up on the sofa, the music videos on TV giving me a false sense of company. Dozing on and off, I fully wake at two in the morning to find that Stella still isn't home and neither is Luca.

I decide to use Stella's phone to text Paolo so I can check on her, but picking up her phone, a series of unread text messages from Paolo catch my eye.

21.38 Stella, call me please. There's been a horrible accident. It's Luca.

I open the history of text messages, my fingers trembling so violently that I drop the phone several times.

21.22 Amore, call me. I need to speak to you ASAP.

21.26 Stella, call me.

21.30 Stella, it's urgent. Call me now.

21.38 Stella, call me please. There's been a horrible accident. It's Luca.

I fall back against the wall, and my body slides down to the floor.

Luca.

I am stone cold; the only reason I know that I'm still alive is because my hands are shaking. My entire body is trembling. I pick up Stella's phone. I dial Luca's number.

No answer. I try calling multiple times in succession, followed by a text message: *It's Mia. I'm sorry. I love you. I'm so, so sorry.*

I call Paolo's number. No answer.

My cab shows up thirty minutes later. I hope I have the right hospital.

Barging through the sterile doors, I fling myself at reception and blurt, 'I'm here for Luca Bonnici.'

'*Si, signorina.* Hold on while I find out where he is,' says the triage nurse. She makes a call to someone while I impatiently tap my fingers on the counter. If he's gone, I don't know how I'll live another day.

Life, you can be so cruel.

'I'm sorry, *signorina*, but he's in critical condition. Only family is allowed, but in the waiting room only,' she says.

'But I am his family,' I squeak.

I am his. He is mine. Please. Please, God, don't take him away.

'*Va bene*, come this way, dear,' she says as she shuffles down the sterile corridor, our footsteps echoing loudly.

The nurse points to the intensive care unit but warns I am not allowed into Luca's room. She tells me that a doctor will be here at seven in the morning to speak with us. She turns the corner and that's when I notice Stella, sitting in a chair, hunched over, hands clasped, head bowed.

'How dare you! How dare you not tell me! Why didn't you tell me? How could you leave me at home like that?'

She gazes up at me in her half-dazed, shocked state. Her eyes are as puffy as mine, with traces of mascara smudged across her cheeks. She blinks at me with eyes filled with the deepest kind of sorrow. My anger is quickly replaced by guilt.

'I'm so sorry, Mia. We didn't want to worry you. We wanted to wait for the doctor first. We thought it best to break it to you gently,' she says. 'I knew how upset and fragile you already were. I was just trying to protect you.'

'Break what to me gently?' I hold my breath, waiting for an answer.

As soon as I ask the question, I regret it. I know that as soon as she answers, life can never go back to what it was before I ruined everything between me and Luca.

Paolo emerges from a nearby bathroom and joins us. Stella starts sobbing, and I turn to Paolo for answers. In his dishevelled state, he, too, looks visibly unsettled.

He clears his throat and takes a deep breath. 'Mia, he was in a bad accident earlier this evening,' he says. 'We don't know much about what happened, but we do know that he lost control going around a bend and hit a tree.'

'No.' I will not accept this. This is not happening. 'Which bend?'

'It doesn't matter,' he says, resting his hand on my shoulder.

The anger rises in my throat. 'Which bend?' I demand, although I think I already know the answer.

'The bend around the corner from the villa,' he says.

This cannot be true. 'What time?'

'We don't know for sure. Around eight o'clock, we think.'

Luca is a skilled driver and rider. There's no way he'd have lost control under normal circumstances.

'It's my fault. He was coming to see me. What have I done?' I ask, my eyes filling up with tears. My hand clasps my chest in an effort to still my racing heart. I'm struggling to breathe, starting to hyperventilate.

'Mia, honey, this is not your fault,' says Stella.

'Stella's right,' says Paolo. 'Don't blame yourself. You know he wouldn't want that.'

'But you said he was upset.'

'Yes, he was. But you know what he's like—he knows how to keep a level head…' The rest of Stella's words trail off into nowhere.

'How bad is it?' I ask finally. My body tenses as I brace myself for an answer I don't really want to hear.

'We don't know,' they say in unison. Neither of them can seem to look me in the eyes.

'Stop lying to me! What do you mean you don't know? You've been here all night! Where are the doctors around here?' I yell.

Stella cringes and turns away.

'They won't tell us anything other than that he's in a coma,' says Paolo.

'*What?!*'

'And that he suffered several broken ribs and internal bleeding. Aside from that, we don't know anything,' he adds.

'Someone needs to call Rosetta,' I say.

Stella still can't look at me. She walks away and sits on a dark blue vinyl chair.

I'm numb.

I take my spot beside Stella and wait.

For the doctor.

For a miracle.

CHAPTER TWENTY-TWO

When the first pink hues light up the sky, I watch the sunrise through the window, praying that Luca will live to see the beauty of such a treasured daily occurrence as this, one that is so often taken for granted. Paolo brings me a coffee. It grows cold by the time I remember to take a sip of it. I fix my gaze on the dated wall clock, watching it tick over and over and over again until the weight of a hand presses on my shoulder.

'He's here,' whispers Stella, nodding in the doctor's direction. He's wearing a pair of blue scrubs, a surgical cap with ties that have come undone at the back and a pair of glasses that have slipped down his shiny nose. Must have been a hard night. He pushes them up when he starts to speak.

'*Ragazzi*, Luca has sustained some considerable injuries. He went into cardiac arrest twice, once in surgery and once post-surgery.'

No.

'There's some swelling on his brain and he's in a coma. This is a touch-and-go situation. I wish I could tell you more, but for now the best advice I can give you is to pray. If you like, I can call a priest.'

Paolo declines the priest and asks what Luca's chances are.

'It doesn't look promising,' he says. 'I'm sorry. I wish I had better news.'

'I want to see him,' I say.

'I don't think that's possible right now, *signorina*.'

'It wasn't a question,' I hiss.

'Five minutes,' he says, after considering me. 'I'll have the nurse call you.'

When I'm finally allowed in, I hover, quivering, in the doorway. Between the swelling, bruising, the ventilator and tubes, he's barely recognisable. There's no sound in the room except for the steady hum of the machines that are keeping him alive. When my brain confirms that it's him—it's really him—I release a moan from deep within, the sight in front of my eyes too unbearable for words. The nurse gives my hand a squeeze.

'*Forza*—you need to be strong for him,' she says.

'Can I touch him?' I whisper.

'Yes, dear. No hugging. He has some broken ribs. Most of his injuries are internal.'

My legs are frozen at the foot of his bed, but my body is shaking. Sensing my hesitation, she hangs her clipboard on the bed and takes me by the arm. She sits me on the chair next to the bed and says, 'You need to pray for him. Tell him you love him and that you need him to come back.'

'What does that mean?' I ask in a scarcely audible voice, and when she doesn't answer, I feel almost relieved. She leaves the room and in the silence, broken only by the beeping of monitors, I start counting the number of tubes connected to Luca.

'Please, Luca. Please come back to me,' I whisper through the tears. I'm holding his hand, kissing it, begging for him to come back to me, over and over again.

Footsteps break the heavy silence. I make out Stella's figure. She stands beside me and gasps when she sets her eyes on him. She stands there, frozen, the colour draining from her face as her hand covers her mouth. Not even I can comprehend the image before me; it's as though a movie is being played before my eyes, and I'm somehow just an observer.

'This can't be…' Her face twists into a pained expression.

'I don't know what I'll do if he—'

'Mia, don't say it, please don't say it.' She looks terrified, as if voicing it will make it happen, as if we somehow have control over it. She flings her arms around me, and I hold onto her tightly. I'm sobbing into her shoulder, and she's sobbing into mine. Eventually, I manage to pull myself away from her.

'Everything was perfect, Stella. We had *everything*. He'd look at me and know what I was thinking. All it took was his smile to make me feel alive each morning. He made me laugh like I'd never laughed before, and when I was with him he made me forget there was a world that existed outside of us. I want our world back, Stella. I need him to make it. He has to make it. I need someone to tell me he's going to make it.'

She looks at me blankly, like she's teetering on the edge of telling me what I want to hear. She blinks a couple of times and then bites her lip. I feel the waves crashing against me again, hitting me over and over in the pit of my stomach.

She takes my hand and gently tugs me away from the bed. 'You need to rest,' she says.

'No. I can't leave him.'

The nurse enters the room and looks disapprovingly at us. 'I thought the doctor said five minutes. That was an hour ago.' My eyes plead with her to stay and she sighs. 'Leave me your number, and I'll call you if there's any change,' she says, handing Stella a Post-it note from her pocket. She scrawls down my number, and that's when I remember I left my phone in Positano. 'Luca's belongings—he would have had a bag with him.'

The nurse nods and arranges for me to retrieve my phone, and I reluctantly leave the other half of myself in the room, fighting for life in a battle that couldn't have been predetermined by any kind of figure. Suddenly, I can't understand why I spent so much time focused on the numbers. Why couldn't I have listened to him? Why couldn't I have trusted? Why did I waste so much precious energy worrying about what could have been, what I couldn't control even if I tried? And why, now that the love of my life is hovering between life and death, does it all seem so clear?

Paolo and Stella spend the rest of the day coming and going from the hospital, but I can't bring myself to leave. My eyelids lock shut at some point after midday, and I doze on and off into the evening. At dusk, Silvio arrives at the hospital, head hanging, shoulders sagging. He's brought food with him. It remains untouched.

Eventually, someone brings me home and tucks me into bed. The young nurse doesn't call. I wake at six the next morning. I take a cold shower in a futile attempt to bring feeling back into my body. It doesn't work. I throw on some clothes and sit on the swing outside with my notepad. I twirl my pencil around until the words begin to surface on the page.

Caro Luca,

I'll never love another the way I've loved you.
    You have to be okay. Please, please, please be okay.

Always yours,
Mia

When I arrive at the Fattoria di Maiano, the waiter recognises me.

'Can I help you, *signorina*?' he asks. It's early and he's just starting to set up tables, their service not commencing until midday.

'Um, I was hoping to have a walk around if that's okay?'

'Of course,' he says, a puzzled look on his face.

I trace the steps of one of our most treasured afternoons together. When I reach the secret lake, I leave the folded note in the carved-out altar in the wall nestled against the Madonna for safekeeping. With my eyes squeezed shut, my mind replays the memory of the two of us frolicking in the water, drying ourselves and laughing as we rush back to the scooter. When I open my eyes, I notice my reflection in the water.

Who are you without him, Mia?

By the time I arrive at the hospital it's past midday. Paolo, Silvio and Stella are sitting together in silence.

'Where have you been, Mia?' demands Stella. 'We've been worried about you.'

'I had some stuff to take care of,' I say, stepping away from them. If any of them try any touchy-feely Italian moves on me, I'm sure it will end badly.

'Any news?'

No answer.

'I asked, is there any news?' I demand, raising my voice. Three pairs of dispirited eyes stare back at me. 'I'll take that as a no.'

I head for Luca's room, and Stella tries to pull me back.

'Hold on, I do need to tell you something,' she pleads.

I shake my arm free and glare at her. As soon as I enter the room, what she wanted to tell me is evident.

There's a priest.

I know what this means.

My eyes widen and my mouth drops. My heart begins to race at the scene taking place in front of me.

'I'm sorry, but this isn't necessary.'

'*Signorina*, the doctors say...'

'We can't lose hope! Stella, tell him!'

Stella starts sobbing.

'Mia, I'm sorry but we need to listen to the medical team just in case this is it. Rosetta insisted they call Father Antonio.'

'No,' I say, shaking my head. 'It can't be…'

Someone comes up behind me and wraps their arm around my shoulders. All I know is that it's not Luca, and I desperately want it—need it—to be Luca.

Later on, a concerned Stella returns to Luca's room with a tub of ice-cream and a spoon.

'I know this is hard but you need to eat,' she says, handing me a spoon.

Like every other time, I know I will never win an argument with Stella, so I reluctantly obey. I'm too numb to care anyway.

Waves of nausea wash over me as I study Luca's expressionless face. I take his hand and plead with him to squeeze it if he can hear me.

Nothing.

I keep asking until I begin imagining twitches. I stroke his face, starting at his eyebrows, stopping briefly at his mouth to remember his beautiful smile, across his jawline to his chin as I have done hundreds of times before.

Nothing. How can there be nothing?

I reach for my phone and switch it on to play our favourite songs.

Still nothing.

The battery dies. I don't want to think about dying.

CHAPTER TWENTY-THREE

At five o'clock, Paolo fills Rosetta in on the latest details as she catches a train to Florence. It's almost eight o'clock before she comes hurrying down the corridor, her overnight bag slipping off her shoulder.

'Mia, it's good to see you,' she says nervously. 'There was a train strike,' she adds, as if she's trying to make small talk and avoid the issue at hand: the fact that her brother is fighting for his life.

'Train strike?' I couldn't care less about a train strike.

She swallows nervously and takes a deep breath. She must be as nervous and distraught as I am—if not more.

'Are you ready to see him?' My voice is flat, void of emotion. Eye contact is too hard, so I walk towards Luca's door. I hold it open for her, expecting her to follow, but when she doesn't walk through it, I glance over and see that she's still standing in the same spot.

Give me strength.

She bursts into tears right there.

'It's okay,' I mouth. She doesn't move. I suck in a deep breath and take the bag from her. She flings herself across my body. With gentle force I pry her away from me and tell her again, 'It's okay.' This time she follows me into Luca's room.

It's so not okay.

I slip into the seat that's practically moulded to the shape of my body, and as if there's a magnet from my chin to my chest, my head drops. Forced to listen to her, my private bubble of hurt escalates with every one of her high-pitched sobs. When I can't stand it any longer, I leave the room without excusing myself. Needing some respite from the hospital room, I run past the nurses and through the main door. On the hospital steps I drop to my knees until a pair of shoes move into my line of vision. Leather. Freshly polished. They belong to a man. He places the weight of his hand on my shoulder, forcing me to raise my eyes to him.

'Please, Signorina Mia, get up. I'm an old man. I don't have the strength to pick you up.'

'I'm sorry, Signor Fiorelli, but please, with all due respect, I need to be alone right now.'

'The people who care about you will help get you through this, Mia.'

'How did you find out?' I ask, looking up at him.

'Stella told me. But it doesn't matter. What matters is that you never lose hope.'

His tired hands reach down to mine and his eyes convey an unspoken plea to my heart. I bring myself to my feet and he slips my arm through his. With an air of grace, he walks me back through the hospital doors. We sit in the waiting room, neither of us exchanging words. I'm grateful for the silence. Once the light moves away from the windows, he stands up and tells me, 'Whatever happens, you should continue painting, even if you feel you can't.'

Somehow I manage to mutter the words, 'Thank you.' When I finally do look up, Signor Fiorelli is gone.

Later that evening, Clara shows up at the hospital, having heard what had happened from Silvio at the bar. The news is spreading, touching all those who hear it, as they drift to me in slow motion. As hard as they're trying to be strong for me, I can smell the fear that lies underneath their tight embraces and squeezes of reassurance.

'How is he doing?' she asks.

'No change. How was your holiday?' I change the subject. I know my thoughts will flicker back to Luca as soon as I stop talking.

'Wonderful. Bert's transfer was approved,' she says, smiling.

'I'm happy to hear that. The boys must be ecstatic.'

She smiles politely with a hint of discomfort, which I attribute to the unpleasant circumstances in which we find ourselves. It's hard to think of happiness in a sterile environment like this when things are so morose.

'I've made a mess of things, Clara.'

'Oh, Mia, what do you mean? Tell me what's on your mind, love.'

'I don't even know where to start.'

'Well,' she says, taking a deep breath, 'sometimes it helps to start with the present. What are you feeling right now?'

'Regret. Sadness. Like I've lost my best friend.'

'I see. And what is your regret, Mia? What's happened to make you feel this way?'

'Everything was perfect, Clara. But looking back, I realise now that, all along, Luca was working so hard to help me see that life should be lived without dwelling on the past or worrying about an uncertain future. And I've been so caught up, held back by my past and what may or may not be in my future, that I lost it all. Him.'

'His accident is not your fault, Mia,' she says.

'I had a cancer scare in Positano. It turned out to just be an infection, but I ended things with Luca. And I can see it so clearly now, now that he's in there, that trying to protect him from a life I thought would be too much for him was only going to hurt him more.'

'I'm sure if the tables were turned, he'd have felt the same way, possibly even reacted the same way.'

'What if I don't get a chance to fix this? What if he doesn't wake up, Clara?' I search her face for answers.

'Sometimes, Mia, when life is uncertain, and the control is plucked out of our hands, all there is left to do is to pray. But know that no matter what happens, life goes on, even when it hurts so deeply that you think it can't.'

She smiles warmly at me. 'Would you like me to call your mother? Perhaps I could arrange for her to be with you during this time?'

'I think that would be a good idea,' I reply, trying to hold back the tears.

Clara reaches into her handbag for a pen and notebook and asks me to scribble down her number. 'Leave this with me,' she says, tucking the notebook back into her bag. She squeezes my hand, and I fold myself in her embrace, sobbing against her shoulder, suddenly aware of just how far away my mother actually is, and how close I'd like her to be.

Clara drives me home and warms up a bowl of soup that Stella prepared earlier in the day. She glances at her watch. 'Do you think your parents will be awake yet?'

'Yes, they'll be awake… though I think I should be the one to call them.'

Clara gives me a nod of reassurance and then lets herself out, promising she'll come by again tomorrow.

Mum answers on the second ring. 'Sweetheart, is everything okay? You don't usually call at this hour.'

'Everything's…'

'Mia?'

'Not fine, Mum. Not fine.' My voice quivers.

'Hold on, honey, let me sit down. Your dad's right here with me. I've got you on speaker.'

'Remember when I went to Positano with Luca?'

'Yes, did something happen there? Are you okay? You're not...?'

'I thought I was sick again, but no, I'm not... and... Mum, I'm so sorry for everything. I never meant to hurt you and Dad by leaving and shutting you out of my life, especially after everything you did for me. I know this was wrong, so wrong, but... I thought that if I wasn't nearby, you'd get used to what it might be like to live without me in case I...'

'Oh, Mia.' She pauses. 'We know all of this has been hard for you. And that it was going to take some time for you to process everything.' She sniffles into the phone. 'We've been waiting for you to come back to us,' she says, choking up.

'We knew you always would, pumpkin,' Dad chimes in. The sound of his voice makes it impossible for me to hold it together.

I take a deep breath and reach for a tissue. 'I didn't know that was the wrong way to be strong. I thought I didn't need you, but I do. And... I can see now... that you and Mum need me, too.'

'Oh, honey,' says Mum. 'We love you so much.'

'What happened in Positano?' asks Dad.

I tell Mum and Dad about the accident, and how much I love Luca, and how uncertain his prognosis is right now.

'You should go over there, Julie. What's the time? We'll sort out your ticket this morning,' says Dad.

'Mia, did you hear that? I'll come right over. I'll get the next available flight.'

'I think you should wait. Until we know more... or how long... or if he...' I try to hold back the tears. 'I want you to come, but not now. Not yet. Not like this.'

'I'm going to pray for him, Mia. Just like I did for you. I never stopped. Never for a single second. I want you to call me... every day. Let me know what's going on, no matter how you're feeling.'

'That's what I want too, Mum.'

We say goodbye and I sit there, staring at the screen of my phone. Despite the physical distance, my parents suddenly feel closer to me than ever.

I haven't been into the basilica since my first day in Impruneta. The next morning, I quietly push the door open and come face to face with Father Damiano.

He looks me up and down before he realises who I am.

'I remember you, dear. Please, come and sit,' he says. I join him in the back pew. 'Your friends—Luca's friends—you're all in our thoughts and prayers. you're all in our thoughts and prayers.'

'Hope is all I have left,' I reply, staring absently at Jesus affixed to the cross.

'What brought you here today?'

'I came to pray for another miracle.'

'Then, *signorina*, will you let me join you?'

His glassy blue eyes plead with me and comfort me at the same time. I lower myself onto the padded kneeler. When I bow my head, he does too.

The pins and needles in my legs signal that it's time for me to go. Father Damiano only moves once I'm fully upright again.

'Remember, God hears everything. Every prayer. Every plea for help.'

As the clicks of my footsteps echo through the basilica and the doors swing closed behind me, I whisper to God, 'Prove it.'

CHAPTER TWENTY-FOUR

There are at least fourteen different ways to describe the beauty of a sun rising. I know this because I have woken early every morning since Luca's accident to watch the sunrise from the swing. Our swing. In the new light of each day, I visit Luca and tell him what made this morning's appearance of the sun so special, and how meeting him, loving him and letting him love me has changed my life. Changed me. Helped me to find me again.

This morning, I don't feel like going to the hospital straight-away, so I take a detour via the Ponte Vecchio. I lean against the edge of the bridge and watch the flow of the river, thinking about the point at which it meets the sea. When does one body of water disappear and become another? Or do they simply get lost in each other? My mind wanders to the old Italian couple I saw on the first day I arrived in Impruneta, walking up that steep incline, arm in arm. I knew that if he fell, she would follow. I don't know how I'll stop myself from falling if Luca doesn't make it. Somehow though, I'll have to.

I reach into my pocket for the love lock, the most meaningful gift anyone has ever given me. My trembling hand twists the key until the padlock flicks open. The intricately engraved words feel cool against my skin. Amongst the hundreds of other padlocks, I find a place for ours and snap the lock shut. Our padlock. Our bridge. Our forever. Blinded by my sadness, I approach the side of the bridge and toss the key over the Ponte Vecchio, into the

Arno. I can't tell whether the moan I feel rise from me is internal or external, but all I know is that it comes from deep inside.

On my way to the hospital, back through the city centre, I pass Signor Fiorelli's stand. He waves and trails after me, unable to keep up with my brisk pace.

'*Cara* Mia, are you okay?' he calls out from behind me. I look at him, past him, beyond him, and respond with a small wave, the words, *I don't think so*, echoing inside me, through me, around me.

When I reach the hospital, Rosetta is in Luca's room.

'Any news?'

Today, like every other day, she shakes her head. She leaves the room and heads back to Luca and Paolo's apartment for a rest. Busying myself with my usual task of replacing wilted flowers with fresh ones, I then take my place on the chair beside Luca's bed. I read pages of Jane Austen and his favourite car magazines, but it does nothing to evoke a response from him. Finally, in the late morning, I set them aside and spend the next couple of hours watching and waiting and reminiscing.

'You have to fight, Luca. Harder than you've ever fought before.'

At midday Paolo joins me. 'It's meant to be one at a time, but I figure he won't mind,' he says.

'Paolo?' I whisper.

'Yes, Mia.'

'Do you think he'll make it?'

He looks at me, and then past me as his eyes stare into the distance. 'I hope so.'

I never want to forget the taste of his lips, the smell of his skin or the way he looked at me when he thought I wasn't watching. I want to remember what it felt like for his smile to take my breath away. If Luca doesn't pull through, all I will be left with are memories. Like all memories, they start out vivid and full of emotion, slowly becoming vague and hazy recollections of what once was. There is only one way I can truly capture the memories while they are still fresh and not subject them to a fate of fading away into a distant past. I break my routine of visiting the hospital after my morning meditation and instead honour the urge to go upstairs to the studio. With considerable force, I manage to open a stuck window for some fresh air. I flick the switch on the vintage radio and roll the dial over the static waves until the pitch is perfect. I gather a bucket, a broom and a bunch of old rags from the laundry. It takes me two full hours to clean the studio.

Under one of the drop sheets I find a rusted biscuit tin. Inside is a stack of black-and-white photographs bundled together with a ribbon. Underneath them is a pile of old letters, worn and faded yellow. I check the postmarks. They coincide with the war. I hold the letters close to my chest, feeling an intense sadness for Signor Fiorelli. Then I sift through the photographs that have captured so beautifully the love he had for Amelia, and I'm reminded of how love has the power to enrich our lives as well as the power to hurt us so profoundly that our lives can, if we let them, be rendered forever damaged. I set the tin aside, and after finding a can of paint in the cellar, I get to work, repainting the main wall of the studio.

And then I sit, watching it dry, as my soul leans into what it feels like to be me. I was lost and broken. Scared and lonely. And then I wasn't. Now, I'm on the brink of heading down the same path, if I let myself. Only this time, for Luca's sake, I am determined to not let the pieces of my shattered self remain fragmented. Because Luca wouldn't want me to live a life that's broken. As much as it stings, I do have a choice. Wallow, wilt and die living, or live by the words he once taught me: *Take life as it comes.*

As I sit amongst the comforting smell of fresh paint while plump raindrops splatter against the open studio window, drowning out the sound of the radio, my mind retraces our steps, our life and the things that made us *us*.

The memories dance around in my mind, until I begin to smile from the inside, and that's when I start painting the first picture.

Us. Piazzale Michelangelo.

I take a card and with a felt-tip pen I write a note to display under the painting.

Our first kiss. *When I was numb, you showed me what it was like to feel again.*

A week later, I have a collection of seven paintings that have captured the memories of my time with Luca.

Us. Our bridge. *You wiped away my tears. You showed me it was okay to be me.*

Us. Sunflowers. *You showed me what it was like to laugh again.*

Us. Our secret lake. *Ti amo... You told me you loved me.*

Us. Bikes. Rolling hills and luscious vineyards. *Taking life as it comes.*

Us. Livorno. A pebble beach and waves crashing. *I never wanted that day to end.*

Us. Shooting stars. *Wishes can come true.*

Two weeks later, I have encapsulated fourteen of our most special memories in my paintings. I head into town, to the local *corniceria*. I hand the shopkeeper one of my paintings and he brings out several different frames for me to choose from. He takes some measurements, and I tell him I need fourteen smooth classic wooden frames with an antique look.

'Fourteen?'

'Yes, please.'

'I'll deliver them to you when they're ready, Signorina Mia.'

*

A few days later, I'm in the studio painting again when Stella knocks on the door.

'Mia, may I come in?' she asks as she gently pries the door open. 'Rocco from the framing store is here. He says he has a delivery for you.'

'Sure, let him in,' I murmur, my eyes fixated on my latest painting.

Rocco places the frames in the corner of the studio and lets himself out.

'You're usually at the hospital by this time,' says Stella, glancing at my paintings sprawled across the floor. 'Oh. Wow. Mia, these are… Are these paintings of you and Luca?'

I nod.

'They're beautiful. These are places you visited together?' she asks, walking closer to admire them.

I nod.

'Where was this?' she asks, pointing to a depiction of us at the *laghetto*.

'It's a secret.'

'What about this field of sunflowers?'

'Near Volterra,' I reply. 'We spoke a lot about making memories. If what they're saying is right… I want to make sure I have something to hold on to.'

She drops her gaze. 'Is this your way of saying you've lost hope, Mia?'

'No, Stella. It's the only way I know how to keep it.'

I turn my head and begin to carefully add the finishing touches to a painting of Luca and me in Positano, by the lagoon. He's standing, reading Jane Austen to me in his sexy Italian accent as I cover my eyes from the glare of the sun, laughing at his narration, my laughter reverberating through our special place.

'A minute later he'll drop the book and scoop me into his arms, twirl me around and throw me into the cool turquoise water with a splash,' I say, staring at the painting.

'Mia, I know how much this hurts. How hard it must be for you, not knowing.'

'I'm trying to make sense of it all, in the only way I know how. I just hope this is… enough to help me keep on living if he doesn't make it.'

She sits down next to me and crosses her legs. She's quiet for a long time before finally telling me, 'Honey, I have no idea.'

And I love her for it. Because she gets it. I bring my knees to my chest and drop my weary head into my hands, my soul aching for those happy times. And when she wraps her arms around me and cries with me, I don't feel so alone.

CHAPTER TWENTY-FIVE

The next day I tell Stella I'll take our rent money to Signor Fiorelli. I want to thank him for coming to visit the hospital.

'*Bella* Mia, where have you been? I've been thinking of you every day, my dear.'

'Thank you, Signor Fiorelli. I've been busy. Painting, mostly.'

'How is Luca?'

'The same.' He holds my gaze, but I need to look away. The words 'the same' mean nothing. No better, no worse, no closer, no farther.

'What are the doctors saying?' he asks quietly.

I shuffle my feet and say the words I've been doing my best to avoid. 'They're saying that it doesn't look promising.'

'You said you've been painting?'

'Yes. It's pretty much one of the only things that's keeping me going right now. I'd like you to come to the villa sometime.'

'Mia, I haven't been home… to the villa… in a very long time,' he says, sighing.

'To see my work, Signor Fiorelli. I'm ready to share it.'

'We'll see, Mia. Did you bring your supplies today?'

'No, I just came to give you the rent money.'

'Keep it. You haven't been working this month.'

'It's fine. Honestly.'

I hand Signor Fiorelli the crumpled envelope. 'Oh, I have something else for you,' I say, handing him the tin of photographs and letters.

It takes a moment before he recognises the box. Gently prying open the lid, he pulls out the photographs and, with his wrinkled hands, slowly unties the ribbon that holds them together.

He holds the photographs to his chest.

'I thought you might have missed them,' I say. 'I know they must be very special to you.'

'Thank you. I very much appreciate this.'

He hands me some brushes and sets up an easel for me. 'Join me.'

'I'd love to.'

I spend the afternoon with Signor Fiorelli, and when I finish my painting he stands back and admires it. It's a painting of a girl, sitting on the edge of the Ponte Vecchio, holding a padlock.

'What's it called?' he asks.

'*The Love Lock.*'

He asks me whether I'd be willing to sell it.

'Oh, I don't know if it's good enough to sell, Signor Fiorelli.'

'Let them be the judge of that, Mia,' he says, gesturing towards the crowd of tourists in the square.

I let him take my painting. Leaving me at the stand, he returns in half an hour with my painting mounted in a wooden frame. He sets it up in prominent view and then takes a fountain pen and a white card from the pocket of his jacket.

'One of a kind. *The Love Lock* by Mia…' He looks up at me. 'Moretti.'

'Two hundred and fifty euros.'

'It will never sell at that price, Signor Fiorelli.'

'Come back tomorrow to collect your money, Mia.'

Three days later, I return to visit Signor Fiorelli.

'You finally came back. I have something for you,' says Signor Fiorelli with a cheerful smile as he reaches into his pocket.

He pulls out a wad of cash and hands it to me.

'Your painting sold within the hour.'

'That's amazing!'

'Mia, look at me,' he says, his crystal-blue eyes fixed on mine. 'You must believe in your abilities as an artist. Your work is selling because your work isn't simply steeped in colour. It's rich with emotion. The kind of emotion that can only be expressed when you've lived what you've lived. Do you understand? You paint from your heart, and with your heart.'

I nod. 'Thank you, Signor Fiorelli.'

'Now, let's paint,' he says, handing me a brush. The loneliness I have been feeling becomes less overwhelming with every brushstroke. It's now October. Summer has passed and so has the *vendemmia*. Grapes at their ripest have been stripped from the vines, ready to be fermented into wine. Before they get ready to fall, leaves start to paint themselves with hues of rich colour as the temperature begins to drop. Even if my heart is immensely grateful for Luca's life, I can't help wondering what next summer will look like for the two of us. That's if there will be a two of us.

I enjoy painting in the company of Signor Fiorelli, hanging onto his every word as he recounts old memories of his Amelia with such passion and vividness. Before I know it, he and I have a routine going. Each day I leave a painting with him, and each afternoon that painting is sold. In the two weeks since I started painting with Signor Fiorelli, I have sold almost 4,000 euros worth of paintings.

On this particular day, I'm about to start a painting when I'm interrupted by my phone ringing.

It's Stella.

'Mia, you need to come quickly.'

My heart skips a series of beats before the rush of adrenaline starts pumping through my body. 'I'm coming.'

I drop my phone into my pocket and Signor Fiorelli looks up at me in surprise. My paintbrush falls to the floor.

'It's Luca! I have to go.'

'Go, *signorina*, go.'

I rush to my bike and pedal furiously, weaving in and out of the pedestrian traffic of the city centre.

Please don't let him be gone.

Please let me make it in time.

I should have been there with him.

I hastily park my bike outside the hospital and bound up the stairs to the entrance, jarring my knee on the way up. When I reach Luca's door, puffed out, legs shaking, my body freezes. I stop to catch my breath. My fingers rest on the door handle. What if he's gone? I'm too afraid to turn it. I don't know what I'll do if I see a bed without his body in it.

Then I hear the sounds of animated Italian chatter, and at first I think I must have the wrong room, because it's not the sombre tone I'd expect to be hearing after losing him. Someone has seen me through the frosted window and opens the door for me as I almost fall through it. All eyes are on me as my gaze moves to the bed.

He's awake.

Alive.

Living.

Breathing.

I let out a loud gasp as my shoulders drop and my hands cover my mouth. If there was ever any doubt in my mind about miracles and wishes not coming true, my living proof is staring me in the face. I stand at the end of his bed, and our eyes meet. I step in closer and reach for his hand. I press my lips against his cheek ever so gently, afraid I might break him. He looks so fragile lying there, still connected to countless tubes. He looks at me and smiles, although I'm confused by the intangible but very real distance between us.

'I love you so much,' I whisper, tears of relief pooling in my eyes. My head falls on his chest and he slowly reaches his arm over to cradle me. Eventually, I resurface and search his eyes for reassurance that everything's okay.

He is silent. He closes his eyes, and I don't know if it's because he's still so weak or if it's what I said.

The energy in the room has shifted and the animated chatter has completely stopped as Paolo, Rosetta and Stella wait for someone to speak.

'Are… are you okay?' I ask.

Luca opens his eyes and nods before turning his gaze away from me. He's lying. This isn't how I imagined this would be. Something isn't right. I'm frustrated that I don't understand.

'What's wrong? Are you in pain?' I ask, my voice uneven.

Why isn't he looking at me?

'It's going to take time,' says Stella, shifting uncomfortably.

'Luca?'

Somebody mutters something about giving us space, and they all file out of the room.

'Luca, *amore*, look at me. Are you okay?' I ask, placing my hand gently on his face. It's overridden with a sadness I've never seen in him before. He might be alive, but he is lifeless. My heart sinks at the realisation that something is wrong, terribly wrong.

'Does it hurt?'

'No, Mia.' His voice is barely audible.

'When did you wake up?'

'Early this morning.'

'You mean this afternoon,' I say, worried at his confusion. The doctors warned there was a risk of injury to his brain. 'I should have been here. I've been coming every day. I was going to come this afternoon—'

'No. I told the doctors to hold off calling you. I'm sorry.' I'm almost sure I see a flash of guilt cross his face.

'What? Why would you do that?' I ask, searching his face for answers.

He doesn't answer me.

'I'm sorry if you're still angry at me. I know I was wrong. I wasn't thinking clearly. I'm so sorry about what happened in Positano. I shouldn't have left you like that. It was so wrong of me.'

He slowly lifts his hand and puts his finger on my mouth to silence me.

'I'm not angry with you, Mia. There's nothing to forgive,' he whispers.

'I don't understand. You're scaring me. Is it the drugs? If you're in pain, they can increase your dosage.'

His face twists into a distressed expression and I feel helpless at not being able to soothe it.

'The doctors say it's spinal damage. They'll know more once the inflammation goes down.'

It takes several seconds for me to absorb the full impact of the news.

'This is all my fault. They said you were upset before coming to see me.'

'No. A car veered onto my side of the road. It wasn't your fault,' he whispers.

'I can't believe this has happened. It's probably just swelling. You just need time to recover. You need to give these things time. Wait for the inflammation to go down.'

'No, Mia. They said there's a high chance I will never, ever walk again.' The second wave hits me, harder than the first. Statistics. Beating odds. Having to be strong. I'm so tired of this. I take a deep breath, letting my lungs expand as I hold it for several seconds before exhaling.

'That you will walk again, you mean?'

He responds with silence.

I swallow the dread and the familiar feelings this messy situation is reviving in me. I lift his hand and squeeze it. He pulls away.

'Don't do this, Luca. I know you're upset, but don't push me away. Please.'

'You were right. It's best if we take a break,' he says coldly.

I close my eyes, not wanting to listen, not wanting to hear what he's telling me. The tables have turned. Karma is here, biting me, and it stings big time.

'I wasn't right. I was all kinds of wrong. I know that now, Luca. Look at me. Please!'

He ignores me and continues, 'The doctors say they'll discharge me from this hospital next week…'

'So soon?' I ask, unsure of how that would be possible.

'But I'll be transferring to the hospital in Orvieto,' he says.

'No way. You can't do that. Stay here. I'll be here—I'll take care of you,' I plead.

I place my trembling hand on his cheek and try to turn his head towards mine.

'No, Mia.'

'No. You can't do this to us,' I whisper.

He closes his eyes and flops his head back on the pillow. I know he's exhausted and needs to rest. I reach over and kiss his lips, lingering there for a heartbeat to see if he'll reciprocate.

Nothing.

I stand up, ripping a tissue from the box sitting on his bedside table, and head towards the door.

'I'd prefer if you didn't see me at the hospital again,' he mumbles as I reach the doorway, his eyes still closed. I know it's because he can't bring himself to look at me. The ice-cold words send a shiver through my body. I'm frozen, ready to shatter if I take a step forward. I stagger through the door and into the bathroom. No amount of cold water on my face can help me. I scan the foyer, looking for Stella so she can take me home. She's chatting with Rosetta. They're discussing the news and their views on his future and whether he'll be able to walk again with some intensive rehab. Stella is telling Rosetta he should stay here, in Florence. Rosetta says she agrees. We all know, though, that it's her brother's decision.

Paolo is having a heated conversation in Italian with the doctor, having stopped him in the corridor.

'What do you mean you don't think he'll be able to walk? Are you sure? What tests have you done?'

The doctor clears his throat. Conversations like this can't be easy, not even for him. The doctor looks as though he's had a lot of experience breaking bad news to families. The muscles in my feet tense up, then my legs, hands, shoulders and jaw. Oh, my aching jaw. I join the two men, and Paolo reaches for my hand. He gives it a squeeze without shifting his attention from the doctor.

'We'll know more when the swelling goes down, but this is the information we have from the latest scans. I know it's a shock, but I've seen enough patients like this, with this kind of injury, to tell you that I am almost positive he won't walk again. I'm sorry.'

I tear my hand away from Paolo's.

'Excuse me, Doctor. Do you believe in miracles?'

He looks at me strangely.

'Do you?' I repeat.

He clears his throat. 'Yes, yes, I do. I've seen a few in my time as a doctor. The mere fact that Luca has pulled through when the odds weren't in his favour is an example of us not getting it right every time.'

'Well, then, I'd appreciate it if you would keep your opinions to yourself.'

'*Signorina*, with all due respect, we need to be realistic about the situation for Luca's sake…' His voice trails off, and I'm immune to the rest of his words. Everything that was once in my grasp is spiralling out of control quicker than I can fathom.

'I'm sorry,' I blurt.

'It can be very overwhelming for patients like this and just as overwhelming for the family. I understand,' he says. 'I hope for Luca's sake that you get the miracle you desire.' Then he leaves us.

'This is going to destroy him,' I say.

Paolo's gaze meets mine, his hand stroking his forehead. 'I know, Mia. I know.'

'We've been so focused on him coming out of the coma that I wasn't prepared for anything like this. I thought we'd lose him or he'd just wake up and things would be... normal.'

'I think we need to give it time. We need to be here for him and support him as much as we can.'

'He doesn't want me.'

'What do you mean?'

'It's his pride. He doesn't want me around if he can't walk.'

'I'll talk to him.'

'He wants to go back home. With Rosetta,' I say.

'We won't let him. We'll do whatever we can to convince him to stay,' he says, placing his heavy hand on my shoulder.

The trip home with Stella is filled with an awkward silence, mainly because Stella usually doesn't shut up. As we take the last bend, that fateful bend that almost took Luca's life, she glances at me, her hands gripping the wheel. 'You know,' she says, 'you were the first person he asked for when he woke up.'

'I was?'

'Yep. And it was only when the doctors ran some tests and realised he'd lost the ability to move his legs that he begged them not to call you. Rosetta told me when I got there.'

I wind down the window and let the cool breeze sting my face.

When we get home, the odour of antiseptic is still on my clothes. I peel them off my body and slip into my comfiest pyjamas. I don't bother joining Stella for dinner. I flop on my bed, not even bothering to slide under the warm quilt.

Stella knocks on my door and delivers me a bowl of penne drizzled with olive oil and a sprinkle of Parmesan. I tell her I'm not hungry.

'I know it's hard, Mia, but he's alive. Surely you can find a way to focus on that?' she says.

'Everything aches, Stella. I just want him back.'

'Sweetheart, I know.'

'I don't want him to be hurting like this. He's there in the hospital, dealing with this on his own. I can't even begin to imagine how he's feeling right now.'

'It's a shock for all of us,' she says.

'I shouldn't have left him in Positano like that.'

'Yes, and he shouldn't be pushing you away either. But sometimes when you love someone, it's only natural to not want them to hurt because of you. But love is about moving through ups and downs together. Letting someone love you can sometimes be one of the biggest gifts you can give that person.'

'Do you think he'll change his mind? About letting me see him at the hospital? I mean, he's so stubborn.'

'Yeah, he is. But he also adores you.'

'That's the problem.' I sigh.

CHAPTER TWENTY-SIX

The following day, trying to distract myself from thinking about Luca in the hospital is impossible. Mum kept me on the phone for over an hour this morning, and while that helped, no amount of washing or ironing, reading or walking or meditating works. I paint for a couple of hours once late afternoon finally arrives, but then I pack up, deciding to visit Silvio at the bar.

Silvio's eyes light up when he sees me. 'Good to see you, Mia.'

I order an Averna. I don't even like Averna.

Silvio raises his eyebrows. 'An Averna?'

'Yes, please.'

'Just one,' he says, pouring me a double shot. He grabs another glass and pours himself one, too.

I cringe as the fiery liquid slides down my throat. I'm not used to drinking liqueur straight like this. Luca usually leaves the last sip of his *caffè corretto* for me.

I miss him so much.

'How's he doing?'

'Well, he's alive. That's a miracle in itself. But…'

'But?'

'He doesn't want to see me. He says it's too hard for him to be with me. He thinks he'll be a burden.'

'Ah,' he says.

'I pretty much called it off with him before the accident, Silvio,' I say, concentrating on the tinkering sound the ice is making as I swish my glass around.

'Why would you do that, *bella* Mia?' he asks thoughtfully. 'You two are so happy together.'

'I got scared.'

'Of what?'

'The cancer coming back.'

'The what?' He finishes off his Averna and pours himself another glass. Fortunately, Matteo is taking care of the customers. 'Wow, Mia, I never knew that.'

'He never told you?'

He stares into his Averna with disbelief. 'Every conversation that guy had with me about you was always to tell me how wonderful you are. He never stopped talking about you—your painting, your jokes, your crazy adventures, the way you made him see life in a different light—but never, ever did he tell me about the cancer.'

'I never expected to find what I did here, Silvio. I found him, and you, and Paolo, Stella, Signor Fiorelli, Clara, the boys… You all have changed my life.'

'So what changed with you and Luca?'

'Nothing. Absolutely nothing. It was fear.'

'When Luca comes to terms with what's happened, he'll let you back into his life. There's no way that man can live without you.'

Our conversation switches to whether we really like the taste of Averna when Paolo joins us at the table. He had to open up the *officina* today, unable to take any more time off.

'Long day?' asks Silvio.

'Don't get me started. We're so behind it's not funny.'

My anxious look says it all.

'But don't worry, I'll manage,' he says, rubbing his chin.

'Averna?' asks Silvio.

Paolo nods and takes a slow sip, as if he's contemplating something, and then he looks at me. 'Stella called me earlier. She was going to tell you when she got home from work. Rosetta is already making the arrangements with the hospital to transfer Luca to Orvieto. As far as I know, if the doctor gives his okay, they'll be transferring him on Sunday. I tried to talk to him—I told him we'd work something out in terms of where he could stay once he's discharged—but he wouldn't listen.'

My lip starts to quiver, and I bite down on it so hard it almost starts to bleed. 'What can I do?'

'I don't think there's anything we can do right now. I've tried, Stella's tried, Rosetta's tried. He won't listen. He's angry, Mia, angry about what happened to him. He needs time to process it.'

I slide my glass towards the bottle of caramel-coloured liquid, motioning for Silvio to fill it. To drink like this is out of character for me, but the numbing feeling it gives during this time of need outweighs my good judgement.

'No more, *signorina*,' says Silvio, screwing the lid back on the bottle.

'Just let her have it, just one more,' says Paolo as he places his hand on my shoulder.

Half an hour later my legs feel like jelly. Silvio and Paolo walk me home, handing me over to Stella, who covers me with a blanket on the upstairs sofa as I drift into a blissful, alcohol-induced sleep.

The next morning I'm at the hospital because I can't stay away. My feet take the familiar route down the linoleum hallway, and when I reach Luca's room I pause. I'm not sure whether or not to knock.

'Mia?'

I turn around to see Rosetta behind me.

'Rosetta! How are you? How is he?'

'He's doing okay. They're still deciding if he's well enough to be transferred to Orvieto later this week. As for me, I'm doing as well as I can. Missing the boys and Francesco, but Luca's alive, and that's all that matters.'

I bite the inside of my cheek. She's right.

'He loves you, Mia. He'll never stop loving you. I can see it in his eyes.'

'With time he'll forget. Eventually, he'll forget what it felt like, what we had.'

'You're different than all the others. He's been asking about you every day. Go on, go in and see him. I'll wait outside.'

I pull the magazines I have brought for Luca close to my chest for some sense of comfort. I gently knock on the door and let myself in. He looks up and a smile begins to spread across his face. As quickly as it appears, it vanishes.

'Hey, how are you doing?' I ask gently.

'You shouldn't be here, Mia.'

'I asked how you were.'

'I can't do this. Seeing you is too hard.'

My face flushes and my words can't keep up with the acceleration of my heartbeat. 'Excuse me? Seeing me is too hard? I know you told me not to come here, but I spent over a month not knowing whether you'd live or die. The last time I saw your eyes open was right before I hurt you the way I did. I didn't know if I'd ever be able to hear your voice again, let alone feel the way I feel when you touch me or smile at me or look at me. How am I supposed to just stay away from you when you're all I can ever think about?'

Luca's face is a mask of agony. 'Mia—'

'No, let me finish. I know why you're doing what you're doing. And I know it's not going to be easy, for either of us.'

'You're making this harder than it needs to be. Even if I was to stay here in Florence, where would I live? I can't live with Paolo. I can't move in with you and Stella—it's a two-storey villa. And the bills? I can't work like this. There's just too much uncertainty around everything right now. I'll probably have to sell my share of the business. You can barely cover your own living expenses on your wages.'

'We'll find a way.'

'There's no way this can work, Mia. Our life changed when I had the accident.'

'I didn't hear you say you don't love me,' I whisper, my voice breaking.

'I'll never stop feeling the way I do about you,' he says, turning his head to look out the window.

'Then let me find a way to make it work.'

He keeps his focus on the window. 'I don't want it to work,' he says softly.

'How can you even say that?'

He shifts his gaze, and the sadness in his eyes cuts right through me. 'I don't want to subject you to a life like this. I'll never be able to carry you in my arms again. I won't ever be able to swim in the ocean with you or do even half the things we've enjoyed doing together.'

I shake my head. 'I don't care. I just want to be with you, no matter what.'

'Come here,' he says.

I place the magazines at the foot of the bed and sit beside him. There's still a tangle of tubes and wires connected to him. He raises his free hand and wipes away one of my tears, opening the gate for more to roll down.

'I don't want to hurt you. Causing you pain is the last thing I want to do, but a little bit of pain now is going to avoid a lot of heartache for you down the track. You'll thank me three, five, ten years from now.'

My bottom lip trembles. 'That's not how this is supposed to work out.'

'This,' he says, pointing to his legs, 'wasn't how it was supposed to work out.' He clenches his jaw and runs his hand through his hair. He eventually looks at me again. Then he places his hand behind my head and pulls me towards him. He kisses the top of my head and holds me close for a few seconds. 'You should go,' he whispers.

'Luca, I can't. I don't want to leave you here.'

'Please, Mia.' He leans back into his pillow, shuts his eyes and slips his hand away. I know the conversation is over, but there's no way I'm accepting that we are, too.

Paolo and Stella are sitting at the kitchen table discussing Luca's prognosis and transfer when I return home.

'Mia, is that you?' calls Stella.

'Yes,' I say, slipping off my coat and throwing it on the sofa.

'Rosetta called. He's going to be leaving soon,' she says. 'In the next day or so.'

'I know.'

'I need to talk to you about our trip. I've been thinking that this isn't a good time to leave you here on your own. Paolo and I have spoken about it, and even though he's okay with closing the *officina* for the month, I think we should postpone it until things get a bit easier for you and Luca.'

I'm horrified at the idea. 'Stella, there is no way you are cancelling this trip on my account. Paolo's never been to New York and you haven't seen your family in over a year. I can't ask you both to give up the money you've already invested in this. You've been looking forward to it for months.'

'I can't leave you here alone.'

'I'll have Clara and Silvio.'

'You would tell me if you needed me, right?'

I take Stella's hand in mine. 'Go and enjoy your holiday.'

Stella nods and points her finger at me. 'Okay, but I'm assigning helpers to check on you.'

'I don't need that. But if it makes you feel better—'

'Yes, it does.'

'Mia, I want to tell you something important,' says Paolo.

'What is it?'

'I told Luca this same thing that afternoon before the accident.'

'What's that?'

'Promise me you won't give up fighting for him.'

My shoulders straighten, and I look him squarely in the eyes. 'I don't intend to.'

His eyes sparkle. 'That's exactly what he said.'

CHAPTER TWENTY-SEVEN

Knocking on the Balduccis' front door again after such a long time away brings a sense of comfort to me, a soothing reminder of what once was.

Clara smiles warmly. 'It's nice to see you looking better, Mia.'

I shift uncomfortably; the twins, as usual, are quick to distract me.

'I know this is a difficult time for you. With Stella away, you're welcome to stay here with us in our spare room, if you'd like. Or I can even arrange for the cottage to be fixed up for you if you'd prefer more privacy.'

'Thank you, Clara, but it won't be necessary.'

'Well, if you don't mind, I'll be checking up on you at home,' she says. 'I promised Stella I would, and I'm sure your mother would appreciate me doing that, too.'

'I've been chatting with my mum every day. I've been missing my parents more than usual,' I admit.

Clara squeezes my hand. 'A little more patience. Things will get easier,' she says.

'We have some new games to show you,' says Alessandro, wrapping his hands around my leg.

'That's great! I can't wait to play them with you. I've really missed you guys!'

The boys drag me to their bedroom, where they show me their new toys and photographs of their trip to Spain. I'm almost envious of how these five-year-olds are so present in their happy, carefree lives. The boys provide just the kind of distraction I need, because it has taken all the strength I can muster to stay away from the hospital and give Luca the space he needs. Despite the distractions in my daily life, it's been hard not remembering Luca in the words, feelings and colours around me. He's everywhere. With me yet not with me.

'Mia! Earth to Mia!' calls Alessandro.

'We've been waiting for hours for you to come and find us! Don't you know the rules of hide-and-seek?' exclaims Massimo.

'Hours?'

'Hundreds of hours!' says Alessandro.

'Okay, you two monsters, let's try again. I'm counting to twenty. Go!'

Luca texts me at lunchtime just before Clara is due to return home. He says he's being transferred to Orvieto at four o'clock but tells me not to come to the hospital. I try calling his phone. He doesn't answer.

As soon as Clara steps foot in the door, I blurt, 'It's Luca. He's being transferred to Orvieto. I need to see him before he leaves. I'll be back before you need to go to work again,' I say, frantically slipping on my jacket.

'Let me give you a lift,' she says.

'I'll take the bus. It'll be fine. It's going to be fine.'

When I arrive, the door to Luca's room is open, and I can hear the chatter of nurses from inside. I knock before entering and they both look up at me with expressions of surprise.

'Can we help you, dear? Are you looking for someone?'

My eyes scan the empty bed. Luca's bed.

'What happened? Where is he?'

The nurses appear shocked. 'I'm afraid he's gone,' says one of them.

My heart starts racing. 'That's impossible. He was awake. He was fine. What happened?'

'You missed him. He was transferred early this morning.'

I inhale sharply. 'What? He texted me at midday,' I say, shaking my head in disbelief.

How could he do this to me?

'Are these his?' asks the nurse, handing me the pile of magazines he's left behind. They haven't been touched.

'Yes,' I reply, accepting them from her.

I try calling Luca's phone. Like earlier, it rings out.

I text him.

Why?

His reply comes seconds later.

Because I love you. I'm giving you the gift of letting you go.

Arriving home to the empty villa, I force myself to set the table for dinner, even though nobody will be joining me. The villa is too quiet tonight. There's no Stella bounding up the stairs, her auburn hair bouncing around her shoulders, her green eyes lighting up as she recounts some amusing story of just another day in Italy. No Paolo calling her repeatedly, teasing her about how terrible she is for leaving her phone on silent. No surprise visits from Luca accompanied by the sound of the wheels of his scooter turning over the pebble driveway, signalling his arrival. I suddenly feel more alone than ever before. There is nobody to text, nobody to call. Clara is at home tending to the boys; Silvio is managing the business at the bar, cracking jokes and pulling shots of espresso; and my parents are in bed, sleeping on the other side of the world.

I'm about to tear open a packet of pasta when there's a knock at the door. It's Silvio, with a tray of lasagna in one hand and a bottle of wine in the other.

'*Ciao, bella* Mia. I know it's kind of late, but I thought I'd bring this around. My mother sends her love,' he says, extending the pan out to me with a smile. 'She made me bring home four trays for you. I have the rest in a freezer at home.'

'Thank her for me. But honestly, there's no need.'

'You're family to us, Mia.'

'Do you want to come in?'

'Sure.'

'Have you eaten?'

'No.'

'Feel like lasagna?'

'Sounds good.'

We eat together, and Silvio tells me he's going to see Luca at the weekend. I stop eating, unable to take another bite, my appetite crushed.

'Do you want to come with me?' he asks.

'I would love to, but I can't. I'm giving him some space.'

'Has he contacted you at all?'

'Not really.'

'I can't believe how stubborn he is. I'll have a word with him. Let's see if I can knock some sense into him.'

Silvio tells me to stop by the bar during my break tomorrow.

'You don't have to do this, you know. I don't need looking after.'

'I'm just trying to keep a promise to a friend.'

'Stella?'

'No, Mia. Luca's been messaging me every day to make sure you're okay. And he made me promise to come tonight. I guess he knew you'd be feeling upset, shall we say?'

The sudden rush of air into my lungs makes me gasp. I want to pick up and leave for Orvieto, but I tell myself another month apart—if it comes to that—is nothing compared to a lifetime together.

'How is he doing?'

'Physically, he's doing well. Considering the trauma he experienced, I'd say remarkably well. He's been sleeping a lot.'

Silvio, sensing my pain, adds, 'I'll tell him you're thinking of him.'

'No need,' I say, feeling despondent. 'He already knows.'

Silvio helps me wash up before saying goodbye, and I head straight into the studio. I sit, back against the wall, legs crossed, window open, in a quiet meditation. Praying, praying, praying. For us. For a solution. For some way to make this work. I eventually fall asleep on the studio floor.

I wake up at some point during the night. I'm not sure if I'm fully awake, or still half asleep, but I hear a voice, soft and reassuring. I can't work out whether it's a man's or a woman's. Maybe it's not even a voice at all—just a feeling. Whatever it is, it's clear, telling me that I must keep painting and never give up. I glance around the room. Nobody's there. I walk downstairs, snuggle up against the pillows on my bed and whisper, 'Whoever you are, I hope you're right.'

The next morning, from the comfort of my outdoor swing, I notice Signor Fiorelli meandering up the path to the villa. At his age, the steps are far from effortless. He appears so unsteady on his feet that I rush out to meet him and loop my arm through his.

'Signor Fiorelli, what are you doing here?' I ask, surprised. 'I mean, I'm glad to see you. It's just that you mentioned it might be hard for you to come here.'

'I have some important business to discuss with you, Mia. And I thought I'd take the opportunity to see that work you were wanting to show me. It's about time I visit my old home anyway,' he says, glancing up at the villa.

'I'll show you. I bought some frames but I haven't got around to framing them yet.'

I help Signor Fiorelli up the stairs, and he pauses to look around when he reaches the top.

'So many memories,' he murmurs.

I lead him to the studio and hold the door open for him.

'I painted these pictures while Luca was in a coma. They're a bit different from my usual paintings, as you can see.'

The fourteen pieces lying on the floor of the studio are more intricate and vivid than anything I have ever painted. I've managed to capture details that surprised me, with techniques I thought myself incapable of previously.

'Goodness, Mia, these are a *capo lavoro*,' he says.

'I'm sorry, I don't understand what you mean.'

'A masterpiece. This is your best work to date, my dear.'

Signor Fiorelli slowly examines each piece, reading the cards associated with every painting. He reaches for his handkerchief.

'Through art you have the power to change someone's life.' He gestures to the paintings. 'As long as he is alive, you cannot live without him. That's what your paintings are telling me.'

'I don't know how to convince him to come home, Signor Fiorelli.'

'Sometimes the answers to our problems lie right before our eyes.'

'You mentioned you had some business to discuss?' I ask, changing the subject.

'Yes, Mia. The buyer of *The Love Lock* wants to know if she can commission a set of paintings from you.'

My eyes widen. 'Commission them? Who is she?'

'It doesn't matter. But this is what she wants,' he says, handing me a piece of paper from his pocket.

Dear Ms Moretti,

Thank you for the beautiful piece of artwork that I had the pleasure of purchasing recently. The Love Lock *will become a treasured part of my own personal art collection. I was most impressed with your style and would like to commission a triptych from you, entitled* The Florentine Bridge, *in which three paintings (oil on canvas) depict the story behind the love-lock tradition of the Ponte Vecchio, for which I can offer you the sum of 15,000 euros. If this proposal is of interest, I will be in touch with further specifications and a twenty-five per cent deposit to begin the works.*

Yours sincerely,
C. Jones.

My jaw drops as the note drifts to the ground. Signor Fiorelli's blue eyes blink at me with shared happiness.

'Signor Fiorelli, did you read this?'

'I didn't need to. She told me about her intentions. Ever since she saw your first painting, she has been coming by to admire your work. She fell in love with it instantly.'

'She's legitimate, then?'

'Oh, yes. And I can assure you, she looks forward to a long relationship with you.'

'When can I meet her?'

'Well, she's quite conservative. She prefers to keep to herself and only likes to meet with an artist after the paintings are completed. She prefers the artist to use his or her own inspiration and not be clouded by any expectations. So what do you say, Mia? Can I tell her yes?'

'Of course! Yes! You can tell her I'd be delighted to take this on.'

'*Benissimo.*'

'This means the world to me, Signor Fiorelli. Now I can truly call myself an artist. It's what I've always wanted.'

'You've always been an artist in my eyes. The recognition of your work by others is simply a by-product of your passion.'

'Do you believe in second chances at life?'

'Absolutely. Why do you ask?'

'Because I was given one. And now I know what to do with it. Through my painting, life makes sense. It's where even the smallest things hold meaning. I know now that if I can pick up a brush and use it to create something out of nothing—even when life looks bleak, when things don't quite fit together as I'd like them to, when my heart's aching—it will always help me to make sense of things. And it's because of this that I know I'll be okay, even if Luca doesn't come home.'

'Spoken by a true artist,' he says. 'Now you have some work to do, young lady. Your buyer needs the paintings by the end of the month.'

'So soon? Oh my goodness! I can't believe this is happening.'

'I can,' he says, a warm smile spreading over his gentle face. 'You're a natural.'

CHAPTER TWENTY-EIGHT

It feels strange to be excited about my work when Luca and I are apart like this, where half my heart is beating outside of myself. It's only been days since I last saw him, but it seems much longer than that. I desperately want to pick up the phone to tell him the news about the commissioned paintings. Having something like this happen, under such unexpected circumstances, forces me to reconsider the way I've been approaching my work and my life. As I take each step through Florence's cobblestoned streets, I know exactly where I'm going. There's an element of peace that fills me up from the inside. It feels as though the City of Art is wrapping its wings around me. Being able to paint for a living is what gives my life meaning. Being with Luca is what colours it, completes it, makes me whole again. As I embark on this new chapter in my life, I know that whatever the future brings, I'll always consider myself Luca's painter girl. I set up my work space, close to our Florentine bridge, with the reassurance that I will always have a small part of myself to come back to, to comfort me when I'm feeling scared or alone, happy or sad, no matter what.

I take out the spec sheet from the anonymous buyer and start prepping my first painting. Soon I have no control over what is appearing in front of me; I'm lost in thought, reliving the emotion of what once was.

Day after day, I return to my place on the bank of the Arno River until my three paintings are done.

I'm in the studio making the final check on my third commissioned painting to ensure it's dry, when Clara calls.

'We're going to Venice for a few days. We're meeting Bert there and we leave tomorrow night. The boys are hopelessly excited about the gondolas.' She laughs. 'Now, while I've got you on the phone, do tell me—on your days off, what is it you've been working on? The boys mentioned you've been working on a big project.'

'I didn't want to say anything until after I'd finished. I was going to invite you over to take a look, actually,' I say, glancing over at my latest paintings of me and Luca.

'I can't wait to see your work,' she says, the enthusiasm in her voice apparent.

I tell her about all the painting I've been doing, as well as the triptych.

'Did Signor Fiorelli mention who the buyer is?'

'A woman named C. Jones. She wanted to be kept anonymous until after I finished the paintings.'

'That's not too uncommon. Sometimes meeting a buyer can make an artist nervous. I'm sure she has every faith in your abilities to create the work she's looking for. Listen, I was hoping we could catch up for dinner this evening. Maybe we can have a proper chat then?'

'Sure. Why don't you come here?'

'Sounds great. I'll bring the wine.'

Clara arrives a little earlier than expected, just as I'm mounting the last painting of me and Luca to the studio wall.

'Come in!' I call out. 'The door's open! Make yourself at home.'

I move my equipment into the corner of the studio. I take a step back and view the wall in its entirety. I've used a soft palette of pastels on some of the paintings, and vibrant hues on others.

Each of these thirty paintings holds a significant meaning for Luca and me.

'Mia, do you need some help in there?' asks Clara.

'Sorry, I got a bit carried away,' I call.

I poke my head out of the studio door. 'Let me get this paint washed off, and I'll be with you in a minute,' I say, making my way to the bathroom. 'You know, I've been thinking that I'd like to enrol in art school,' I say to her from the bathroom.

'You should absolutely do that, Mia. Your work... oh my goodness, it's truly breathtaking.'

I walk out of the bathroom and dry my wet hands on the back of my jeans. Clara is standing in the doorway of the studio, her mouth slightly ajar, her eyes wide, as she takes in the artwork displayed on the walls.

'I literally just finished the last one this afternoon,' I say, pointing to a painting of the early twentieth-century antique carousel, run by the fifth generation of the Picci family, which lights up Piazza della Repubblica. Luca and I stood there arm in arm, gelatos in hand, mesmerised by the golden lights bouncing in and around it as the painted horses gently swayed to and fro, eliciting smiles of glee from small children. As the music hummed away, their laughter tickled us, and for a few short minutes we enjoyed the taste of innocence and simple pleasures that life has to offer.

'Delightful.' When she finally tears her eyes away, she looks around the room and says, 'Look at what you've done to this room. It was never like this before.'

'You've been here?'

'Yes, Signor Fiorelli has done many paintings for me over the years,' she murmurs, her attention focused on a painting of me and Luca walking along the beach.

'It's called *Once-in-a-Lifetime Tuscan Love*. It's our story...' I say, my voice trailing off. She seems so enthralled in the paintings that I doubt she's heard a word I've said.

'Go on,' she murmurs without shifting her gaze.

'It started out as fourteen paintings when he was in hospital, and I haven't been doing much else except for painting and looking after the boys this month,' I confess. 'So that number grew to thirty.'

Clara is silent for what feels like hours as she admires the wall from afar, then steps towards each painting, one by one, as if viewing them in a gallery. She traces her fingers across the framed labels. Once she's finished she turns around and looks at me. 'My goodness…'

I raise my eyebrows, unsure of how to interpret her response.

'Like them?' I ask shyly.

'I'll give you sixty thousand euros for all of them.'

'Excuse me?' I say, certain I've misheard her.

'Make it ninety.'

'Pardon?' I blink several times in a futile attempt to play back what I think I have just heard.

'It's the most incredible story depicted in contemporary artwork I have seen in my entire career.'

I'm absolutely speechless.

'These pieces are magnificent. The way you've captured the emotion, the depth. It's extraordinary. Especially given your age and experience. Are these paintings all based on real events? Things you did together?'

'Yes,' I whisper.

She reaches over to the painting of me sitting at the bar, sketching Luca, who's working in the *officina*.

'I have at least four buyers I know who would be interested in this work,' she says, her eyes glued to the painting.

'But nobody knows my work. How will you convince anyone that it's worth their consideration?'

'You let me worry about that,' she says, her eyes sparkling. 'I've been in this business long enough to recognise a gem when I find one. And believe it or not, I'm very familiar with your work.'

My eyes question her.

She breaks out into a smile. 'I'd hoped to remain anonymous until after you'd delivered the triptych. It seems like a good time to let you know I'm the one who commissioned it.'

I can't believe what I'm hearing. It all feels too surreal. 'You're C. Jones?'

'Yes, Mia. Jones is my maiden name.'

'Oh my goodness! I had no idea.'

'That's how it was supposed to be. I wanted you to show me your work in your own time. I happened to be visiting Signor Fiorelli when I saw your painting. My office is around the corner from the Uffizi. Signor Fiorelli was telling me how talented you are. I didn't realise the painting was yours until I saw your name on the card beside it. By then I'd already offered to buy it. Every afternoon I'd stop and see more of your paintings. I showed them to my partner, Joseph, and, well, here we are now.'

'I'm very grateful, Clara.'

'You're a true artist. Knowing I'm helping you in your career is an honour. This is just the beginning. That is, if you'd be happy for me to help you.'

'Of course,' I say.

'So, would you consider selling these paintings?'

I think back to how hard it was to pick up those paintbrushes when I was unwell, and how the paintings in this room are so much more than a love story. They're painted by a girl who turned pain and fear into love and hope. A girl who was given a second chance at life but was scared to take it; however, once she did, she found herself.

'Consider them sold.'

She claps her hands together, an infectious smile creeping across her face.

'Here, let me show you your paintings,' I say, gesturing towards the corner of the studio where a drop sheet sits over the commissioned pieces. I lift the cover to reveal the three works. I've painted one picture of the Ponte Vecchio at sunset, one of a couple tossing their key from the bridge, and another of an elderly couple sitting on a park bench admiring a panoramic view of Florence. 'I hope they're what you were looking for.'

'No, they're not.'

I'm unsure of how to respond.

When she turns to look at me, she's beaming, letting me know in a voice as smooth as honey, 'They're much more than what I'd hoped for. They're brilliant.'

Once we're downstairs, Clara opens the bottle of wine she brought over and tells me about her plans for the paintings. She'd like *The Florentine Bridge* triptych to be displayed in London for three months for an upcoming art exhibition featuring contemporary artwork by Florentine painters depicting the city. She needs to make several phone calls regarding the paintings she has seen today but tells me it's likely they will be sold as a collection at auction. I'm still reeling at the events that are unfolding when Clara interrupts my train of thought.

'Are we ready to start dinner?'

'No, I think we should eat out tonight, Clara. On me.'

The following morning, I wander into Impruneta, trying to make sense of the conflicting emotions within me. The overwhelming joy at yesterday's news, dampened by the incessant longing to be able to share it with Luca. My eyes rest on the *officina*. I can almost hear the roller door being shut, causing the ache within me to grow heavier. I watch a young couple cross my path, stopping beside a parked scooter. He smooths her hair and gently wipes under her eye. He holds his finger out in front of her and she blows a puff of air over her loose eyelash.

What would you wish for, Mia?

To never be apart from you.

My phone rings, nudging me back to the present. It's Clara.

'I'm outside the villa. I thought I'd come to say goodbye before we head to Venice. Will you be long?'

'I'll be there soon,' I reply, tearing my gaze away from the *officina*.

Clara emerges from her car, and together we make our way to the front door. As I turn the key in the lock, I hear the sound of car doors opening and closing. I turn around and narrow my gaze. Emerging from Clara's car are my parents.

'Hello, pumpkin,' says Dad, smiling. 'We thought we'd surprise you.'

Mum rushes towards me. She runs her hands through my hair then rests them on my cheeks. 'You're beautiful,' she whispers, her eyes damp.

I throw my arms around her, inhaling the familiar floral scent of her perfume. I turn to Dad, who locks me in a tight embrace, an embrace I didn't realise I'd missed this much.

'When did you arrive? And how did you…?'

Clara smiles. 'Told you to leave this with me. You've been so strong, but I thought a reunion might make things a little easier for you.'

I smile in appreciation.

'I suggested your parents could stay in my cottage, but I assume you'd like them to stay here with you, at least until Stella returns from New York.' Then, almost as an afterthought, she adds, 'I was thinking, actually, that the cottage could be perfect for you and Luca. We could arrange whatever modifications might be required. I'll leave you to think about it. Now, I need to dash, but we'll spend some time together once I return from Venice. I promised your parents a personalised tour of Florence.'

*

Mum and Dad unpack and settle in while I set up the spare upstairs bedroom for them.

'I'm so proud of you,' says Mum, watching me smooth out the sheets. 'Your life here… it's so different to what it was like for you at home. It's like you've grown up overnight.'

'I love it here. Actually, I've been meaning to tell you that I've been thinking of staying in Italy. To study, that is. I'd like to study at the academy…'

Mum nods, showing me she understands. 'Clara filled me in on all the details about your paintings. I think if that's what you want to do, you should do it.'

'Even if I don't get accepted… I still want to stay here though. With Luca…'

Mum lowers herself onto the edge of the bed and pats the mattress for me to sit down beside her. She turns her body to face me and takes my hand in hers. 'Why aren't you with him, honey?'

I shrug. 'He wants space.'

'Does he?' She questions me with her eyes.

'That's what he thinks he wants. He thinks that because he can't walk he isn't enough for me. The thing is, he's more than enough. He's everything to me.'

'Oh, Mia. You're so young to be dealing with something like this. I know you love him, but are you absolutely sure this is what you want?'

'Let me show you something.' I lead Mum into the art studio.

I show her the paintings of me and Luca, telling her about each one. She listens, moving from one piece to the next, taking everything in.

Finally, she speaks. 'Has Luca seen these? Have you shown them to him?'

'No. Not yet.'

'Darling, I really think you should.'

Instantly, my heart knows exactly what I need to do to bring Luca home. Maybe Signor Fiorelli was right. Sometimes the answers are right in front of us.

Mum and Dad fit into life in Italy seamlessly. We've been spending bursts of time together sightseeing, and since she returned from Venice, Clara has been spoiling Mum with visits to century-old villas, appreciating all they offer in terms of architecture and design. Dad's made himself at home at Silvio's bar every evening, where he plays cards with the locals. He's there tonight, while Mum and I spend a quiet night in at Clara's. I'm lost in my own thoughts, thinking about the best time to visit Luca, who still isn't answering my calls.

'You seem a little distant tonight,' says Clara. The boys are in bed and we're standing in the kitchen drying dishes together.

'I was thinking about the paintings, and showing them to Luca,' I say, rubbing my tea towel over an already dry plate.

'You should go see him,' says Mum.

'You and Dad have only been here a little over a week. I can't just leave you.'

She winks at me. 'It's not like we'll be bored without you. It's Italy! Besides, we'll be here when you get back. We'll be here as long as you need us to be.'

'I'll make sure your parents have plenty of ways to occupy their time while you're away,' says Clara.

'What if he refuses to come home?' I twist the tea towel into a knot.

Mum takes it off me and folds it. 'Well, sweetheart… at least you'll know you tried.'

Clara chimes in. 'She's right, you know.'

I take a deep breath. 'Clara, you know the offer you made about the cottage… I was wondering if that still stands?'

*

Later that evening, Mum and Dad slip into bed and I return to the studio. Memories of me and Luca dance around my head amongst the silence of the studio, one of the places I know I can count on for solace. I cast my mind back to the day we visited the Boboli Gardens, where everything was green and luscious and in bloom, the time we ate so much gelato on the beach that we both felt sick for hours afterwards, the time we wished upon our shooting stars.

I set up my paper on an easel and start to paint. Luca. Standing near the outdoor table, shades in one hand, squinting to get a better look at that girl on the swing. Once I'm finished, I take a card and let the ink flow: *Where it started.*

Then I reach for a sheet of notepaper and start writing.

Dear Luca,

I'll never forget our first kiss. In that moment I knew my life would be forever changed. You showed me that love knows no time, and that one of the greatest gifts we can give ourselves is the permission to let go and listen to our hearts. When I was scared and broken you showed me that it was safe to trust in life. You showed me that what we feel is just as important as what we think. I know now that allowing you to love me and to be with you no matter what the future might bring is okay, safe and right. If there is love, there is acceptance, and true love allows for unity in the face of uncertainty. I know now that if we can take life as it comes, together, everything will be okay.

I'm not a girl of many words; my brushstrokes are my words and these paintings are for you. This is us. This is our love. A once-in-a-lifetime, what-are-the-chances-of-us-ever-

meeting kind of love. This is what we had and what we stand to lose if we remain apart. There are 195 countries in the world, with over seven billion of us in it. But there's only one person I want to be with, and I belong to him as much as he belongs to me.

Please come home to me.

Your painter girl,
Mia

CHAPTER TWENTY-NINE

As I stand on the platform waiting for the train bound for Orvieto, I think about the way drops of watercolour pigment can run and bleed into each other across the surface of wet paper. They do this amazing thing: they bloom. When I was learning to paint, I was taught that good blooms, the kind you can control, are something to be embraced, because they add vibrancy and excitement to a piece. Bad blooms, on the other hand, are considered messy, appearing in all the places you don't want them to, and are to be avoided at all cost. These days, when I take brush to paint and intentionally work with this technique for fun, I know that I'm consciously creating a work of art because I get to choose the colours I want. Ultimately though, the drops do what they want. I observe my painting once I'm done and think of how beautiful it is, in all of its loose and messy imperfection. Even in those places where the colours are muddy, it's still more perfect than I could have ever imagined it to be.

I step through the sliding doors of the train and find a spare seat. After six failed attempts at reading the same page of my book over and over, I spend the rest of the trip gazing out the window, watching out for the right station, my body tense at the thought of seeing Luca again, not knowing how he might react to seeing me.

Only a handful of people disembark at Orvieto train station, mainly tourists. I wander around for about fifteen minutes before I need to ask for directions on how to reach Rosetta's apartment.

'Excuse me, could you tell me where I can find Via della Fonte?'

'Not too far from here, *signorina*. Take the first left and then your second right,' says the passer-by.

I follow his directions and stop outside the apartment, realising that I'm more nervous than I thought I was. My heart starts racing as I reach for the doorbell, knowing that in a few minutes I'll be seeing Luca again.

'Si?'

'Uh, Rosetta, it's me, Mia.'

The intercom goes quiet for what feels like forever. Somehow, I convince myself that Luca has found out it's me waiting for him here and has told her not to open up. I turn around and begin to walk away. It's then I hear the click of the metal door and Rosetta's voice calling after me.

'Mia, wait!'

I turn around to see Rosetta standing there, smiling at me. She walks towards me and locks me in an embrace.

'I'm so glad to see you,' she says.

She makes small talk, telling me her boys are out with her husband, Francesco, and that the weather is unusually cold for this time of year. She asks how I got here and if I came alone. Finally, we speak about Luca.

'Mia, I want you to know that I tried so hard. I begged him so many times to call you, to let you in, to reconsider, but he refused. I know this isn't what he wants, though, and I wanted so badly to call you, to let you know how he was doing, but he made me promise not to. Please forgive me,' she says.

'It's okay. I mean, it's not okay, but I understand. How is he?'

She's searching for the words. 'The same, really. The rehab facilities here are pretty average, and it's hard to notice any improvement.'

'Where is he now?'

'Upstairs. Come, I'll take you to him.'

As we ride the lift up to the apartment, I ask Rosetta how Luca manages to get in and out of the flat.

'He doesn't go out much. Just for rehab. He was only discharged from the hospital two weeks ago, and that was only because he insisted on coming home,' she says. 'But what worries me the most is that Fiorentina played Juventus last week and he wouldn't even let me turn on the TV.'

'But he loves soccer! Fiorentina is his favourite team. He never misses a game.'

'I know,' she replies, sighing.

She leads me to the living room and smiles with reassurance before leaving me to stand there alone. He hasn't seen me yet. He's facing a window that overlooks a narrow street. Aside from a few passers-by going about their day, and some sheets hanging on a washing line, there isn't much to look at. It feels so wrong, so unfair, to see him sitting there in a wheelchair, lost in his own thoughts like this. I think about how bittersweet it is to feel such immense gratitude for life on these kinds of terms, and how not being able to make something better for someone in the way that we want to can cause so much angst if we let it.

'Luca?'

His hands reach for the wheels of his chair, and he slowly turns around to face me. It's the same Luca in so many ways: the same olive skin, the same defined cheekbones, the same impeccable style in clothing. Except he's in a wheelchair. He has a wounded demeanour that almost rips my heart open.

Our hearts collide somewhere in the middle of the room when our eyes meet. And there they hover uncertainly until he averts his gaze, and I'm unsure whether to move forward towards him.

I clear my throat. 'How are you?'

'I'm okay,' he says flatly. I wait for him to continue speaking. He doesn't. Rosetta pokes her head through the door and tells us she has some errands to run. Sensing our discomfort, she says, 'Would you like to maybe take a walk outside?'

Luca flips his head up. 'That would be great, Rosetta. There's only one small problem,' he says through clenched teeth. It's so out of character for him to snap at someone—anyone. I cringe at his callous behaviour.

I decide not to spend one more second in the unbearable silence. 'I think that's a great idea. Let's go outside,' I say.

'Fine,' he says.

I hold the door open in the lift until he manages to wheel himself in. We ride in silence, only speaking once we reach the cobblestoned road outside. It's cold on the street, and I suddenly wish I'd brought a jacket with me. I cross my arms as we walk up the inclined street that Luca's arms are working hard to navigate.

'You shouldn't have come here,' he says breathlessly.

'I wanted to see you.'

'I thought I made things clear.'

'Please don't treat me like I'm a stranger,' I say, my voice uneven.

He doesn't answer me and keeps propelling himself up the hill, tiny beads of sweat forming on his forehead. We take a spot outside at the closest café in the piazza and sit across from each other.

'Um, I should go order us something to drink. *Corretto*? Double shot?'

He nods, looking as though he's in discomfort.

'Does it hurt? Are you in pain?' I ask.

'My body's fine.'

I order our coffees and return to the table. Luca grabs his cup but doesn't take a sip.

'I wanted to call you, to tell you how sorry I am. I told you in the hospital, but I thought you might have been angry with me for leaving—'

'I'm not angry with you, Mia. You've done nothing wrong. It's me. This. All of it,' he says.

'This isn't your fault. You can't help what happened to you,' I say.

He shakes his head.

'Why can't you look at me?' He keeps staring at his cup, and this time I can't help raising my voice. 'Please, Luca, just look at me!' The group of tourists sitting at the table beside us glance over and pretend to not have overheard me.

'Because it hurts,' he whispers.

I draw a deep breath. 'I hate this so much. I hate being apart from you. I hate the way things have changed between us. I hate that this has happened to you—to us.'

'Stop, Mia.'

'No! I came here because I want you to come home. I miss you. I can't stop thinking about you.'

'Please don't do this.'

'Why won't you hear this? Why won't you let me in?'

'Why? I can't walk, Mia! There are no guarantees I'll ever walk again.'

'I know you're angry that this has happened. That you haven't accepted it yet. But you almost died. You were this close to dying, Luca,' I say.

'This is not what you want. Trust me. I'm no good for you anymore.'

'How dare you even think that!'

'I can't do this to you. You deserve more, so much more. You don't deserve this.'

'You're a hypocrite of the worst kind,' I say, the blood rushing to my cheeks. '*You* don't deserve this, Luca. What do your days look like right now? Rehab followed by hours of staring blankly out an apartment window while life goes on around you, while the person who loves you more than anything in the world is a hundred miles away thinking of you every second of every day, aching just as much as you are? My heart knows what it wants.'

'So does mine.'

'You're lying,' I say, my voice cracking as my eyes fill up with tears.

His chocolate eyes flash with hurt.

'I know you think you're doing me a favour, but you're not. I accept you for who you are and for whatever the future brings. And this is what the future brought and yes, it's completely shitty and horribly unfair. I wish I could change it for you. But love—love is something that knows no boundaries. You don't just fall out of love because someone can't walk,' I say.

'One day when you're married with kids of your own, you'll be enjoying a life without these kinds of limitations or obligations, and you'll thank me.'

'No,' I say vehemently. 'Don't even go there. I will never thank you for pushing me away like this. Never. No way. You told me I was your forever. I want you to be my forever. I don't want this.'

'Yes, Mia,' he says softly.

'Okay, so if you ever learn to walk again, what happens then? Is that when I'll get a call from you? Or maybe the next girl who comes along who accepts you for who you are can have you, but I can't?'

'That's not fair. You know I'd do anything for you, *bella* Mia. But not this. You have to know I'm not doing this because I don't love you. I'm doing this because you're the single most important thing that ever happened to me.'

The tone of his voice makes my heart feel heavy, knowing that all of this has been much harder on him than it has been on me. He places his hands on the wheels of his chair.

'No, don't go. Please don't go.'

'This conversation is finished. I'll get Rosetta to take you home,' he says.

'We were happy, Luca.'

His Adam's apple bobs up and down as he swallows.

'Look at me,' I whisper.

'I can't.' His face tightens and he bites his lip.

'Look at me, Luca.' My hands reach out to frame his face and we hold each other with our eyes for what must be seconds. Seconds that feel like hours because I've missed this so much. I lean forward and press my lips against his so softly that it almost feels like we aren't touching. Instantly it doesn't hurt anymore. Luca pulls me deeper into the kiss, into that place where we completely lose ourselves, that place where we are whole again. This is us. It's over way too soon.

He gently pulls away.

'No,' I whisper. 'That feeling, Luca? It isn't based on whether or not you walk.'

He takes a deep breath. I reach for his chest and feel the rapid beating of his heart.

'You do feel it,' I murmur.

His hands glide over his unshaven face.

'Look, I know you're hurting, but what has happened to you doesn't make you any less able to care for me. Not being able to walk doesn't change the fact that you are perfect for me.' I grab the photo book containing the pictures I've taken of the paintings of us from my bag. 'These are snapshots of what we had,' I say, dropping the book on the table. 'Us. Our story. Everything we lived and what we stand to lose if we remain apart. We made those memories. I kept those close to me when I didn't know if I'd lose you. You changed me, Luca. You're everything I never knew I was looking for and more,' I say, wiping the tears from my eyes.

He looks up at me, his own eyes filled with tears, and says, 'Mia, I'm so sorry.'

'I'm checking into a hotel,' I say as I glance around the square. 'Right over there. That's where I'll be. Until you're ready. I will be there for a day, a month, six months or a year. I'm not going anywhere until you come home. Otherwise, I'll make this my home.'

*

The room service I ordered goes cold under the dome of its metal cover. I'm too busy contemplating how precious life is, how much trust is truly required of us in order to live life fully, especially in times of uncertainty when we feel the overwhelming need to control or move away from anything that might hurt us or those close to us. I decide that if I do lose Luca, that this gift of insight and deep knowing is something I will carry with me for the rest of my life, no matter how long or short it ends up being. Luca gifted me so much more than his unconditional love. He gifted me a fresh pair of eyes.

From the balcony, I watch couples fill tables in restaurants; streetlights illuminate the piazza and outdoor heaters take the chill out of the air. I pull myself away from the balcony and go to run a bath when the hotel phone rings.

'Ms Moretti, there's a gentleman by the name of Luca Bonnici insisting on seeing you.'

'Please let him up,' I reply.

A minute or so later there's a knock at the door. He's shaved and is wearing his favourite pair of jeans and a cotton shirt. There's a bunch of roses on his lap.

'Come in,' I say. I sit on the edge of the bed so that we're at eye level and he moves as close as he possibly can, our knees almost touching.

'I can't hurt you anymore, Mia.'

'I don't know what you mean by that.'

'I'm sorry I made you find an empty bed at the hospital. I knew that if I saw your face, heard your voice, felt your touch, I'd never be able to leave. I asked about you every day. Every single day.' He takes a deep breath. 'That letter, and those pictures—how do we ever get back to that?'

'Everything's changed, but the important things have stayed the same.'

He bites his lip.

'I've wanted to tell you that I've been painting—a lot.'

'I saw. They're beautiful.'

'You haven't seen half of it, Luca. My work has been selling. I've been working on commissioned paintings.'

'Really? That's amazing. How did this happen?'

'I'd been painting with Signor Fiorelli. It was good for me—for both of us. Anyway, he sold a few paintings for me, and then Clara bought one, and then she commissioned three pieces of work. I didn't know it was her at the time because she stayed anonymous, but she offered me a lot of money for them.'

His eyes widen as a smile spreads across his face. 'That's great—really, really great,' he says.

I nod happily.

'That's enough to cover your tuition for the academy,' he says.

'It's also enough to cover our living expenses until we can work things out with the *officina*.'

Luca's smile fades. 'I want this more than anything, Mia—to be with you, to start a new life with you—but I need to be able to work it out first.'

'You don't need to do anything. You just need to trust.'

'I'm supposed to be the one looking after you.'

'Just come home and we'll work out the rest later—together.'

He takes a deep breath.

'I've already arranged a place for us to stay. Somewhere you'll be comfortable, and if you do happen to find yourself staring blankly outside the window, the view is pretty special.'

He shakes his head. 'You're unbelievable.'

'I told you—I'm not going home without you.'

There's a long pause, and he lets out an exhale.

'Say yes, please just say yes,' I whisper. 'I promise you this will be okay.'

Prendi la vita come viene.

I hold my breath, watching Luca's expression, trying to work out what he's thinking.

'I don't want to live another day without you.'

'Is that a yes?'

'*Sì.*'

'Stay with me tonight?'

'I'm not going anywhere. Ever.'

CHAPTER THIRTY

Paolo unloads a box from his car and sets it inside the cottage. 'That's the last one, Mia.'

'I think that should go over there,' says Mum, directing Dad to the corner of the living room, where he places a lampshade. She steps down from the ladder she's standing on and admires the painting she's just affixed to the wall. 'All done, sweetheart. Now it looks like a home.'

While Paolo and Dad have worked on making the modifications the cottage needs to make things more comfortable for Luca, Mum has infused it with all the trimmings a new home needs, and it's evident she's enjoyed every minute. She's even converted one of the spare bedrooms into an art studio for me.

Dad shakes Luca's hand and pats him on the back. 'Tomorrow night, Silvio's bar. We're watching the Grand Prix,' he says. He turns to Mum. 'You and Mia should come too, Julie.'

Mum raises her eyebrows, her face illuminated by a playful smile that makes me realise how much I'm going to miss her when she and Dad return to Melbourne.

With some encouragement from Paolo, Luca's been convinced to go back to work in the new year. While he won't be able to do everything he used to, Paolo's reassured him he'll be able to do enough to ensure he won't have to sell his share of the business. Rehab starts on Monday; I'm due to start studying at the Academy of Art next spring.

Luca grins. 'Thanks for everything,' he says.

Mum bends down and gives him a kiss on both cheeks.

'See you tomorrow night,' says Paolo, holding open the door for Mum and Dad.

Luca and I wave them goodbye and retreat back inside.

'We're all set now, *amore mio*.'

Luca flashes me a smile, the kind of spectacular smile with enough power behind it to make your whole day sing. 'Some mail came for you today,' he says, motioning to a few letters on the windowsill.

I pick up the letter and slowly tear it open.

Sender: Jones & Frazzetto Art Dealers of London

Dear Ms Moretti,

It is with great pleasure that we enclose the remaining balance for the commissioned works for The Florentine Bridge. *In addition, we are pleased to inform you that your collection of paintings recently sold at a London auction. Several other potential buyers have expressed an interest in further commissioned works from you. We are proposing a series of paintings based on Signor Giovanni Fiorelli's photographs. We have enclosed the details of this request and look forward to hearing from you should you be interested in this proposal.*

Yours sincerely,
Clara Jones & Joseph Frazzetto

I fold the letter in half and tuck it back in its envelope, a smile spreading across my lips as my eyes fixate on the view of Florence in the distance, an idyllic sea of terracotta-coloured rooftops visible from the window of my studio.

'Life will lead us to where we need to be,' I murmur.

'What's that, *bella mia?*'

'Sometimes we just need to believe that everything's going to work out exactly as it should.'

I feel the warmth of Luca's hand on the small of my back and the reassuring awareness of being held—not just now, always; not just by him, but from within—anchors itself deep inside me. Just underneath that rests a feeling of looseness and tranquillity.

'You know, when you were in the hospital and they weren't sure if you'd make it or not, I prayed so hard that you'd live to see the sun rise and set again. I'd watch the sun come up every morning, and then I'd come to the hospital, where I'd sit by your bed and describe how beautiful and special it was.'

Luca swallows as if something has caught in his throat.

'I took our padlock to the Ponte Vecchio before you woke up. I thought you'd want me to.'

He lets out a small cough and says, 'I'm glad you did that.'

'Do you remember anything about the coma or the accident?'

'I just remember the headlights of the car veering towards me. But right before I lost control and came off the bike, I thought of you. And as for the coma, the only thing I remember was hearing your voice—you were begging me to come back to you. I came so close to dying, Mia. It makes me think about how brave you really are. I was unconscious; I didn't have to fight like you did.'

'It was a different kind of fight. Your fight to stay strong and accept what's happened starts now.'

He nods, blinking slowly. 'You know what, *amore mio?* I think we should visit our bridge,' he says, pointing out the window towards the city centre. 'If we leave now, we could make it before sunset.'

I walk beside Luca as we make our way towards the Ponte Vecchio. From the other side of the piazza, Signor Fiorelli tips his hat and

I wave back. The cobblestoned streets are uneven, and Luca's working hard to handle what is far from a smooth ride.

'Let me push you?'

'I've got it.'

'I know you have, but—'

He stops pushing his chair and looks up at me.

'I'm sorry,' I say.

He smiles at me reassuringly. 'On the way back,' he says, winking at me.

When we reach the centre of the Ponte Vecchio, we stop under the middle arch and admire the reflection of the bridge glistening on the mirror-like surface of the Arno. Here we watch tourists come and go, snapping pictures they'll file away and look back on with fondness in weeks, months or years to come. Enamoured couples bend down by the statue of Cellini and snap their locks shut around the gate, despite the warnings not to. I hope they'll remember the way it felt to be here, on a bridge over a river that holds the energy of hundreds of lovers before them.

A cool breeze brushes against me and I pull my coat around me. My thoughts sift their way through all the events that unfolded since Luca and I first came here and the last time we were here together. I let all those memories knit themselves together: the laughs, the tears, the smiles and the blissful silences, the intoxicating highs and the devastating lows. The softness of a touch and the euphoric high of a kiss. When Luca reaches for my hand and looks at me in that way nobody else does, I'm almost certain he's been thinking about the same things.

'I want you to know that no matter what, I'll always be here, Luca. No matter what happens to you or to me.'

He pulls me onto his lap and I nestle my head against his body as we watch the colours in the sky trickle away while the sun disappears. When Luca moves his face towards mine at the exact same time I move mine towards his for a kiss, everything clicks back into place. In this world of uncertainty, one thing I know for sure is that tomorrow morning that same sun will rise again, beaming light and warmth upon us as it marks the beginning of a brand-new day.

'We're going to be okay, aren't we?'

Luca strokes my cheek and smiles. 'This bridge is like us, Mia: it can withstand anything, no matter what life lobs its way.'

'*Prendiamo la vita come viene.*'

A LETTER FROM VANESSA

Dear Reader,

I hope you enjoyed reading *Her Tuscan Summer* and spending time in Tuscany with Mia and Luca!

If you are interested in learning about my upcoming releases, you can sign up for my newsletter here. Your email address will never be shared and you can unsubscribe at any time.

www.bookouture.com/vanessa-carnevale

Her Tuscan Summer is the first adult novel I sat down to write, many years after I returned to Australia after having lived in Florence for several years. My time in Tuscany provided me with lots of inspiration. For years I'd kept notes about the places I'd visited and the Italian culture I love so much. I hope that this story reminds readers of what a special, once-in-a-lifetime kind of love can feel like, and how important it is to be able to trust in times of uncertainty.

I love hearing from readers, and if you've enjoyed this book, please consider leaving a review or saying hello! You can reach me via Facebook, Instagram or my website, where you can also sign up for my newsletter updates.

With love and best wishes,
Vanessa

www.vanessacarnevale.com

vanessacarnevalewriter

@vanessacarnevale

vanessacarnevale

ACKNOWLEDGEMENTS

To my fabulous editor, Lucy Dauman, and the fabulous Bookouture team, thank you for your ongoing enthusiasm for my books, which really means so much to me.

Heartfelt appreciation to Laura Brown, Natasha Lester and Mary Lovelien, who provided feedback on an early draft, as well as ongoing support as I navigated the world of writing and publishing.

To the most supportive friends a girl could ever wish for: Amanda Ingrosso, Jane O'Keefe, Katrina Agius, Lucinda Westerman and Stav Catalano—big love, and even bigger thanks. I'm also fortunate to have some amazing friends who made sure my children had a blast in their care when I needed to squeeze in some extra writing or editing time. Amelia Rambaldi and Giuliana La Valle—*grazie mille*!

Thanks to Anjanette Fennell, for seeing something in my work before I ever did. You told me it was a matter of 'when, not if' and then somehow you made me believe it.

To Heather Waring, my primary school library teacher, who, through her immeasurable love of books, inspired me to hold onto the dream of one day becoming a published author.

Thanks also to my wonderful family in Italy for all your love, support and encouragement: Peppino, Vincenza, Diego, Angela, Anna and Pino.

Thanks to my mum, who always bought me books as a child and turned a blind eye when I stayed up past my bedtime to read them, and my brother, who read a draft of this book on the bus to work, pretended not to cry, and thereafter encouraged me, with unwavering faith, to pursue one of my biggest dreams in life.

Finally, to Fabio, Christian and Alessia, you are my world, my everything. *Vi voglio un mondo di bene.*